Books by Tracie Peterson

THE HEART OF CHEYENNE

A Love Discovered

PICTURES OF THE HEART

Remember Me
Finding Us
Knowing You

THE JEWELS OF KALISPELL*

The Heart's Choice

LOVE ON THE SANTA FE

Along the Rio Grande
Beyond the Desert Sands
Under the Starry Skies

LADIES OF THE LAKE

Destined for You
Forever My Own
Waiting on Love

WILLAMETTE BRIDES

Secrets of My Heart
The Way of Love
Forever by Your Side

THE TREASURES OF NOME*

Forever Hidden
Endless Mercy
Ever Constant

BROOKSTONE BRIDES

When You Are Near
Wherever You Go
What Comes My Way

GOLDEN GATE SECRETS

In Places Hidden
In Dreams Forgotten
In Times Gone By

HEART OF THE FRONTIER

Treasured Grace
Beloved Hope
Cherished Mercy

THE HEART OF ALASKA*

In the Shadow of Denali
Out of the Ashes
Under the Midnight Sun

SAPPHIRE BRIDES

A Treasure Concealed
A Beauty Refined
A Love Transformed

BRIDES OF SEATTLE

Steadfast Heart
Refining Fire
Love Everlasting

LONE STAR BRIDES

A Sensible Arrangement
A Moment in Time
A Matter of Heart

LAND OF SHINING WATER

The Icecutter's Daughter
The Quarryman's Bride
The Miner's Lady

---

*Beyond the Silence**
*Serving Up Love***

*with Kimberley Woodhouse
**with Karen Witemeyer, Regina Jennings, and Jen Turano

For a complete list of Tracie's books, visit TraciePeterson.com.

1

THE HEART *of* CHEYENNE

A LOVE DISCOVERED

TRACIE PETERSON

BETHANYHOUSE

a division of Baker Publishing Group
Minneapolis, Minnesota

© 2024 by Peterson Ink, Inc.

Published by Bethany House Publishers
Minneapolis, Minnesota
www.bethanyhouse.com

Bethany House Publishers is a division of
Baker Publishing Group, Grand Rapids, Michigan

Printed in the United States of America

Library of Congress Cataloging-in-Publication Data
Names: Peterson, Tracie, author.
Title: A love discovered / Tracie Peterson.
Description: Minneapolis, Minnesota : Bethany House Publishers, a division of
    Baker Publishing Group, 2024. | Series: The heart of Cheyenne ; 1
Identifiers: LCCN 2023037696 | ISBN 9780764241079 (paperback) | ISBN
    9780764242694 (cloth) | ISBN 9780764242700 (large print) | ISBN 9781493445301
    (ebook)
Subjects: LCGFT: Christian fiction. | Romance fiction. | Western fiction. | Novels.
Classification: LCC PS3566.E7717 L676 2024 | DDC 813/.54--dc23/eng/20230920
LC record available at https://lccn.loc.gov/2023037696

Scripture quotations are from the King James Version of the Bible.

This is a work of historical reconstruction; the appearances of certain historical figures
are therefore inevitable. All other characters, however, are products of the author's
imagination, and any resemblance to actual persons, living or dead, is coincidental.

Baker Publishing Group publications use paper produced from sustainable forestry
practices and post-consumer waste whenever possible.

24 25 26 27 28 29 30   7 6 5 4 3 2 1

1

November 1867
Independence, Indiana

I t seems all I ever do is attend funerals," Marybeth Kruger murmured as the cemetery caretakers began shoveling dirt over her father's casket.

Just days ago, all had been well. She and Papa had been talking about the coming of Christmas. Papa had agreed to freight a load of grain to Evansville from a farm thirty miles out. A snowstorm blew in and made the conditions worse than anyone had seen in years. The sheriff told Marybeth that Klaus Kruger was nearly to his destination just beyond Pigeon Creek when tragedy struck. The horses got spooked by the wind and snow, and the wagon ended up upside down at the end of the bridge. The doctor said Papa had broken his neck and died instantly. Marybeth supposed that was better than lingering in pain and suffering. But best would have been if he hadn't had the accident at all. Her little sister, Carrie, wasn't even two years old, and at the age of twenty with no husband or living relatives, Marybeth had no means to support her. What were either of them to do?

She felt someone touch her shoulder and turned. It was Edward Vogel. Her dearest friend in all the world. She saw the dampness in his eyes. He and her father had been close. She and Edward's wife, Janey, had been lifelong friends, but Janey's was another tragic death that weighed heavy on Marybeth.

"You ready to go home?" Edward asked her.

"I feel like I have no home." She looked across the cemetery. "I keep thinking of all the dead. There are so many. Our lives have been short moments of joy encompassed by sorrow and death."

He looked toward where Janey and his son were buried, and Marybeth couldn't help but follow his gaze. He'd married Janey after returning from the war. And then Janey had delivered a stillborn son and died herself shortly after. Marybeth had been devastated by Janey's death. They had been so very close.

They were surrounded by the graves of their departed loved ones. Marybeth's mother had died seven years earlier. Marybeth's stepmother, Sarah, had died after giving life to Carrie. Now her father was gone as well. For Edward, there was Janey and his son, his mother, and two brothers who'd died in the war.

"Marybeth, I was hoping to have a word with you."

She turned to find their pastor. She gave a nod. "Thank you for such a nice service, Pastor Orton."

"Your father was a good man and trusted friend, Marybeth. We were blessed to have him as an elder."

"Yes. He loved our church." She didn't know what else to say. A neighbor had offered to have Carrie over to play with her children while Marybeth attended the funeral, but she still needed to get home.

"I know this is a delicate matter and perhaps a poor time to bring up such a subject, but have you considered what you will do about your sister?"

Marybeth frowned. "What do you mean?"

The pastor's expression was one of compassion. "Well, you and she are alone now, and you have no means of supporting her, much less yourself."

"I'm sure there must be a better time to talk about all this," Edward piped up. "The grave isn't even covered."

"Yes, I know. I feel terrible for it, but on the other hand, I cannot allow for a babe to go hungry," the pastor replied.

Marybeth looked at the older man. He had been pastoring at the little Methodist church for as long as she had memory. He had presided over her mother's funeral and her stepmother's.

"Carrie isn't going hungry," Marybeth said in a barely audible voice. "The house is full of food. People haven't stopped bringing food since the accident."

"But that will only last a few days. In time she may well starve," the man said. "That is why I'm suggesting you give her up. Let her be raised by a family who can provide for her. I've been speaking with Thomas and Martha Wandless. They're quite well-off, as you know, and would be happy to take Carrie as their own."

"But she's not their own. She's mine. I've raised her from birth and done a good job, if I do say so myself." Marybeth's ire grew. People always seemed to think they knew what was best for other folks, but Pastor Orton was the worst of all for trying to arrange people's lives.

"Now, Marybeth, no one is trying to suggest you haven't taken good care of your sister, and while your father was alive and providing for the both of you, no one would have suggested things go on any other way."

"I should say not. Papa would have torn into the man who suggested he divide his family." She fixed the pastor with a glare. "He would have despised the interference or suggestion that he couldn't take care of his own."

"And would have well been within his rights. But, child, you have no husband and no other relative to provide a living for you and your sister. Winter is upon us, and you'll need money for heating and food. Where will you come by it?"

"I'll help her." Edward's voice was reassuring. "I'm sure others will as well."

"For a time," the pastor said, nodding, "as good Christian folks should do, but it won't be possible to continue forever."

"I'm sure it won't need to continue forever," Edward replied.

"Edward!" They all glanced up at his name being called. It was his sister, Inga Weber. She waved and called out again. "Edward, could I speak to you for a minute?"

He turned to Marybeth. "I'll be right back."

He moved toward Inga, leaving Marybeth feeling deserted. How was she to fight for her sister without his support? Pastor Orton had always intimidated her, and she was sure he knew it. She glanced back at him and squared her shoulders. She would just have to be strong.

Pastor Orton shook his head. "You must think of poor Carrie. She has now lost her mother and father. The Wandless couple could provide her with that and give her a life of ease. They have plenty of money, and Carrie would live a life without want."

Marybeth finally found her voice. "I'm her sister and the only mother she's ever known. I could never give her away as if she were a doll I'd grown bored with. I pledged to my stepmother and my father that I would always care for her."

"Marybeth, you need to see reason. You have no way to provide for Carrie. I'm sure you wouldn't want the law to be involved."

"What are you saying?" Marybeth fixed the older man with narrowed eyes.

"I'm saying that those who know better might become involved and take matters out of your hands legally. After all, we just want what's best for your sister. She's only a babe."

"I'm what's best for her, and she's what's best for me. We belong together. We've lost everything else. How could you be so cruel?"

"It's not meant to be cruel, Marybeth. If you were to calm a moment, you would see that for yourself." He reached out to take hold of her arm, but Marybeth pulled back. "Please, I'm only trying to help. Soon you'll have to find a job, and you won't be able to do that and care for your sister. There's a family with the will and means to provide for Carrie. They can give her what you cannot, Marybeth. I'm sure they'd allow you to visit."

Edward returned just then. "We need to be going." He took hold of Marybeth and turned her from the pastor's intense face. "Afternoon, Pastor."

He led Marybeth to where the wagon stood, horses stomping in the snow and blowing out great clouds of breath.

"Are you all right?"

"He wants to take my sister from me. After everyone else I've lost. He wants to take her as well." A sob broke from her throat, and Marybeth pulled her woolen scarf to her face. "Why did God allow this to happen?"

"I've asked myself that over and over about a lot of things." He helped Marybeth up onto the wagon and then followed her. "He still hasn't answered me."

"It's not my fault or Carrie's that Mrs. Wandless is barren. I've long felt sorry for her, knowing that she wanted children. I've even prayed for her. People have suggested they adopt before now, but she's always put that off, hoping to have her own baby. I don't know why she suddenly feels the need to rob me of a sister."

Edward picked up the lines and released the brake. "Busybodies. That's what they are. Pastor Orton has always stuck his nose in where it wasn't wanted. He thinks just because he pastors a church that he has the right to be in all the details of his flock's life."

"I know what he's saying makes sense to him." Marybeth let the tears run down her cheeks. The cold air stung, but she didn't care. "He's right that I don't have any way to provide. Once the money Papa saved is gone, I honestly don't know what we'll do. At least he owned the house outright."

"Then that will come to you and Carrie. I'll talk to my brother-in-law, if you like. He can handle legal stuff for you since he's a lawyer. I don't know if your pa had debts, but I doubt it. He was pretty firm on paying cash."

"Yes, he was, and I know of nothing that he owed. He wouldn't even let me run a tab at the grocers'." Marybeth wiped her face with her scarf. "Oh, Edward, I know you're hurting too. Pa always said you were like the son he never had."

"He was always good to me. My pa said he was the best man in Independence."

"They were good friends. Right to the end," Marybeth admitted. "I appreciated that you and your pa were pallbearers. I appreciate even more the way you helped Pa when he was alive."

"He was easy to work with and good to teach me about

things I didn't know." Edward shook his head. "He always understood my desire to work as an officer of the law. He encouraged me when my pa started nagging me about quitting that work and coming back to help him with the horse farm."

"Pa had a talent for seeing what a man was cut out to do. He often spoke of what a great deputy you made."

"I wish my pa could understand like yours did. Raising horses is just not my calling. Inga loves it. Her boys love it too, so there will be someone to continue the family business. But I intend to go on working in law enforcement. I like being a part of the police department in Evansville."

"That's because you're good at it." Marybeth sighed and huddled down in her woolen coat. "I was sure hoping it wouldn't turn so cold so soon."

"Me too. People get mean when it gets cold. You'd think they'd go find a place to stay warm and keep inside, but instead it seems to make them seek attention out of boredom. We arrested three different groups of folks yesterday for fighting."

They turned down the street where Marybeth's father had purchased the family house over twenty-two years ago. Back then, the town of Lamasco, as it was called, was only about eight years old. Situated on the west side of Pigeon Creek across from Evansville, Indiana, this community had attracted a vast number of German immigrants, including Marybeth's mother and father. Marybeth had been the first of their family to be born in America. Her first six years of school had been given in English and German, so she spoke both fluently.

In 1857, the parts of Lamasco that had overflowed to the east side of Pigeon Creek had been incorporated into Evansville, but on the west side of the creek, folks had decided to remain independent of Evansville and changed their name to Independence. Some of the older folks still called it Lamasco, but no one seemed to mind much.

Marybeth remembered when their house had been only one of a handful. Now houses were built side by side, block after block. It had been a wonderful place to grow up, and she'd hoped to give that life to Carrie, but now she wondered if that could still happen.

She looked over at Edward. Their talk of the horse farm seemed to have brought him even lower. "I'm sure your father will understand in time. He loves you."

Edward brought the horses to a stop and glanced her way. "It's of no matter right now. You've just lost your pa, and it's not right to focus on anything but that. Look, I'll be by tomorrow to bring you some more wood. Do you have plenty for tonight?"

Marybeth nodded and jumped down from the wagon. "I do. I'm gonna go stir up the stove and get a fire going in the fireplace before I head over to pick up Carrie. Thanks again for standing by me at the funeral. I know Pa would have been grateful for your support and all that you're doing for me and Carrie."

He smiled for the first time that day. "I'm honored to help. You and your pa got me through the worst of it when Janey and the boy died." He always referred to his son as "the boy," since he and Janey hadn't picked out a name for him. Edward had buried them together, with the boy safely tucked in Janey's arms. The gravestone simply read *Jane Vogel and Son*.

"That's why God gave us to each other," Marybeth said, letting the finality of the moment settle on her. Papa was really and truly gone. She glanced at the house and trembled.

"Best get in out of the cold. I'll see you in the morning." Edward slapped the reins and headed on down the street.

Marybeth had never felt so alone.

Edward made sure the horses had adequate feed, then went into the house. He and Janey had rented this place at the edge of town when they'd married. That was shortly after he'd come home from the war. Of course, he'd needed time to finish recovering from a wound he'd taken at the Siege of Savannah. A ball cored a hole through his side and out the back in the blink of an eye. Loss of blood had nearly killed him, but thankfully nothing vital had been hit. Little by little, Edward had recovered enough to be sent home just after the first of the year in 1865.

Inga had been his nurse since their mother had mourned herself to death over the loss of his two brothers. She had died that September after news that Jacob had been killed in August at the Battle of Atlanta. Their brother Gunther had taken a minié ball two years prior to that at Shiloh. Mother had been convinced that she would lose all three when the brothers had enlisted to join Evansville's Twenty-Fifth Regiment of the Indiana Infantry. And she'd nearly been right. Edward might have died but for the fact that after being wounded, he'd mistakenly been transferred with some special patients—sons of congressmen and senators—to a hospital in Washington. There, he'd received quality care that wouldn't have been available on the battlefield. Most likely it had saved his life. Inga called it God's provision. Edward sometimes wondered, however, if he had cheated death and that was why Janey and the boy had to die.

Once inside the cold house, Edward made a fire in the

hearth and sat down to enjoy the warmth before heading out for his night shift. They'd been outside for far too long in the growing cold. He probably should have talked Marybeth into canceling the graveside services, but it hadn't occurred to him at the time. Thankfully the wind hadn't been blowing.

Catching sight of the letter he'd left unopened on the table, Edward got up and grabbed it before settling back down in front of the fire. It was from his former commanding officer, Major Henderson. The man had written only once before. That letter had come to congratulate Edward on his marriage and to offer hope that Edward was fully recovered.

Edward looked at the letter for a moment. Major Henderson had always had plans to go out west after the war. Like Edward, he was a law enforcement officer with a strong desire to keep the law and order of a frontier town. Edward had always figured to get enough experience in Evansville that one day he could go west and take up a position standing guard over an entire community. He and Henderson had discussed it quite thoroughly once.

He opened the letter and read the contents. Henderson was a man of few words, always getting straight to the point. This letter was no exception.

I'm sure this letter takes you by surprise, but I have an offer to make.

2

After getting home from work the next morning, Edward decided to eat breakfast before going to see Marybeth. All through the night, the wind had picked up until it was howling like a banshee and blowing around anything that wasn't tied down. The only good thing was it kept folks off the streets and made Edward's night fairly quiet. The wind finally calmed just before dawn, and by the time his work was done, it seemed back to normal.

He built up the fire in the stove and set the cast-iron skillet atop the burner. He cut a hunk of side pork and dropped it in the pan. It crackled and sizzled immediately, sending a pleasant aroma into the air. Next, he ground some coffee and filled the pot with water. He'd done for himself most of his adult life and found it a comfortable routine. He'd joined the army at eighteen after just a few months of working for the Evansville Police Department. His superiors had noted that Edward had a talent for getting in and out of places unnoticed, so Major Henderson recruited him for reconnoitering. Sometimes that meant several days out on his own—doing for himself.

Of course, marriage to Janey had provided him with a loving companion who saw to his every need. Janey was one of those women who took pride in seeing him well cared for. It wasn't until she was bedridden trying to bear their son that Edward realized just how much she did. When she died, Edward was back to doing for himself, and he did his best not to think about what was missing in his life.

His brothers . . . his mother . . . Janey and the boy. What good did it do to think about them and how much he missed them? It served no good purpose and just left him all the more melancholy. A man could lose his mind that way.

He flipped the pork and went to slice himself a couple pieces of bread. Only then did he allow himself to think of the letter he'd received. Major Henderson wanted him to come west to an end-of-the-rails town called Cheyenne. The great transcontinental railroad was being built from coast to coast, a marvel to be sure, given all that they were up against: weather, natives, rugged mountains, and desert. It seemed that the crew working from east to west planned to stop for the winter in Cheyenne—so named after the local Indians.

Edward finished with the bread and went to the table, where he'd left the letter. He picked it up again and scanned the few lines.

Because of your being a family man, married and surely by now you have children, I want to invite you to join us in the growing town of Cheyenne. We need family men to settle this town. I can offer you a job on the town's police force, and with that comes a fine salary and a town lot on which to build your own house.

But Edward wasn't a family man. Janey had died and taken his chances at a family with her. The offer sounded like everything Edward had ever wanted, however. He was tired of Evansville and death. A new start in a new place sounded like heaven.

He'd even prayed about it long and hard before heading to work. Then that evening walking his beat, he still thought and prayed, despite the annoying weather. Marybeth and Carrie kept coming to mind, and with their predicament, a plan had started to form. He could marry Marybeth. Platonically, of course. He wasn't about to marry another woman and risk her life by being intimate and getting her with child. Marybeth was a good woman, and her nature was the kind Edward appreciated. He could explain the situation, and he was almost certain she would see the sense in it. Then he would have his family-man status, and she would have a husband and provider. No one would worry about taking her baby sister then.

The pork was starting to burn, so he hurried to the stove and took it up. He poured most of the grease into a can, then plopped the two pieces of bread he'd cut into the frying pan. They browned up fast and easy. The coffee wasn't yet done, but that didn't stop Edward from throwing the side meat between the two pieces of toast. He bowed his head and blessed the food, then added a prayer that Marybeth would be receptive to his proposition.

Marybeth had just finished helping Carrie with her oatmeal when a knock sounded on the front door. She wiped her sister's mouth but left her in the feeding chair with a small piece of toast and jam before heading to the door. Who would be calling at this hour?

She opened the door to find Pastor Orton standing there. The man beside him wasn't someone she recognized.

"Marybeth, I apologize for the earliness of the hour, but I wanted to see how you and Carrie are doing. I've also brought a friend, Judge Perkins." The pastor nodded toward his companion. "Might we come in?"

She gave a sigh. "Of course. I was just feeding Carrie." She left them at the door to fend for themselves and made her way back to the kitchen.

The pastor and judge followed. Marybeth didn't miss the way each man seemed to inspect every inch and corner of the house.

"You keep an orderly house, Marybeth," the pastor had to concede.

"My father was always well pleased." She took a seat at the table beside her sister's chair. Carrie had already devoured the jam and toast, so Marybeth prepared her another small piece.

"Might we sit?" the judge asked.

"Yes, of course. I don't mean to be a bad hostess. I simply have a lot on my mind," Marybeth told the stranger. "We only buried my father just yesterday."

"Yes, Pastor Orton relayed that information to me." The man took a chair, and the pastor did likewise. "My condolences."

"Thank you." Marybeth didn't bother to look up.

"Marybeth, I brought along Judge Perkins so that we might discuss the situation regarding your sister. I thought if you had questions about how things might proceed, the judge could give you answers."

"I thought I made it clear that I wasn't interested in deserting my sister." Marybeth handed the toast to Carrie, who squealed in delight.

"Tanks you," Carrie told Marybeth.

"You're welcome, little one," Marybeth said, smoothing back Carrie's baby-fine blond hair.

"I know this is a hard thing for you to consider, Marybeth, but you must be reasonable." The pastor glanced at Judge Perkins. "You are a single woman with no means of your own. Your father wasn't a wealthy man to leave you a large inheritance."

"We did all right, and my father did set aside some money for me. I have enough."

"Perhaps for the time being, but the almanac says it will be a hard winter. That money will be eaten up in fuel and food. And what will you do if you come down sick? Who will care for your sister then?"

"I don't intend to come down sick, but I'm sure if I did, we would work it all out." Marybeth watched Carrie rather than look at the men.

"Young lady, I am not of a mind to impose my will upon you, given that you've just lost your father," the judge began. "I'm sure that your heart is quite overcome with sadness and the desire to stifle further change, but I must keep in mind the welfare of your little sister. She's much too young for you to care for alone. You will have need of working to support her, and where will she stay while you seek that employment, much less when you take it on?"

Marybeth drew a deep breath and pushed down her anger. How dare they come here the day after the funeral and try to force her to give up Carrie? Pastor Orton would never see her grace his congregation again.

"I know that the situation looks rather worrisome to you both, however, I believe that we will be just fine. Several of our friends have promised to help with providing wood and coal if we need. And Papa had already laid in a large supply, so we might not have to bother anyone. There is also a nice nest egg that Papa saved. Our needs are quite small, and I can take in mending or laundry to earn extra money. I've given it a lot of consideration and know that God will provide for our every need."

"It's remarkable that your faith is so strong," Pastor Orton said, smiling. "But don't you see it would be so much better if you had only yourself to worry about?"

"And given that there is a childless husband and wife who would be happy to provide for your sister, don't you think it would be best for her?" The judge gave her a look that suggested maybe Marybeth hadn't even considered the possibility.

"Carrie is my responsibility, and not only that, but I'm the only mother she has ever known. Have either of you thought of that? She's quite attached to me and I to her. Would you rip a child out of my arms to put her with strangers who know nothing of her likes and dislikes? To me that sounds quite cruel."

"Marybeth, those things can be learned," Pastor Orton said. "Carrie has never had another set of parents, that is true. But because she is so young, she will learn and soon forget this life."

"But I don't want her to forget," Marybeth said a little louder than she'd intended. "I don't want her to forget our father nor her mother. I don't want her to forget how much I love her. Please understand that the matter is closed. I do not intend to throw away my sister or push her off on someone else. I have prayed about this and know what my role is in her life. I made my father and stepmother a promise, and I intend to keep it."

Marybeth got to her feet, and at first neither man moved. Finally, they stood.

The judge frowned and shook his head. "It would seem that the matter may well have to be taken out of your hands. The welfare of the child is much more important than your feelings."

Looking to Pastor Orton, Marybeth kept her temper in check. "I am thankful for your concern, but until you can honestly see that there is a problem, why not allow the Lord to move as He will in this matter? You have, after all, preached on many occasions that God is in control and will have His way."

The pastor stood silently for a moment, then looked at the judge. "Let us go and discuss this elsewhere. In time, I'm sure we can convince Miss Kruger of how severe this situation is."

They headed for the door, and Marybeth forced herself to follow them rather than scoop up Carrie and run in the opposite direction. She nodded at their good-byes and quickly closed the door and locked it behind them. Leaning against the jamb, she felt tears come to her eyes and let go the hold she'd maintained on her emotions.

"Oh, Father, please protect us from these men. Don't let them take Carrie from me. Haven't I lost enough?"

A knock sounded on the door behind her, and Marybeth jumped. Surely, they hadn't come back to cause her grief. She turned and reached for the key, then paused. She could leave the door locked and refuse to open it. Maybe she could tell them that Carrie needed her for something.

She opened her mouth to speak, and the knock sounded again. Marybeth bit her lower lip and prayed for strength.

"Marybeth, it's me. Edward."

She hurried to unlock and open the door. She wiped at

her tears as he stepped into the house. "I'm sorry. I thought Pastor Orton and the judge had come back."

"What judge?"

She sighed and headed back to Carrie. "Pastor Orton came with a judge to convince me to let them have Carrie. I told them no. They weren't very happy with me, and I feared they'd come back to just . . . well, take her."

"I'm sorry. I know that must have upset you a great deal."

"They're never going to leave me alone. Mr. and Mrs. Wandless are determined to take my sister for themselves. What am I to do?"

"That's why I've come."

Marybeth stopped midstep and turned. "You have an idea?"

"I do. Come and sit with me for a moment."

Marybeth motioned to the table. "We can sit here. Carrie is just finishing up with breakfast." She dropped onto a wooden chair at the table and looked at Carrie, who was laughing and smearing jam around the tray of her chair. Papa had just bought her one of those new contraptions with the tray that raised up and lowered down once the child was seated. It was such a nice thing to have, and Marybeth had been so grateful for it.

Edward sat across from her at the table. He took the same seat Pastor Orton had vacated. It was so nice to have her friend there in the older man's place.

"I know this may sound like a strange proposition, but hear me out," Edward began. "I received a letter from my former commanding officer, Major Henderson. He's asked me to come to Cheyenne. It's several hundred miles west of here in the Dakota Territory. The big transcontinental railroad will go through there, and they've nearly reached Cheyenne. They plan to stop there for the winter. I went and talked to a fellow at the railyard in Evansville. He says that the Union Pacific Railroad intends to make Cheyenne a big headquarters for the line. Cheyenne is bound to become a big city."

"You're going to leave me?" Marybeth felt her heart sink, and her stomach began to ache.

"No." Edward pierced her with a look. "I want to take you and Carrie with me."

Marybeth shook her head. "How?"

"That's the part that may sound strange. Look, they want family men. Men who are married and settled down, hopefully with children. They want to civilize the area, and . . . well, I guess to their way of thinking married men are able to do that better than single men. You know as well as I do that women are often looked at as a stabilizing factor." He gave her a halfhearted smile. "We fellas probably wouldn't even worry about silverware or takin' showers if not for you ladies."

"So you want us to go along and pretend to be your family?" She thought on the matter momentarily. It would get her and Carrie out of Pastor Orton's hands.

"No, I don't want to pretend. Look, you know that I never intended to marry again. I won't kill another woman by getting her with child. I just won't. And you told me you didn't know if you'd ever find a husband who would accept Carrie. Well, I would. We could marry—in name only—and I'd be a pa to Carrie. She already knows me." He reached over and waggled his fingers at her as if to tickle her side. Carrie squealed and giggled, squirming as if he'd already touched her.

"She does love you," Marybeth admitted. She considered all that he'd said. "I do too. You've been so dear to me ever since you married Janey."

"And I love the two of you," he replied. "This would help us both out, but . . . unfortunately, the major wants me out there as soon as possible. Do you suppose you could make your mind up right away?"

"I'll put it to prayer immediately." Marybeth couldn't imagine she would have a better solution, but the idea of marrying Edward without the kind of love that was intended in a marriage left her feeling strangely empty.

"I'll come back tomorrow for your answer."

Marybeth nodded. "I'll have one."

She didn't bother to show him out of the house. Instead, she looked at her baby sister. Carrie was oblivious to what had just taken place. She had no way of knowing her entire future was on the line. Either choice Marybeth made would completely alter Carrie's life. Her own as well.

Marybeth cleaned Carrie up and guided her to the front room, where her toys awaited in a small wooden box Papa had made. Carrie immediately found things to occupy herself with, and Marybeth sat on the floor beside her and watched.

She'd begged God for a solution, and it would seem He had delivered one. Edward had wanted to go west for as long as Marybeth had known him. Janey had wanted that too, but Marybeth had never planned to leave Independence.

"Cheyenne is a long ways away," she murmured. Carrie looked up for a moment, then returned her attention to a rag doll.

There was really nothing left for her in Independence. There was no family. Most of her extended relatives were still in Germany. She didn't know any of them, and neither Mama nor Papa had ever really spoken of them. She had a few friends in the neighborhood that she would miss, but otherwise there was no one who really cared about her and Carrie staying on.

An image of Janey on her wedding day came to mind. Marybeth had been her maid of honor. She had been so happy for Janey and Edward. They were perfect together, and Janey had confided that she had never known such happiness— Edward was her all.

What would she think of Marybeth marrying her husband? Would she mind for the sake of saving Carrie from being taken away?

"Janey, I don't know if you can hear me, but I never coveted your husband. Edward has always only been a dear friend. I wouldn't have even met him but for you. I've always enjoyed his company, and he is a good man, but I know he loved you . . . and he'll never love anyone else."

She felt a sad resignation waft over her. Was it acceptable to God to marry a man for the sake of anything other than love?

"Lord, You know the situation, and I've been praying for a solution. This would definitely resolve the matter, but is it all right?" She almost immediately thought of stories from the Bible where marriages were arranged. People did marry without being in love. It gave Marybeth a sense of peace and assurance that she wouldn't be going against God if she moved forward with Edward's proposal.

If they married, she would commit herself wholly to him, and if the time ever came that he wanted a marriage in deed as well as word, she would willingly give herself to him. But could she live her entire life without the true love of a husband?

She looked at her little sister. Carrie deserved security, and Marybeth wanted no further threat of losing her. Surely that was worth the price of giving up on falling in love.

3

I'm glad you came out to see us," Inga said, bringing Edward a large slice of cake. "I made this a couple of days ago when I made the cake for Marybeth and Carrie."

"Hello, son. What brings you out here?" his father asked, coming into the kitchen.

The family farm wasn't that far from town, but it had been a while since Edward had graced their doorstep. Inga and George had taken up residence here with Father and seemed quite content to raise their family here, while a part of Edward always felt odd in returning to his childhood home. With Mother gone, it never felt quite right to him.

"I need to tell you both something." He took the cake and fork that Inga offered and put them down on the kitchen table. "It can't wait."

"Sounds serious," his father replied.

Inga put another piece of cake on a plate and handed it to her father. Then she grabbed the coffeepot with a potholder. "Sit, Pa, and I'll pour you a cup."

He did as she said, and she saw to it that he and Edward each had a steaming mug to go with their dessert. Once that was done, she sat down beside her father. "So what's this all about?"

Edward took a sip of the hot coffee, then put the cup down before speaking. "I had a letter from my old commanding officer, Major Henderson. He wants me to come west to Cheyenne. It's a new town in the Dakota Territory. The transcontinental railroad is going to go right through there as they build west. He wants me to work for him policing the town."

His father held the coffee to his lips but hadn't yet sampled it. "Seems a long way off to go for a job when you've already got one."

"They're planning big things for Cheyenne, and they want married men with families." Edward held up his hand. "I know what you're going to say but hear me out. Marybeth is having no end of trouble with some folks who want to take her sister away from her. I want to marry her and give her and Carrie protection and the ability to stay together."

"Who would want to take Carrie away from Marybeth?" his sister asked.

"Pastor Orton. He's been talking to Thomas Wandless, and apparently he and his wife want to adopt Carrie. Pastor even got a judge to come talk to Marybeth. Scared her to pieces. I figure if I marry her, then the matter is resolved. Pastor is worried she won't have any way to provide for Carrie and herself, but if she's married to me, she'll have provision. Carrie knows me as well as she knew her own pa, and I figure I can be a good father to her."

"Sounds like you've given this quite a bit of thought," his father said, finally taking a long sip of the coffee.

"I have. Prayer too. You know I've wanted to go west for a long time. This opportunity can't happen for me unless I have a family. Major Henderson stressed the need for married men with families. With Marybeth and Carrie, I get a wife and a child."

"But I thought you were never going to marry again," Inga said in a whisper.

"I wasn't. It'll be a marriage in name only, and Marybeth understands that. I won't be the cause of another wife dying."

"Son, you know that isn't always the way it works. You can't go blaming yourself for Janey's death. There was obviously something wrong with the boy. The doctor said it sickened Janey as well. That was why she died."

"I know what he said, but I won't risk it happening again."

"I've had four boys, Edward," his sister spoke up. "I would risk my life over and over, if necessary, but all went well, and we came through it without harm. That's the normal way of things. The way God put us together."

"Well, it didn't work out that way for Janey and the boy, but that's beside the point. Marybeth must have a way to keep Carrie safe, and this will solve the matter for us both."

"But Marybeth shouldn't have to give up the love of a husband in order to save her sister," his father said, frowning. His brow knit together as it usually did when he was considering a difficult situation. "Have you thought of the sacrifice you're asking of her—giving up love?"

"Never expected my father to be the romantic of the family," Edward said with a shrug, "but the fact is, she won't be without love. I've loved her for a long time. She's like family to me. Carrie too. It may not be the kind of love a husband gives a wife, but she'll have it, and I'll see to it that she has everything else she needs."

Pa shared a look with Inga, then shook his head. "One day you're gonna see it won't be enough. I hate to think about what it will do to the both of you when that time comes."

Edward ignored the sense of truth that came with his father's statement. He couldn't offer Marybeth more. This would just have to be enough.

"You know you'll be alone out there. No family to help you along." Inga reached over and gave his arm a squeeze. "You'll only have each other."

"And the major and his family. I'm sure we'll make friends quick. I'm to be given a piece of land as part of my agreement to come. The railroad has portioned out certain lots for the town. They want to attract families west, and the sooner folks settle and build houses, the better for the railroad."

"And the railroad intends for this to be a big town, eh?"

"Yes, Pa. It's situated in such a way that it will be like a crossroads. Go south and you hit Denver. East and west and you're going to go coast to coast. Eventually, north will take you all the way to Canada. They plan for there to be at least a dozen tracks converging on Cheyenne. It's going to be quite the place, and trains from all over will have to go through there. It'll be like Chicago."

"Well, I suppose if your mind is made up . . ."

Edward could hear the concern in his father's tone. Whether it was worry over the distance or over his son marrying a woman he didn't intend to fully make a wife, Edward didn't know. And frankly, he didn't care. He knew this was what he had to do. There would never come a better opportunity, and Marybeth was desperate for help. He couldn't just leave without seeing her needs met. Janey would never want him to do that.

"It is. Now I need to go see Marybeth."

He got up from the table and turned to Inga. "Would you

get George to come over first thing in the morning to Marybeth's house? She's gonna need him to handle settling her father's affairs and selling the house. I'm hoping to get us out on the late morning train, so he'll need to come early."

"You're leaving tomorrow?" Father asked. His eyes widened, as did Inga's. She remained wordless but nodded.

"I think it's for the best." Edward leaned over and gave Inga a hug. "Pray for us."

"I will," she said, holding him tightly. "And I'll tell George."

Edward let her go and moved over to his father, who had already gotten to his feet. "I don't know what to say, son."

"Just say you'll pray for me."

"I will do that." They embraced, and Edward tried not to think about how it might be the last time he'd see the older man. There had been too much loss already. He pulled away and smiled. "Horses are needed in Cheyenne same as here. You all might find yourselves wanting to relocate."

"It is a thought," Inga said. "I know George has spoken of it before."

Edward smiled. "See there." He looked at his father. "They say there's land enough for everyone. Thousands of acres available. Imagine what you could do with that kind of range."

"It is tempting," his father said, smiling. "But I think I'll wait and hear what you have to say about it. Might be the winters are worse and land dryer. Go live on it awhile and then tell me how great it is."

Edward nodded and headed for the door. He paused only long enough to take up the uneaten portion of his cake. "This is mighty good, sis. I'll tell Marybeth to be sure and bring your cake with us on the train west."

He was grateful that Inga didn't break into tears. Thankful, too, that his father had been so pleasant about it all. He could see the worry in his eyes, but the fact that he kept most of it to himself was a credit to the older man. Pa knew it wouldn't change Edward's mind, so why speak about it until they were fighting over the matter?

On his way to Marybeth's, Edward stopped by the cemetery. It was the last thing he needed to do before seeing Marybeth. He tied his horse off and made his way across the drifted snow. The wind had blown over any sign of those who had attended the graveside services two days before.

Edward bent down and brushed snow from the headstone he'd arranged for his wife and son. For a few moments, he stared down at the writing: *Jane Vogel and Son*. He supposed he should have given the boy a name. Maybe God had one for him.

"I'm leaving Independence, Janey." Edward gazed across the headstone to the rows of stones that marked other graves. "I'm sorry to have to leave you both behind, but Major Henderson has called for me to join him in Cheyenne."

The sun's brilliance offered no real warmth. The air was still plenty cold, and Edward stomped his feet in the snow to keep some semblance of warmth.

"I'm gonna marry Marybeth Kruger. It's just to take care of her and her sister. I know it's what you'd want me to do, and I promised you I'd marry again. Of course, if folks in heaven know everything about what's going on down here on earth—and I don't know that they do, but if so—then you know it's just a marriage in name. I just can't risk losing her like I lost you. I know you understand, and I won't explain again. Still, sometimes I can't help but wonder if my survivin' the war came at the price of losing you. I know Pa said God doesn't work that way, but I can't help but think I should have been the one to die."

Edward blew warm breath against his gloved fingers. "I guess that doesn't much matter now. Marybeth and Carrie need me. I suppose in my way I need them too. They've been seein' me through the bad times—the lonely times. Klaus did too, but now he's gone. You've probably already welcomed him up yonder." Edward shoved his hands in his coat pockets.

"I just wanted to come by and let you know. I know it sounds silly. You aren't here. I get that. You and the boy have a heavenly home that's better than anything I could have given you, but . . . well, just know that I miss you. Him too."

There was an aching emptiness in Edward's arms. He longed to hold his family close and feel their warmth—have their lives go on. He frowned and turned back to his horse. There was nothing more to be said, and he suddenly felt rather silly standing out there freezing to death and talking to a grave when he needed to be speaking to Marybeth.

Marybeth was anxious to see Edward again. She feared he might have changed his mind. Maybe upon reflection he realized how ridiculous it was to just up and marry his wife's best friend so that he could take them hundreds of miles west to start a new life.

"Oh, Lord, please don't let him have changed his mind."

Pastor Orton had already been by the house earlier. He had knocked on the door for nearly ten minutes, but Marybeth had pretended they weren't home. Carrie was sound asleep in the back room and didn't so much as whimper as Marybeth sat beside her bed praying the man would leave them alone. When everything went silent, Marybeth breathed a sigh of relief and thanked God that the man had gone on his way.

Then she began to pray in earnest that Edward would come and assure her that he intended them to marry.

After praying about the marriage, Marybeth had had a peace about it that she really couldn't understand. She kept waiting for there to be a nudge or uneasy feeling, but the more she considered what she was about to do, the more it seemed right.

They would marry as friends, determined to care for each other's needs. If something more grew out of the arrangement, then it would come because God ordained it. They weren't lying to each other or to anyone else. They would love and honor each other in sickness and health, for richer or poorer, and remain true to one another. That was something Marybeth knew she could do without hesitation, and she felt confident Edward could manage it as well.

When Edward showed up an hour later, Marybeth stood ready and able to give him an answer.

"I will marry you. I will be true to you and love and honor you until my death." She smiled, and he did as well.

"Let's go see the justice of the peace in Evansville right now. I told him we might be coming," Edward said, glancing around. "Where's Carrie?"

"She's next door. I asked Mrs. Parker to keep an eye on her and not let anyone know she was there. I needed to pick up a few things in town after I talked to you. I guess I hadn't expected that we'd marry today, but it suits me just fine."

"I let my family know," he replied and reached for Marybeth's coat where it hung by the door. "George is gonna stop by in the morning to set things up for you with the house."

"When do you think we'll leave?"

"Tomorrow, late morning. I've checked on the train schedules. It's perfect."

Marybeth nodded, but instead of coming directly to him she went to the fireplace and took down a tin box. She opened it and revealed a stack of bills and coinage.

"I want to give you this money Pa saved. It's nearly a hundred dollars and will help on our trip. I just ask that you also take this drawing I made of Carrie's feet and get her a pair of boots for the trip. She's almost outgrown all of her shoes, and a pair of lace-up boots would be good and sturdy."

"Keep it, and we'll stop to shop after we marry. I trust you with the money, Marybeth. You've never been the type to be frivolous. Keep your pa's money. We'll need it soon enough."

She took out some of the larger bills and folded them with the drawing. "I'll take this along, then." She put the lid back on the tin and set it up on the mantel. "And you said George will come by tomorrow?"

"Yes, he'll figure out what is needed to help you with the house. Do you want to rent it out or sell it?"

"Selling it makes sense. We can use the money to buy another place in Cheyenne. I know you and Janey were renting, so if you prefer that, it's all right."

"I figure we'll probably have to rent at first, but Major Henderson said that a piece of land comes with my job. I have some money saved, and maybe in the spring we can save up enough and build on it."

"Maybe George can have this place sold by then, and we can use that money as well."

Edward nodded. "Maybe we can."

Marybeth smiled. "It would seem God is providing for all of our needs."

"It would seem."

He helped her with her coat. "Have you heard any more from the pastor?"

"He came by earlier. I saw him open our front gate, and I hurried to the back room where Carrie was napping. I hid in there while he knocked on the front door. Thankfully Carrie slept through it."

Edward frowned. "I don't like that you felt you needed to hide. I don't like that at all. A woman ought to feel safe in her own home. He needs to know this is out of his hands now. First chance I get, I'll go talk to him."

Marybeth did up her coat buttons and grabbed her hat and scarf. "I would appreciate that very much. He frightens me. I know I shouldn't let him, but I can't help it. Carrie's all I have left."

"No, you have me now. You'll have me for the rest of our lives." He paused, and his expression softened. "I promise I'll take good care of you both. I've loved you both for a long time, and that won't change. I know it's not what you deserve, Marybeth, but I'll work hard to try to make you happy with what I can give you. Just don't ask me for what I can't give."

Marybeth swallowed the growing lump in her throat. If they didn't get a move on, she very well might start crying. She nodded. "I won't. I promise."

The ceremony was short and simple. There were no flowers. No well-wishers except for two rather stodgy-looking men who worked with the justice. There was really nothing at all that suggested they were participating in a wedding rather than a court case.

Marybeth tried not to let it make her sad. She, like most girls, had dreamed of her wedding day, and this was nothing like that.

Once the judge finished, they signed the papers, and Edward took their copy of the marriage certificate and folded it up.

"Let's get the shopping done and then head home," he said as he carefully tucked the paper into his inside pocket.

Marybeth nodded and took hold of his arm. "Then what?"

He glanced at her for only a moment, then fixed his gaze straight ahead. "We go to our houses and pack. Take what's important for setting up our household. I'll come with the wagon in the morning and bring a couple of empty wooden crates. We can't take much in the way of furniture, but we'll try to take what we can. Hopefully we can buy stuff in Cheyenne."

"I want to take Carrie's feeding chair. Can we manage that?"

"We will," Edward replied. "We'll do whatever we have to do to make this work."

Whether he was talking about the chair or their situation, Marybeth wasn't sure.

4

Marybeth woke well before dawn to finish her packing. She had already managed to put together a stack of household goods that she felt were important to bring. Then there were a few things that she hoped to never be parted from: her mother's favorite dishes, a couple of quilts her mother had made, as well as one Marybeth had made for Carrie.

There had been so much food left over from people bringing it after her father had died that Marybeth urged the neighbors to come and get what they wanted after she packed a basket with items for the trip. They were happy to oblige. None of the folks around her were very well-off, and the extra was much appreciated. Once the food was cleared out, Marybeth washed and dried all the dishes. She would arrange with George to get them to Inga, who could then see that they got back to the women in the church.

After breakfast, Mrs. Parker's oldest girl had come to get Carrie. They had arranged for her to play next door while Marybeth did her final packing. It seemed there was still so much to do and so little time. Thankfully, she had done up all of the laundry the day before the funeral. It had kept her too busy to think about burying her father and now freed her up from a lot of last-minute washing.

She folded up the last of Carrie's clothes and put them in a small leather suitcase. She would keep this with her on their trip. It contained all that Carrie would need, including some warmer clothes they'd purchased along with the new shoes.

After this was done, Marybeth assessed the stacks of things in the living room. She had towels, washcloths, and linens for the bed—things that they would need for their new home. With those, she added two cast-iron skillets, a large soup pot, and two smaller pots, along with various kitchen utensils. She had done her best to keep things to a minimum and pack things inside of other things so as to take less space, but it was imperative they have the things that would help them establish comfort in their new home.

Last night she had repacked her sewing basket to include everything she thought she might need in order to mend and make clothes. In a second basket, she gathered bandages, ointments, and other items that would be useful when someone came down sick. She supposed there would be such things in Cheyenne but couldn't be sure. Cheyenne was in the wild frontier, and even with the train now reaching them, supplies might be very limited.

She knew they would have to pay extra for each piece of freight and wanted so much to pack only what was absolutely necessary. Especially since she had no idea of what Edward would be bringing along.

When a knock sounded at the front door, Marybeth figured it would be Edward and went to open it without worry. Instead, she found Pastor Orton with Thomas and Martha Wandless. But this time, rather than be afraid, Marybeth smiled.

"Good morning." She glanced at each person.

"Please forgive the early hour, but I worried that we might not catch you. I stopped by yesterday, and you were apparently gone. We've come to talk to you about Carrie. May we come in?" Pastor Orton asked.

"You may, but I haven't long to discuss any matter. I'm leaving soon."

"This needn't take long."

Marybeth stepped back from the open door and allowed the trio to enter. When everyone was inside, Marybeth closed the door and joined them. They all seemed quite interested in her stacks of goods.

"What's going on here?"

Before Marybeth could answer the pastor, the door behind her opened, and Edward entered the house. His action surprised her. Usually, he knocked and waited to be invited in, but this time he just walked in as though he owned the place. Marybeth smiled. She supposed he did, now that they were married.

"Pastor, Mr. and Mrs. Wandless." He gave each a nod. "I figured to stop by your place. What brings you around so early?"

"I was just telling Marybeth that we didn't want to miss seeing her as we did yesterday," the pastor replied. He frowned slightly. "Are you accustomed to just walking in unannounced?"

"I wasn't, but yesterday Marybeth and I got married."

Marybeth went to Edward's side and looked back at the pastor. "We did."

Edward seemed to anticipate that the older man might not quite believe him and pulled out the marriage certificate. "You can see it for yourself."

The pastor took the paper and read it. "I must say I'm quite surprised."

"Well, sometimes God has plans that surprise all of us," Edward said, taking back the paper.

"I suppose I'm glad that you're here, since we've come to persuade Marybeth to allow Mr. and Mrs. Wandless to adopt her sister, Carrie."

Marybeth tensed, but Edward gently took hold of her arm. "I'm sorry, folks, but Marybeth and I have no intention of giving Carrie up. She's a part of our family."

The pastor cleared his throat. "Now, see here, you two are just getting started and will no doubt have a family of your own. But Carrie needs a family too. Mr. and Mrs. Wandless are the perfect couple to raise her. They can offer her every comfort."

"But that isn't necessary," Edward replied.

"Adoption is a wonderful thing," Marybeth added. "I'm sure the orphanage in Evansville has other children in need of homes. Carrie, however, isn't in need. She has a home and is much loved. I'm sorry, but the answer is no. I will not give up my sister."

Mrs. Wandless looked to her husband and then to the pastor. "I thought you said that she wanted a better life for her sister." Tears formed in her eyes.

"We have intruded where we should not have come. Pastor Orton, I will speak to you about this later," Mr. Wandless said, taking hold of his wife. "Come, dear."

"Wait. I'm sure we can make some sort of arrangement," the pastor called out.

Mr. and Mrs. Wandless didn't even look back. They headed for the front door as Mr. Wandless handed his wife his handkerchief.

Marybeth caught up to them. "I'll pray for you," she murmured as they exited the house. Pastor Orton was to blame for all of this, after all. It wasn't the fault of two people who longed for a child. They were misled by the pastor, plain and simple.

"You two are not seeing reason. That poor couple is most desperate for a child, and you have denied them that dream. You should be ashamed," Pastor Orton began.

Edward shook his head. "And you were bargaining with something that didn't belong to you. I don't know what you stood to get out of the entire arrangement, but you're the one who should be ashamed."

The man sputtered as he struggled to reply. "I . . . well . . . you have . . ." He stopped and shook his head. "I only wanted to help Marybeth and Carrie in their time of need."

"And perhaps Mr. Wandless in turn would help you build that new church you've been dreaming of?" Edward asked.

Marybeth was surprised by that. She'd never considered that Pastor Orton might have an ulterior motive.

"If Mr. Wandless chose to show his appreciation in such a fashion, there would have been nothing wrong with that." The pastor shook his head again. "You were wrong to marry, and you know it. It's the reason you didn't come to me for the job. You knew I would remember our conversation of just a few weeks back when you told me you'd never marry again because you could never love again. I know you didn't marry for the right reasons." He looked at Marybeth. "I presume you talked him into this so that you could selfishly keep your sister. God doesn't honor such things. You've brought a curse upon yourself."

Marybeth felt a tingle go up her spine. Had she done that?

"You preached not long ago that Jesus became a curse for us so that we need never come under such things," Edward interjected. "You said that if we belonged to Him, we needn't fear curses."

"I did," the pastor replied, "but it's clear that you don't belong to Him."

"And how do you figure that? I gave my heart to Jesus some years ago. Marybeth did too. Who are you to judge us?"

"I'm your pastor, and I have that right."

Marybeth could feel Edward tensing. She longed to put an end to the situation and gave Edward's arm a pat. "We don't have too long before we need to catch our train. Did you bring the crates?"

"George is on his way with them and my things." Edward seemed to calm. "Pastor, we need to bid you farewell. Marybeth is right. We have a train to catch soon."

Edward opened the front door again. "In fact, George has just come."

"You two didn't marry for the right reasons," the pastor repeated as he followed Edward to the door. "God won't honor that. You're living in sin."

Marybeth felt overwhelmed by the things he was saying. She'd never seen Pastor Orton act in such a manner. Was this truly all about money and a new church? She had once held such respect for the man, but now he was like a stranger to her.

Pastor Orton headed down the walk in a huff. He didn't even bother to acknowledge George Weber as he passed him on the way.

George glanced over his shoulder as he reached the front door. "What's with him?"

"I'll tell you inside," Edward replied. "Let's go get those crates so we can finish packing."

The men worked together to bring in two rather long wooden boxes. Marybeth was relieved to see their size. With the small boxes she already had, there would be plenty of room for all she needed to take.

"So what's wrong?" George asked as they set the last box down.

"Pastor wanted to force Marybeth to give up Carrie to Mr. and Mrs. Wandless. I'd heard something that suggested Wandless was going to provide the money for a new church. I'm thinking this was part of the deal. Pastor Orton didn't admit it, but it seems likely."

George gave Marybeth a sympathetic smile. "Sorry he would put you through all that."

"Now he tells us we're cursed and living in sin," Edward added before Marybeth could speak. "The man is obviously upset over something more than Carrie."

"It sounds like you're probably on the right track thinking that he's losing out on something. He's been trying to talk the wealthier congregants into building a new church for a long time. He probably saw Marybeth's situation with her sister and figured that would be the way to secure Mr. Wandless."

Marybeth went to the first of the wooden crates and pulled off the lid. "Did you bring nails to secure this after I pack it?"

"I did," George said, pulling a handful from his pocket. "I figured you'd have a hammer."

"I do." Marybeth picked up a stack of newspapers. "After I line the box, I'll fetch it."

"I know where it's at, Marybeth," Edward said. "You go ahead with what you're doing."

George went to help her by picking up a smaller box. "This is heavy. What's in it?"

"My mother's dishes. They're breakable, so I wrapped them in dish towels and put them in that box, hoping the shipping crates would be big enough to hold it. I figure we can pad the smaller box inside with towels and rag rugs."

"That sounds good. Once you get the paper down, let's

put one of the rugs down. We can spread it out in such a way to cushion everything."

They were just getting to the rug when Edward returned with the hammer. "Might as well take the hammer too. Can't have too many tools."

"Papa's tools are mostly in the shed out back. If you want to go through them and take what you think we'll need, that would be wonderful. I had forgotten all about them."

"I've got a bunch of my own but let me go see. George, did you bring the papers you need Marybeth to sign?"

"I did. Marybeth, these papers will basically give me the power to handle the house and your father's estate. Is that what you want?"

"Yes." She glanced up and smiled. "It will be a great relief to know you're taking care of everything."

"And what is it you want me to do exactly?"

"Sell everything. I'm taking what's important to me and Carrie. We've got some things from each of our mothers, as well as everyday things I figure we'll need, but the rest can be sold. All the furniture and what tools Edward doesn't want, as well as whatever else I've left. If you see something you want, George, feel free to take it as well."

"Not without paying you for it. I'll hold an auction and sell stuff that way. Then I'll put the house up for sale. I think it will sell fast. Your father kept it in good shape."

"Yes, but some folks are still hurting for money after the war. It's only been two years, and it's not been easy on anybody, even in the North, and we're situated right on the edge of the South. Seems like folks around here suffered more loss than some."

"There was plenty of misery to go around, but things are improving."

Marybeth nodded. "I hope it will sell fast, because we'll need the money to build our own place, but if not, perhaps you could arrange for it to be rented out."

"I'll do my best for you." George placed the box of dishes in the cushioned spot they'd made. "This should keep it pretty safe. We'll have them mark it fragile at the station. Hopefully that will keep any zealous handlers from tossing it about."

It wasn't long before Edward returned with a dozen or so tools. "I'll put these out in my crate with the other tools."

"Oh, I almost forgot. I know Pa would have wanted you to have this." Marybeth hurried into her father's bedroom and returned with a rifle and ammunition. She handed it over to Edward. "I'm sure there's room to pack it."

Edward looked the rifle over and nodded. "I'd be honored to have this to remember your father by." He tucked it into a fold of blankets, then added the ammunition. "I'm sure we'll be glad to have it. Did he teach you to shoot, Marybeth?"

She smiled. "He did. He worried that the war might come this far north, and I might need to protect Carrie and myself. I don't do too bad if I do say so."

George chuckled. "Well, from what I hear you'll need such skills where you're going."

Marybeth frowned. "I know it's awfully wild out west, but I hope I won't have to rely on my shooting."

"We'll rely on God," Edward reminded her.

"Of course you will," George declared, taking up the last of the pillows. "Let's get these in there."

"Oh, wait, I still have the coffee- and teapots." Marybeth hurried to the kitchen and came back with the items. Edward took them and tucked them into the box.

"That all?" he asked.

"Except for what we'll carry with us"—she turned to observe every corner of the room—"it's all in the crates."

Edward helped George secure the lids and nailed them shut. Marybeth watched with a sense of finality. It was almost as if they were nailing closed a coffin.

"That just leaves our bags," Marybeth said, glancing around the room again. This was the last time she would be here—the only home she'd ever known. She gave a heavy sigh. "I should go get Carrie while you two load the wagon."

"See if that neighbor of yours can come and stand as a second witness for the signing of the papers," George said as Marybeth pulled on her coat.

Marybeth nodded and hurried next door. She had never been outside of Independence and Evansville in all of her life. Now she was about to leave all she knew for a vast open world that still had Indian wars. What would become of them all?

Father, please don't let this be a mistake.

Edward and Mrs. Parker witnessed Marybeth signing the papers, then George had him sign a separate set just to cover any legalities with him as Marybeth's husband. When George was completely satisfied, they headed to the train station in Evansville.

Carrie bounced up and down on Marybeth's lap as they entered the busiest part of the city. She was excited about all that she saw.

"Lookie. Lookie," Carrie declared over and over. The night before she'd done that with her new boots.

Marybeth laughed at her sister's antics, and Edward found himself doing the same. Carrie was good for the soul. She delighted in so many things. Hopefully she would help Edward and Marybeth keep their sense of wonder and humor during what were certain to be hard days ahead.

A brief wave of guilt washed over him. Was he doing the right thing, taking them west? Their life in Cheyenne was going to be so much harder than what Marybeth had known here in Independence. She'd never even experienced anything outside of her little circle. He'd gone to war and had seen the horrific grief it caused. He had experienced such things that he prayed she'd never know, and yet with the Indians still quite active in the west, wild animals running amok, and other dangers, he might be taking Marybeth and Carrie to their deaths.

He glanced back at the boxes they'd packed. He had to admire Marybeth for her frugal choices. They had talked about the need to choose wisely, and she had. She had given up so much for him. He would find a way to make it up to her. He'd see they built a house as soon as possible. Of course, the money would probably come from the sale of her father's house, but Edward had a nice nest egg to add to hers. And he would work hard to raise whatever money they needed to see the job done. Even if he took on an extra job or two.

Only momentarily did his thoughts go back to what the pastor had said about them being cursed and living in sin. There was no truth to that. Edward was confident that they had done the right thing. He was certain this was what God wanted for them.

Wasn't he?

He lowered his head to ward off the wind and whispered a prayer. It just had to be the right thing.

Please, God, don't let me have just made things worse.

George brought the wagon to a stop near the baggage and

freight platform at the train depot. He jumped down and immediately hailed a couple of men.

Edward looked to Marybeth. "Why don't you and Carrie wait inside the depot? George and I will get this taken care of."

She nodded. "Will you bring the bags when you come, or should I try to take them?"

"George and I can bring them. Just get inside and get warm."

He took Carrie from her arms, then helped her down from the wagon. Carrie was still quite excited about all that was happening. She bobbed up and down trying to see everything at once. The brim of her woolen bonnet knocked against Edward's left eye.

"You're wilder than a bag full of cats." Edward kissed her nose. "I can tell you're going to love going on the train."

"Train!" Carrie repeated and clapped her mittened hands. "Go, go, train."

Edward laughed in spite of his concerns. "Yes, we're going to go, go, train."

Marybeth took her sister in hand. "Let's go inside, Carrie. We'll get warm and wait for . . ." She looked at Edward. "We haven't talked about what she should call you, but I suppose it should be Papa."

Edward felt a tightening in his chest for just a moment. "We can figure that out later. Go on before you freeze."

Marybeth met his eyes and nodded. She understood. She was so compassionate, and he felt overwhelming gratitude for that. One way or another, he was going to see that this worked for all of them. He owed her that.

5

By the time they arrived in Omaha, they had changed trains three times and wrestled Carrie for miles on end. As they disembarked from the train, Edward carried the bags, and Marybeth held her sleeping sister. It was just past suppertime, and Marybeth felt famished.

"Do you suppose we could get something to eat?" she asked, shifting Carrie to her right shoulder.

"That was my thought. First, though, let's see about a room. Then I can leave off our bags, and maybe you and Carrie could wait there while I find something for us to eat."

"I'd like that," Marybeth said. "I don't know whether I'm hungrier than I am tired or the other way around, but I would love to be able to put Carrie in a bed."

"I understand. She has been a handful. I never knew a little girl could have so much energy."

Marybeth gave Edward a smile. "You handled her perfectly. I've never known anyone but Pa to have such patience with her."

As they exited the train depot, Edward looked up one side of the street and down the other. "Looks like there's a hotel that way. Let's stop and see if they have any rooms. Seems like a nice place—at least on the outside."

Marybeth nodded and followed him to the three-story building. She gave a silent prayer for provision. The last thing they needed was to be traipsing around Omaha looking for a place to stay.

The wind picked up as Edward opened the hotel door and ushered Marybeth inside. She sighed in relief at the warmth that washed over her. Thankfully, Carrie didn't even stir.

"Evenin' folks. Lookin' for a room?" a balding man asked from behind the reception desk.

"We are," Edward replied, putting the luggage down.

"You're in luck. I have just one room left. That'll be two dollars. Just sign here." The man turned the registry book around and handed Edward a pen.

Edward signed the book and paid for the room while Marybeth did her best to stay on her feet, holding Carrie. She hadn't realized just how very tired she was. The train had been noisy and exhausting. Dirty too. It was hard to keep Carrie clean since she wanted to crawl around on the floor and explore under the seats.

"It's on the second floor at the end of the hall," the proprietor told Edward as he handed him a key. "Room number is on the key, and the bathroom is just next door."

"Is there somewhere I can get some decent food and bring it back here to the hotel?" Edward asked. "My . . . wife and daughter are exhausted."

"We have a dining room here. I can arrange that for you if you like and have it sent up," the man replied. "Get you big beef sandwiches and some of the best apple pie you'll ever sink your teeth into. Maybe some milk for the little one."

Edward looked to Marybeth. She nodded. Anything sounded

good at this point. Edward paid the man for the food and took up the bags once again. He led the way upstairs, and Marybeth followed. Carrie felt ten pounds heavier than she had just moments before. It would be so good to be able to put her to bed and relax.

They reached the room and made their way inside. It was quite nice. The full-sized bed was framed with a wooden head and footboard. The mattress looked thick, and there was a nice quilt atop it with two additional blankets folded across the foot of the bed. Two dollars had seemed an outrageous price, but the accommodations were better than expected.

"Those pillows look comfortable," Edward said, pointing to the head.

"I thought the entire room looked amazing." She placed the still-sleeping Carrie on the side of the bed farthest from the door, then began to unbutton her coat.

"She's completely done in," Marybeth said as she moved down to untie Carrie's bootlaces. "I hope she'll sleep through the night."

"Won't she need something to eat?"

"No, remember you got her that glass of milk earlier? She drank it all and ate the last pieces of cheese and bread. I'm sure she'll be fine. I wish we could both have a bath, but I'll wash her up in the morning."

Marybeth set Carrie's boots aside and slipped her out of the coat. She went to one of the bags Edward had lugged upstairs and opened it. After retrieving Carrie's nightgown, Marybeth grabbed a large piece of waxed canvas and a thick towel.

"I'm completely done in as well. Who would have thought sitting on a train would wear a person out?"

"It wasn't the train. It was the little girl who wanted to

be everywhere at once on the train," Edward said, smiling. He glanced around the room. "This should suit the two of you well. I'll wait until the food comes and then see about finding another place to sleep."

"No!" Marybeth hadn't meant to reply quite so loudly, nor in such a desperate tone. "Please don't go," she said more calmly. "I would be afraid to be here alone. Can't you stay?"

He nodded. "I can stay. I just didn't know if you'd be comfortable with me here."

"You're my husband, Edward. Of course I'm comfortable having you here. I don't even mind sleeping in the same bed. After all, Carrie can be there between us."

"I can sleep on the floor. The place is clean, and with a couple of blankets, I should be just fine."

Marybeth didn't argue with him. She was just relieved that he would stay. She spread open the waxed canvas and positioned it and the towel under her sister in case she had an accident in the night.

"I didn't realize Omaha was this big," Edward said, looking out the shaded window. "I suppose all the towns along the transcontinental railroad line will have the potential for such growth."

"I suppose so," Marybeth replied. She pulled the quilt and sheet up around Carrie's shoulders. As she straightened, Marybeth couldn't help but rub her shoulders.

"Want some help with that?" Edward asked as he cast his coat aside.

"Oh . . . well . . . if you like."

He came behind Marybeth and began massaging the knots in her shoulders. Marybeth could have cried. It felt so good to have the muscles worked over. Carrying her sister around all day had really been too much.

"That feels so much better," she said with a sigh.

"You can do the same for me sometime," he replied.

"No time like the present. You're taller, though, so I'll need you to sit on the edge of the bed."

Edward hesitated, causing Marybeth to turn and gaze into his eyes. "Come on. The food will be here soon. Might as well feel better."

He didn't say a word but did as she instructed. Marybeth put her hands on either side of his neck and started there. She pretended she was kneading bread. The muscles of his neck were taut. It took quite a few minutes of rubbing and pressing her palm into them before they started to loosen up. She worked her way down his shoulders and into his upper back, feeling him relax a little more.

The knock on the hotel room door caused them both to jump. Marybeth couldn't help but giggle.

"Goodness, we're acting like children caught stealing cookies."

Edward actually smiled at this and went to the door. He opened it to find a steward with a tray.

"Your order, sir."

"Bring it in," Edward said. He glanced around the room. There was a small dresser across the room. "Just set it on top over there."

The man nodded and did exactly that. Edward dug in his pocket for something to tip the man. "Here," he said as the man headed for the door. "And thanks."

The man took the coins and smiled. "Thank you. I hope the food is enjoyable."

With that he left and closed the door behind him. Edward looked to Marybeth. "I'm sorry we don't have a table and chairs."

"I'm fine sitting on the floor." She went to the tray and looked things over. "Oh, it looks wonderful. They even sent water and a glass of milk."

"I'll get the tray. You go ahead and sit where you want." Edward picked up the food as Marybeth sank to the floor.

"This is as good a place as any." She leaned back against the wooden footboard of the bed. "I just hope I can stay awake long enough to eat." Edward positioned the tray between them and sat on the floor opposite Marybeth.

She lifted the cloth napkin. "Looks like there are two sandwiches and two pieces of apple pie. I'm sure I won't need a whole sandwich or piece of pie. You can have what I don't eat as I'm sure you'll be able to polish it off and then some."

Marybeth cut her sandwich in half. Eating in silence, she wondered if Edward was sorry yet that he'd included her and Carrie on this adventure. It would surely have been easier to travel west without them.

"Good eats," Edward declared, easily downing the roast beef and bread. He didn't balk at all when Marybeth pushed the other half of her sandwich toward him.

They said very little as they ate. Marybeth figured he had no more energy left than she did. She sampled the pie but found she was already more than full.

"I'm going to save the milk for Carrie in the morning. If you don't mind."

"I think that's wise. We'll need to catch the train early."

"What happened to our crates?" Marybeth began cleaning up as Edward dug into the pie.

"They went on to Cheyenne. I arranged for them to lock them up at the station. We'll get them the day after we arrive—or rather, later in the day. The train won't arrive in Cheyenne until around three in the morning."

"I remember you saying that. It's still impressive to imagine getting on the train in the morning and getting to Cheyenne in only twenty hours or so. That's nearly five hundred miles."

"I know. I was told it could take forty to fifty days by wagon."

"And we'll get there in mere hours. Just imagine when they'll have the entire railroad in place and you'll be able to go from one coast to the other in just a matter of weeks instead of months."

"Probably less time than that. It will be a wonder."

Marybeth suppressed a yawn. "I'm going to get ready for bed. Would you put the milk on the dresser? I think the room will be cool enough that it'll keep just fine."

"If not, I could put it on the ledge outside the window."

She shook her head and yawned again. "No, it'd freeze. It'll be okay."

After gathering her nightgown and robe, she glanced around the room trying to figure out how best to change. It dawned on her that the clerk had said the bathroom was next door.

"I'll step next door and clean up a bit . . . and change."

Edward nodded. "Keep our door open. That way I'll hear and see if anyone tries to cause you trouble."

Marybeth hadn't thought of something like that. She smiled and gave a half nod before heading out. There was so much of this arrangement they really hadn't considered.

She looked at her reflection in the mirror. Her face seemed paler than usual. Thinner too. She supposed she hadn't eaten much since Papa died. Her attention had been focused on making sure Carrie ate. People from the church as well as neighbors had brought food to the house for days, but Marybeth couldn't remember any of the meals.

Pulling the pins from her hair, she couldn't help but wonder if Edward regretted his decision. Did she?

"It was the only thing we could do," she murmured. Trying to fight off the pastor and Mr. and Mrs. Wandless by herself would have been impossible. Pastor Orton had already gotten a judge involved. They would have taken Carrie from her without delay.

She looked again to her reflection. No matter what happened, she vowed to make things as easy on Edward as possible. He was the hero in her story—hers and Carrie's. No matter what the future held, she promised herself then and there that she would do whatever she could to make certain Edward didn't regret his decision.

Edward awoke early the next morning. It wasn't even light outside, but then again, dawn came later and later as the calendar pushed toward the end of the year. He stretched, surprised at how well he felt. That massage Marybeth gave him the night before had really done the trick with his stiff neck and sore shoulders. She had a touch.

He got up and cracked the hall door open to check his pocket watch. Four forty. They had a little less than three hours before they needed to catch the train. He glanced over his shoulder and saw that Marybeth and Carrie were still sleeping. He opened the door a little wider to let more light filter in. Carrie had snuggled into Marybeth's arms, and they'd pulled the quilt tightly around themselves. Marybeth's blond hair mingled with Carrie's, making it almost impossible to tell where one left off and the other began.

For a long time, Edward just stood watching them. He'd used to watch Janey that way. She seemed so angelic in sleep.

He'd told himself when she was laid out for the funeral that she was just sleeping. Nothing more. It was the only way he could keep from rushing to the front of the church to take her into his arms as people paid their respects.

Memories flooded his mind. Janey sleeping late because he'd failed to wake her up. Her chiding him for it because she had things that needed to be done. Usually, it was laundry or baking. Janey always made the very best bread. Marybeth's bread was just as good. He couldn't help smiling. The girls once had a contest baking pies to see who should enter their pie into the county fair's judging. Edward and his father, along with Marybeth's pa, had been the judges. They'd sampled each pie, then told the girls they'd have to sample them again. They put away four pieces of pie each before admitting that both were equally delicious, and they couldn't pick just one. The girls gave them such a hard time. That year at the fair Marybeth and Janey tied for first place, vindicating the men's inability to decide.

Edward nearly laughed out loud, and when he looked at Marybeth again, he saw that she was awake and watching him.

"Good morning. You look mighty happy for a man who spent the night on the floor," she said as Carrie began to stir. "Would you light the lamp?"

"I was just remembering that time you and Janey had us judge your pies before you entered them at the fair." He went to the bedside table and found the matches. He lit the lamp and turned the wick up.

Marybeth chuckled. "That was something else. They'd never had a tie at the fair, but the head judge told me they had never had two pies taste equally delicious right down to the flaky crust." She pushed back the quilt and sheet and sat up.

Her straight blond hair splayed out around her shoulders and down her back. Edward imagined it feeling like corn silk. She rose and took up her robe. Only then was Edward aware of her state of undress. He turned rather quickly on his heel to close the door.

"Sorry. I wasn't thinking."

"I'm completely covered. No need to worry," she replied.

Edward peeked over his shoulder and saw that she was wrapped in the robe. Carrie rose up on her knees and held up her arms. "I wet."

Marybeth nodded. "I figured you might have trouble since we didn't take you to the bathroom before bed last night. Thankfully, I made provisions. Hopefully the top sheet isn't too bad. Come along. We'll get you cleaned up."

"I'll take care of the bed," Edward said, figuring he should do his part.

"I'll take the mat and towel with me. You might check and see if she got anything else wet." Marybeth gathered all the things she'd need and headed with Carrie to the door. "How much time before we catch the train?"

"Just under three hours."

She beamed a smile. "Plenty of time to take care of everything."

He marveled at her serenity and ease of managing the situation. She really was quite special. Janey had always said that Marybeth's calm in the face of a storm or bad time was inspiring. He supposed he'd seen some of that over the years. Now, however, it seemed far more personal and evident. He'd just taken her away from all the comforts of her home and still she awoke with a smile and kind word. She was quite the woman.

6

Marybeth didn't know what she'd really expected of Cheyenne, but arriving in the wee hours of the morning and finding it still very active took her by surprise. Gambling and dance halls, saloons, and brothels were open, and what looked to be hundreds of people still milled the streets.

On the train from Omaha, Edward had spoken with an older gentleman who sat just across the aisle. He was involved in the town planning for Cheyenne and told Edward that he would be glad when the railroad moved down the tracks to build elsewhere and left Cheyenne behind.

"We want a nice town with good people like yourself and your family," he had said, smiling at Marybeth and Carrie. "Right now, you'd think it was something from the pits of hell itself, but I hope that won't keep you from considering its future."

His description continued as he spoke of railroad men so rough and crude that they'd make sailors blush with their language and comments. It seemed the main focus of Cheyenne as a town was vice, and the godlier folks were determined to rid themselves of it as soon as possible.

"The hotel is just a block over on Sixteenth," Edward told her. "Let's get a move on so we don't find ourselves mixing with the wrong folks."

Marybeth nodded and stuck close to his side. Carrie, thankfully, slept through the ruckus. She had stirred several times, but her day of climbing up and down the seats and running the aisles when given a chance left her once again exhausted. Marybeth could only hope she might sleep well into the morning.

At the hotel, she changed Carrie into nightclothes and put her to bed. The room was quite small, but at least it was private. Edward told her most of the clientele slept in a communal room with as many as thirty men stretched out from wall to wall. They shared one common bathroom with brushes, combs, and razors shared as well. There were only five private rooms in the entire hotel, and they rented for much higher than the communal room. The small bathroom they shared with the four other rooms on the first floor wasn't much, but it was clean. Marybeth could only imagine the filth of the community bathroom upstairs.

There wasn't much space for Edward to stretch out on the floor so when Marybeth suggested he share the rather large full-sized bed, he agreed. The bed had been pushed up against the wall, so Marybeth took her place there, and Edward moved Carrie into the middle of the bed between them. He blew out the single candle they'd been given for light and eased into the bed in the dark.

Marybeth felt the bed dip down as Edward added his weight. She hadn't been at all uncomfortable having him with her in the room, but having him in her bed, even with

Carrie there, caused her some unexpected concern. What if they all ended up huddled together in the middle? Being together that way might become all too personal. As it was, Marybeth hadn't changed out of her clothes, and she didn't figure Edward had either. They really should have thought the practicalities through more thoroughly before striking out on their adventure.

Marybeth thought of their situation for a long time after Edward began the deep breathing of sleep. Things had moved so fast that she really hadn't had time to consider everything, but here she was hundreds of miles from home, living in a town that was known for being dangerous and foul, married to a man who didn't love her as a wife.

She glanced to the side in the dark. She couldn't see him but knew that Edward was there. She could hear him breathing . . . could feel his warmth. It was nice to have the latter, as the room was quite chilly.

What is going to happen to us, Lord?

She had prayed off and on throughout the trip, but this was the first time she had really worried about their outcome. In a town like this, the dangers were bound to be high. How could she keep Carrie from harm when it sounded like it was all around them? What would she do if something happened to Edward?

When she woke up hours later, Marybeth sat up with a start. Carrie was still asleep, but Edward was gone. Knowing him, he probably felt the need to find his friend and let him know they'd arrived. She eased out of the bed and looked around the room. It was then that she noticed there weren't any windows, and the room was more like a large pantry or washroom than a bedroom.

She dressed quickly, sorry that her preparations for the

day couldn't include a bath. She wondered when that luxury might be hers again. She took the pitcher and went to the bathroom, happy to see that it was deserted. There was a small copper tub and a stove with a large reservoir of water. Hot water. She could have cried at the sight.

Marybeth filled the pitcher and took up a washcloth and towel and hurriedly returned to their room. Carrie slept on. Marybeth used the time to clean up and arrange her hair. By the time she'd secured the last pin, Carrie was awake and asking to go to the bathroom.

"You did so good not to wet the bed," Marybeth said, taking her sister by the hand. "You're a big girl!"

"I big girl," Carrie repeated proudly.

Once Carrie had relieved herself and Marybeth had been able to clean her up and ready her for the day, the little one started complaining of hunger.

"Pease wanna eat," she said, looking to Marybeth hopefully.

"I do too, but I'm afraid we have nothing here. I think we'll have to go find a grocer and buy some food."

"Buy food," Carrie said, clapping and dancing around. "Buy food."

Marybeth laughed and grabbed her sister's coat. She helped Carrie into it and did up the buttons. After that, she found Carrie's discarded bonnet and snugged it onto her head. It was almost too small. It seemed the child was growing every day.

When she went for her own coat, Marybeth found a note left to her by Edward. "'Went to find the major. Be back soon. Edward,'" she read aloud. She looked at Carrie. "Well, that explains where Edward went."

"We go now." Carrie went to the door and tried to open it. Thankfully, she was too little to grip the handle.

Marybeth tucked the note into her coat pocket and went to her sister. "You must hold my hand. It's dangerous outside."

Carrie did as she was told but seemed completely oblivious to what Marybeth had said. It wasn't likely she understood, but Marybeth knew she would have to get it across to her in time. Carrie needed to stick close to Edward or Marybeth, especially with all the rough characters the man on the train had described as regular citizens of Cheyenne.

Retracing her steps from the earlier hours, Marybeth found the clerk at the front desk. "I need to locate a store where I can buy a few cans of milk for my . . . ah . . . a few cans of milk—maybe some bread and cheese."

The bearded man smiled. "Of course. Armstrongs' is just a short walk away. Go out the door and turn left. Follow the street up a block. It doesn't look like much from the outside, but they have a good selection."

Marybeth nodded. "Thank you so much."

"You might want to wait for your husband, missus. Just to be safe."

"I'm afraid I don't know how long he'll be and my . . . the baby is hungry." She and Edward still hadn't talked much about how they were going to present Carrie. Was she going to just be their daughter, or were they going to make an effort to explain the past?

"You'll wanna keep an eye out for trouble," the man told her. "Most of the really bad characters have gone to bed and won't be on the streets to bother you, and the railroad men have reported to work, but there might still be some troublemakers."

"Thanks. I'll keep my eyes open." Marybeth lifted Carrie in her arms and headed for the door. "Thank you again."

She stepped outside into her new world and paused to take

it all in. Dirt streets edged with some boardwalks. Unpainted, newly built businesses alongside tents that advertised every- thing from palm reading to hot baths lined the way.

Freighters were out moving supplies from the train sta- tion to various locations, and people began to appear from various shops. Marybeth glanced at Carrie, who had grown quite wiggly.

"Are you excited?"

Carrie clapped her hands. "'Cited."

Marybeth nodded. "Me too."

Edward had little trouble locating the jail. The two-story building was brand-new, and inside he found his old com- mander finishing with some paperwork.

"Major Henderson."

The man looked up and smiled. "Edward Vogel, as I live and breathe. You're a welcome sight."

"Glad to be here, Major."

"No, no. Call me Fred. The war is over, and I'd just as soon put that part of my life to rest."

"Fred it is."

Henderson pointed to his ledger. "There were seventy fights to break up last night. Seventy. I try to keep a record of each one, but it's impossible. There were burglaries and murderous threats, and even a killing that everyone swears was self-defense, so nothing further will be done."

"No law west of the Mississippi, eh?" Edward looked around the room. "It's not at all what I expected."

"Cells are behind us, and court is upstairs. Ed Melanger was elected city marshal, and the police magistrate is an old frontiersman named John Slaughter whom most of us just call Judge. We hope to have a city police force of at least a dozen by next year. You and I will be a part of that."

"And that's the law in Cheyenne?" Edward asked.

"That and about seventy men—maybe more, seems the number grows daily—of a special police force who like to take matters into their own hands."

"Vigilantes?" Edward met Henderson's rather blank expression.

"Call them what you will. They're local businessmen and citizens who are striving to clean up Cheyenne. It's been troublesome at times, but it is saving the city a lot of money in dealing out justice swiftly and to the point. Sometimes the vigilantes drop off miscreants to be dealt with here at the jail. There's always a detailed list of each man's crime. We collect the fines and turn them loose or lock them in chains and turn them over to the army for manual labor."

"What about hangings? I've heard vigilantes in the West are notorious for that."

"They are." Henderson heaved a sigh. "However, for hanging offenses we've always had multiple witnesses, sometimes entire crowds, who've given sworn testimony in each case. Like I said, it's saved the town a lot of money not to have to hold court and trials. I've been informed to look the other way and see the vigilantes as a useful group who are on the same side."

"I don't know how I feel about that," Edward replied. He shook his head. "Seems a town ought to be run by the book."

"Except for one thing, Edward. There isn't a book to go by out here. We have had some help from the local army at Fort Russell. They're just a few miles away and put prisoners to work from time to time. The railroad had some of their own police, but now that the town of Cheyenne is formed, we're doing our best to create law and order as we go. We're writing the book, so to speak. The vigilantes are basically good men who care about Cheyenne. And they're getting results. They push in and get the facts, then hang the guilty or arrest them, and it sends a real message to scum and lowlifes. There's a lot of fear and trembling when someone finds a notice posted on their door demanding they leave within twenty-four hours by order of the Vigilance Committee."

"I suppose a place like this has to take whatever help it can get."

"That's the way I look at it. Like I said, we're seeing good results, and there are just way too many bawdyhouses, saloons, gambling halls, and such for a handful of deputy marshals to see to. There are thousands of people in Cheyenne, with more coming in every day. The city marshal figures it's something like a thousand men to every deputy. By spring we'll see the numbers cut at least in half, if not by two-thirds, but that doesn't help us now."

"Why will the population drop so much? I thought this was a division headquarters for the Union Pacific?"

"That's always the way it is at the end of the line. When the railroad moves west and sets up another end-of-the-tracks town, all the supplies will go there, and the vice will follow. Most of the men who aren't dealing drinks or cards are working for the railroad, and most of the women are working for themselves. That's why I stressed the importance of wanting married men with families."

"Yeah, I could tell by what you said that single men weren't exactly wanted."

"Now, that's not true, but you must understand, women civilize a place. Families serve to make it even stronger. Schools and churches are needed when you have families, and those two things bring about more law and order than a dozen police stations. I'm looking forward to meeting your wife and daughter. I was never so glad to get a telegram in all my life as when I got yours saying you were coming to Cheyenne. I know your character better than most of the men who served under me. I'd trust you with my life."

Edward noted the admiration in Henderson's expression. He couldn't lie to him . . . not now.

"I need to explain something. Just between you and me." Edward glanced around. The cell behind them contained several prisoners. They were guarded by a deputy who conversed with them as if they were all old friends. Some of them probably were. A few of the men played cards together and gave an occasional protest of being cheated, but most of the men slept.

Edward lowered his voice and leaned in. "My wife Janey died trying to bear me a son. They are both buried back in Indiana. I married a good friend who was in dire need. Her father passed away leaving her and her baby sister orphans. When you said you needed family men, I figured this was a good way to help her and myself."

"You sure didn't need to do that. I would have taken you anyway," Henderson said, frowning.

"It served us both."

"Marriages of convenience usually do," Henderson replied with a shrug. "Stranger things have happened. Folks marry complete strangers out here all the time. Next thing you know they have ten children and are pillars of the community."

"No, that won't happen with us. I won't risk another woman that way. Janey was my world, and knowing I had a hand in taking her life just about caused me to take my own. Had my faith in God been less, I don't know what I would have done."

Edward hurried to continue. "Look, I'm just being honest with you. You deserve that much, Major—Fred. That was a year ago, and I'm in a better place now. Marybeth did a lot to see me through my loss. She was Janey's best friend and over time became one of mine as well. She's got a good head on her shoulders, and when folks started threatening to take her sister from her, I knew I had to help her out."

"Why would they take her sister?"

"Why do folks ever stick their noses into other folks' business? They thought they were being helpful while gettin' something they wanted for themselves. A couple of rich folks wanted a child and couldn't seem to have one, and Marybeth had no means of supporting her sister. She didn't want to give up Carrie, and a judge got involved, so by marrying her, I could prevent that and have the family you requested. I think it's all gonna work out fine."

His friend gave a slow nod. "I suppose it might at that." He pushed back his paperwork. "Why don't you come with me? I'll give you a tour of the town. I managed to secure a spot for you to rent. It's in a decent location on the east side. Just about as far from Chicago as I could get."

"Chicago?"

Henderson laughed. "That's what we call the west side of town, although we might as well just call it hell."

Marybeth entered the Armstrongs' store with Carrie in her arms. The almost-two-year-old immediately started babbling and pointing. Marybeth had to admit the warmth of the store, as well as the surprising selection of items, caused her to want to point as well.

"Howdy," a woman said, coming to Marybeth's side. "I'm Cynthia, and this here is mine and my husband's store."

"I'm Marybeth Kru—Vogel," she replied. "And this is Carrie. My husband and I and . . . well, we all just arrived last night on the train from Omaha."

"I'll bet that was a trip and a half with a little one. Joe and I came up from Texas. When we heard about this place, it just sounded like somewhere we'd like to live. No children, though. Ours are grown and gone."

Marybeth considered the woman a moment. She looked to be in her forties. But maybe older. Her expression bore a hardness that left her looking plain and careworn. Her brown hair was braided and pinned up, and her attire was a simple skirt and blouse with an apron worn over them.

"We ran out of food, and Carrie is hungry, so I asked about a store at the hotel."

"We have a good selection," Cynthia Armstrong said, motioning Marybeth to follow her. "I don't have fresh food right now. That's hard to get here, especially in the winter. We had some decent produce this summer whenever the railroad and freighters could coordinate. That was before the tracks reached Cheyenne. They've just finally managed to get us connected. There was quite the celebration last week."

"I wasn't expecting fresh food. Carrie will drink canned milk."

"That I have. I also have some bread I baked yesterday, if you'd like to buy a loaf."

"That sounds perfect. What about crackers and cheese?"

"We have those, as well as some canned foods. Occasionally, one of the local women will do some baking for me to sell here. Men will pay almost anything for a dozen freshly made cookies." She smiled, and it softened her expression.

"They can't get away from their mamas fast enough, but when the chance for some homelike comfort comes along, they're first in line."

"I can understand that. I miss my mama."

"Yeah, me too." Her voice bore unexpected sorrow.

Marybeth didn't want to make her feel worse. "I'll take a few cans of milk and some crackers and cheese. Oh, and the bread."

Cynthia nodded but gazed past Marybeth as a couple of men entered the store. Marybeth turned and saw one push the other.

"Hank, you're always bossin' me around, and I ain't gonna take it no more," the younger of the two men declared.

"You ain't smart enough to get through the day without me tellin' you what to do." The older man reared back and slugged the younger man in the jaw. The man went reeling and hit the floor. Almost immediately he jumped up and plowed into the man he'd called Hank.

Marybeth had seen men fight before but never inside a store. When Cynthia touched her arm, she turned, still completely caught up with the men who were now throwing additional punches.

"You'd better come back here with me." Cynthia pulled her along behind the counter. "Joe will take care of this, but it might get messy."

"You two know better than to come in here causing trouble," the man behind the counter at the other end of the store declared. "Take your fight and get out."

The men ignored everyone but each other. They continued to slam into the counter and other displays, sending items crashing to the floor. Joe came from behind the counter with a rifle. He leveled it at the older of the two.

"I said take your fight outside."

Hank looked at the younger man and then back to Joe. "My fight ain't with you, Joe."

"That's good. Then take it outside." He stood his ground, fixing Hank with a hard look.

"Come on, Emory. Let's go." Hank gave the younger man a backhand into his gut. "I'll take this up with you later, Joe."

"Ain't nothin' to take up, Hank. I don't care if the two of you knock each other senseless, just don't do it in my store."

The man grunted something and exited the store, dragging Emory with him. Marybeth looked back to Cynthia.

She shrugged. "Those are two of the worst examples of mankind in Cheyenne. The Garlow brothers are just plain bad." Her soft Southern drawl helped Marybeth to relax.

"I'm not used to such scenes to be sure."

"Well, in all honesty, most of the decent women in Cheyenne know better than to go out alone. Most even have their help do the shopping or hire a boy to come get what's needed. This isn't a safe town . . . not yet."

"My husband is hoping to help on that end," Marybeth said, forcing a smile. "He's one of the deputy marshals."

Cynthia frowned and looked away. "I hope he has better luck than some of the others."

7

T his is the tent I managed to secure for you. I paid the deposit and first week's rent," Fred told Edward.

"A tent? In the middle of winter." Edward could see there were a dozen or more tents set up in rows.

Fred chuckled. "I know you aren't used to frontier living, but this is the way it's done. At least at first. If you get to looking around town, you'll see folks who have added log bottoms or attachments to make their tent living a little more comfortable. Those are people who own their tents of course. Others have brought over buildings from Julesburg. That was the last end-of-the-tracks town to the east of here."

"They moved the whole building?" Edward asked in disbelief.

"Sure. They've done that all along the line, and they'll keep on doing it until the owner decides to settle in one place or another. Railroad will move 'em for free. It helps to establish the next town."

"I'll be. That's just amazing as far as I'm concerned." He looked the tent over and shrugged. "Guess I should see the inside."

"Not much to see, but go ahead." Fred pulled back the first set of flaps. There was another set of netting below this. He tied those back. "You'll be glad for the net come summer. It gets hot here, and the bugs are vicious."

Edward followed him inside. The entire tent was about ten by ten with a small cookstove vented out the top of the tent just to their right. Beside the stove was a box with a few pieces of coal.

"It doesn't look like much, I know."

"I'm just afraid Marybeth may think it dangerous for Carrie."

"Why don't we go grab some lunch—my treat—and I'll let you know more about where to get the supplies you'll need. My wife and I have some things you can use. A couple of old army cots and extra blankets and such."

"I don't figure Marybeth and Carrie have had anything to eat since last night. I should go see to them first."

"Let's go together, and you can introduce me to your wife. She and your daughter . . ." He paused and looked at Edward as if for correction. When none came, Fred continued, "can come with us to lunch. I'll let her know how things are around here. From what you've told me about her, I'm sure she'll be able to manage."

"I know she will." Edward gave a halfhearted smile. "She's always been that kind of gal. She won't complain."

"Sounds like you got yourself a keeper."

They closed the tent back up and made their way to the hotel. Fred filled Edward in on the various places he could get the things he'd need, including coal for the little stove. Edward tried to keep everything perfectly ordered in his head. He was still worried about what Marybeth would think of their situation.

At the hotel, Edward led the way to the tiny room. When

Marybeth, holding a piece of bread, opened the door, Edward had to smile. "Figures you would have already found food."

"Carrie was hungry." Marybeth looked beyond Edward to the stranger.

"This is Major Fred Henderson, my commanding officer in the war." Edward stepped inside, and Fred followed.

"Mrs. Vogel, I'm quite pleased to meet you."

"Call me Marybeth, please."

"And you call me Fred." He smiled, and Edward saw Marybeth's apprehension melt away. "Like I told Edward, the war is over, and there's no more 'Major.'"

"Where'd you get the bread?" Edward asked.

Marybeth crossed the room to deposit the bread with some other food at the foot of the bed. "I bundled Carrie up and went to the Armstrongs' store. I asked the front desk clerk where a good place to buy food might be. He recommended them. It was probably a mistake, though. Two men came in fighting, and Mrs. Armstrong told me I shouldn't go out shopping alone. Her husband dealt with the men and got them to leave, but it did make me aware that perhaps I should wait until you're able to go with us."

"The Armstrongs are good folks, although Joe wasn't always," Fred said. "He was a gambler who got saved at a revival last summer. Found Jesus and got a whole lot easier to deal with. Who were the men that were fighting?"

"Hank and Emory Garlow," Marybeth replied.

Fred's eyebrows drew together. "Two meaner, more ruthless men were never born. Those two brothers have caused more trouble in this town than anyone. I'm actually surprised they haven't been hanged before now."

"Mrs. Armstrong said they were bad."

"*Bad* is an understatement." Fred shook his head. "They're

the very reason you should never go out alone, especially with the baby."

At this, Carrie made her way over to inspect the new man. She never knew a stranger, unfortunately, and held her arms up to Fred. "Up, pease. Up."

Fred didn't hesitate. He lifted Carrie into his arms and held her to his shoulder. "Hello there."

"Hello." Carrie smiled at him but offered nothing more. She touched the brim of his felt hat and then gave a pull on his beard.

Fred pretended it hurt and gave a howl. Carrie looked at him in surprise for a moment, then giggled and reached for the beard again.

"She loves everyone," Marybeth said, shaking her head. "I don't know how I'm going to teach her not to be going after strangers."

"Children seem to have good horse sense. They can usually tell if a person means to cause them harm," Fred replied. "But I understand your concern. I have children of my own."

"You do?" Marybeth seemed excited by this. "Please, tell me about them."

"I have Samuel, who is four, and David, who I suspect is about the same age as this little one. He's two."

"Carrie will be two the end of December. The thirtieth, to be exact."

"David just turned two, so they ought to have a lot to talk about." Fred put Carrie back down, and she ran to where she'd been eating cheese and bread.

"Fred showed me the tent he's reserved for us to live in. It's about ten by ten. We're going to collect our things at the train station and take them to the tent, then we'll come for you and Carrie." Edward watched her face for any look of alarm.

"A tent in winter sounds quite cold," Marybeth replied, looking to Edward and then to Fred. "But if that's how it's done, I'll give it a go."

"It's done quite well here. There's a nice cookstove you can use to heat and cook. It'll keep the place warm, believe me. Eve and I used one when we first came to town with the boys." He paused and added, "Eve's my wife."

"I'll look forward to meeting her."

Edward stepped forward. "The tent is actually a little bigger than this room."

"And there's a community outhouse for this group of tent dwellers. A lot of folks use the old chamber pots for nighttime and dump them in the morning," Fred offered. "Even on the east side of town, it's best to keep inside at night. It won't always be that way, though, so don't lose hope. Once the tracks move on west, things will calm down considerably."

"When do you expect that will happen?" Marybeth asked.

"Come spring. Things have slowed way down for the winter. They'll focus on building up things here in Cheyenne. This is to be a division headquarters, so there will be shops for repair and a roundhouse. They've already put up a couple of warehouses, and they're stuffing them with supplies for the spring push west. Some of the men will be hired to go into the mountains and cut timber and make ties. There's always plenty of winter work."

"I see. Well then, we shall make the best of it and trust God to watch over us."

"Yes, ma'am. That's our thought as well. Eve just told me the other night that being as spring was only a few months away, she could manage. Figures she can do almost anything for a few months." Fred smiled. "I think you two are going to like each other a great deal. Now, however, Edward and I were going to get some lunch, and we thought you and the baby might like to come along."

"Oh." Marybeth looked to Edward and then to Carrie. Her sister seemed quite content eating her cheese and crackers. Still, the lure of hot food made Marybeth consider the situation carefully. After Carrie ate, she was going to be tired. They'd already had quite the morning.

"I think we'll just stay here. That will take less time and trouble for you two. I'll get things packed up while Carrie naps, and when you're ready for us at the tent, just let me know."

Fred nodded. "Of course. It won't be long. Things continue to move pretty fast around here, even in the daylight."

Edward stepped close to her, and Marybeth lifted her gaze to his. "Are you sure you'll be all right?"

"We'll be fine. The really bad folks are sleeping, or so I've been told. We'll stay put. We learned our lesson."

Edward pulled on his hat. "Let's get on with it, then."

Once they'd gone, Marybeth considered all they'd said about the tent. She couldn't imagine anyone wintering in a tent. How in the world could that work? The temperatures were already quite frigid. The hotel room hadn't even been all that comfortable. Even now she had Carrie wearing extra clothes. What would happen when January came, and the temperatures lowered even more?

She gathered the things she'd washed earlier and checked to see if they were dry. They were. Marybeth started folding them. How would she cook meals for them on a tiny cookstove? At least it must be tiny, she surmised. The tent was only ten by ten.

How were they supposed to live in a tent?

A sense of panic welled in the pit of her stomach. Nothing was right. Nothing was as it should be. A tent was where they would live, but it wasn't a house. She was married to a man but wasn't a wife. She cared for a child but wasn't a mother. They had come to a place that people equated with violent men and sinful women. That was no place to make a home. Had she misunderstood God? Had she acted out of fear and leapt at the first solution offered? What if they *were* cursed for having married without the true love of a husband and wife? Had she brought down God's wrath upon them?

Marybeth wrapped her arms around her body and closed her eyes. Overwhelmed with a sense of grief and fear, she pleaded with God to still her roiling spirit.

If I did wrong, Lord, please forgive me. Don't make us to suffer the evils of sinful men who don't care about the needs of good people. Help us, Lord. Help us please.

She opened her eyes, and her gaze immediately went to the head of the bed where she'd left her Bible. She went there and curled up much like a child. Opening the Bible, she went to Scriptures that she had read time and time again in moments like this.

"'Be merciful unto me, O God,'" she read aloud. "'For man would swallow me up; he fighting daily oppresseth me. Mine enemies would daily swallow me up: for they be many that fight against me, O thou most High. What time I am afraid, I will trust in Thee. In God I will praise his word, in God I have put my trust; I will not fear what flesh can do unto me.'"

Carrie came to the edge of the bed. "I read."

Marybeth smiled. "Of course." She pulled Carrie up on the bed and tucked her safely against her. "This is Psalm

Fifty-Six, and we will memorize verse three. You say it after me. 'What time I am afraid . . .'"

"What afraid," Carrie repeated in her own way.

"'I will trust in thee,'" Marybeth said.

"I trust me."

"No, silly." Marybeth laughed and pushed back Carrie's straight blond hair. "We get into trouble when we put our trust in ourselves. When we're afraid, we need to trust God."

"I trust God." Carrie said it in such an assured voice that Marybeth could only kiss her on the forehead.

"Yes, that's good. I trust God. 'What time I am afraid, I will trust God.'"

"I will . . . trust God." Carrie giggled. "Read more."

Marybeth felt her spirit calm. "I think you're absolutely right, sweetheart. We need to read more of the Bible. It's the perfect help for our worry."

By the time Edward returned for them, Marybeth felt completely at peace. She knew putting her trust in God was the only hope she had of being able to face the future. And even when they came to a stop in front of the duck canvas tent, Marybeth whispered a prayer of thanks to God and smiled.

"So this will be our home," she said. There were several other tents similar in fashion to theirs. Most had other things scattered about, but the outside of this tent was clean.

"We got the fire going, and Fred helped me get extra coal, so we should have plenty. We got everything inside too."

"I must say I'm impressed. That was a lot to get into the tent."

Edward shrugged. "We really didn't bring that much."

"I know." She drew a deep breath. "But it will be enough. We're going to be just fine here. For as long as we need this tent, I know it will serve us well. I've prayed about it and feel complete confidence in God."

"I'm glad to hear you say as much. I'm afraid my faith has wavered today."

"Mine did too, but Carrie and I read the Bible." Marybeth turned to help Carrie down from the wagon. "Can you tell . . . Papa . . . what we read in the Bible, Carrie?"

"I trust God," Carrie said proudly.

Edward's lips curled ever so slightly. "That's a good one. I trust God," he repeated.

"It's from Psalm Fifty-Six: 'What time I am afraid, I will trust in thee.'" She smiled. "Seems like a good verse to know out here in the middle of nowhere."

8

Marybeth decided rather than worry anymore about it, she would get to work. Edward bid her good-bye after seeing that she had what she needed and knew where the pump and privy were located. Taking Carrie by the hand, she went inside the tent and surveyed the situation. Carrie was already trying to check out the stove.

"No, Carrie," Marybeth gave a stern command. "You mustn't touch. Hot. Very hot."

Carrie pulled her hand back and looked at Marybeth. "Hot." She repeated the word as she glanced back at the stove. "Hot."

"Yes, and it will burn you and hurt you bad. You mustn't ever touch." Marybeth took Carrie by the hand. "Come on, let's look over here."

The men had somehow managed to loosen the tops of all the crates. Marybeth took advantage of this and removed the wooden lid. It was one of the larger crates, and her thought was to empty it out and put Carrie in it to play. It wouldn't be the perfect situation, but if she put a blanket on the bottom, at least Carrie would be warmer than on the dirt. And being confined, she couldn't risk touching the stove.

On top was one of the rag rugs Marybeth's mother had made. Most of the rags she'd used were in shades of blue, green, and brown, so it was dark and perfect for the dirt floor. With a little difficulty, Marybeth maneuvered the rug from the box and spread it on the open floor as far away from the stove as possible. She had to move the crates around as she arranged the piece, but in time most of the rug was in place. It covered nearly half of the tent floor, and Marybeth knew she had another the same size for the other half. She wouldn't worry about it, however, until after she emptied more of the crates.

Next, she pulled out blankets and bedding, towels, and Carrie's feeding chair. She moved everything to the far side of the room on the clean rug and went back to finish emptying the crate. When that was done, she positioned the crate on the rug and spread one of the blankets inside. Then she got Carrie's toys from the suitcase and put them in as well. By this time, Carrie was excited about what was to come next, and when Marybeth picked her up and lowered her into the crate, Carrie giggled and wiggled in excitement.

"Now, you play here while I work."

"I play," Carrie agreed. She immediately took up her doll and sat down to explore what other items Marybeth had put down.

With that taken care of, Marybeth returned to unpacking the crates. She considered the situation carefully, hoping that Edward wouldn't mind that she was arranging his things as well. She left the tools in one of the smaller crates and arranged his meager belongings in a stack. Like herself, Edward hadn't brought very many personal items.

She stood back at the door flap and looked again at the room. She could put the crate where Carrie was playing as a sort of divider. On one side they could have their living area, and the other side could be for sleeping. The now-empty crates could serve as their furniture. The two smallest could be turned over and used as chairs, and one of the bigger ones could be a table.

The problem with using the crates as a table and chairs was that she had no real place for the towels and dishes. She frowned. Perhaps if she resecured the lids, she could store items in the crates and sit on them as well and, wih the table crate, she could turn it on its side and maybe put a little curtain across the opening. If Edward could put a shelf inside, that would do nicely for a pantry.

Remembering that Fred and Edward had gotten a pail of water for her before leaving, Marybeth found the teapot and filled it with water. She knew putting it on the stove would not only provide water for the hot tea she was craving but would also add steam to the rather dry air. She added a little more coal to the stove, then went back to work.

For beds, they would have to sleep on the floor. There really wasn't any other choice. She could put down a blanket or two on the rugs and then another couple of blankets on top. She had four pillows, but nothing else with any kind of cushioning. Studying the bottom of the tent, she could see where the owner had secured it to the ground with more than the scant number of tent pegs that would have ordinarily been used. Marybeth had heard from the man on the train that the wind could be quite bad. It would have been nice if the tents had had some sort of flooring, but that wasn't the way of it. It was little wonder that people had a lot of things around the outside of their tents. It hadn't dawned on Marybeth that the debris might be a way of protecting their tents from the wind and snow.

She had just finished with the makeshift beds, setting her and Carrie up in the far corner and placing Edward's pallet nearer the flap opening, when she heard someone call a greeting.

"Yoohoo! Are you home?" called a feminine voice.

Marybeth pulled back the flap and found a young woman with long brown hair flowing free beneath a wide-brimmed felt hat. She held a covered plate in her hands.

"Hello, I'm Melody. I live in the tent next door with my father, Clancy Doyle."

"I'm Marybeth Vogel. Come in." Marybeth stepped back and waited until Melody was inside before closing the flap. She didn't bother to tie it. "I just put some water on for tea. Would you like to stay for a cup?" she asked the petite woman.

"No, I just wanted to stop by and bring you some cookies I baked." She pulled back the towel that covered the plate to reveal a half-dozen sugar cookies. "I also thought I'd see what you might need and if you had any questions."

Marybeth chuckled. "News travels fast. Thank you for these." She took the plate and transferred the cookies to one of her own dishes before handing it back. "I wouldn't want anything to happen to this."

"And one less dish to wash," she said with a smile. "Have you been in Cheyenne long?"

"No, we've just arrived from Indiana. My, uh, husband, Edward, has come to be a deputy marshal."

The young woman frowned. "It's a lawless place, to be sure. My da gets in a fight at least once a week and usually gets banged up something fierce. Of course, he's Irish, and to him that's just good sport. For me, however, it means trying to wash blood out of his clothes and patch him up. I wish your husband good luck in his job. The menfolk around here won't make it easy."

"It scares me, I have to admit. The response is pretty much the same with everyone. As you can see for yourself, I've been doing my best to settle in, but I can't imagine being warm enough or safe in nothing but waxed duck canvas for shelter."

"The tents aren't so bad. We've lived in one all along the line. Started in Omaha and have made it this far."

"So is it just you and your father?"

Melody nodded. "It is. My mother died when I was just a wee one. There's never been anyone else. Just my da."

"What a life. I can't imagine being one of the only decent young women in a vast sea of criminals and loose women." Marybeth clamped her hand over her mouth.

Melody laughed. "Don't worry. You haven't offended me. You spoke the truth. There are only a handful of church-going women in this town. Although there are more coming every day. Most of the men wouldn't dream of bringing their wives and children west as they build the rail line. Until the towns are actually established, decent women want little to do with them. It's far too dangerous."

"But you've managed."

"That's because my da is dangerous. Few would dare try to take liberties with me, and those who did try paid a pretty price. Most end up permanently damaged, and word gets around fast that a man is takin' his life in his own hands if he wants to court me."

"That must be difficult for you. I mean, if you met a fellow you cared for, would your father understand and show some restraint?"

Carrie came to the edge of the box and raised her arms to Marybeth. "Up. Up pease."

"No, you must stay put until I have things better arranged," Marybeth said, leaning down to kiss Carrie on the top of her head. "You play."

She did as she was told but kept eyeing the two women as if trying to figure out their conversation.

Melody smiled and gave her a wave. "Your daughter is so cute. She looks just like you."

Marybeth said nothing but instead checked on the water.

Melody leaned toward the stove. "We're at six thousand feet here, so you'll have to learn to change how you cook. That is, unless you were living in the mountains in Indiana."

"No. No mountains. At least none that I know about."

Melody continued. "Water boils at a lower temperature here because we're higher, but food takes more time to cook." She shook her head. "Da explained it all, but I don't understand it really. I just refigured the time for baking and such, and I do all right."

"I never thought about anything like that being different from place to place." It was one more thing Marybeth would have to deal with.

"There's definitely a lot to consider. And to answer your earlier question, my da would love for me to find a decent fella to love. He worries that I'll never take love seriously because of takin' care of him, but in truth I haven't found anyone I care for." Melody waved again at Carrie, who was smiling in return.

Marybeth thought Melody sounded rather wistful. "How old are you?"

"Twenty-five. You?"

"Twenty." Marybeth shook her head. "I never would have thought you were older than me. I guess I'm feeling old, what with my responsibilities."

"Being married with a child naturally ages a woman," Melody replied with a shrug. "And movin' here won't help one bit. Be careful of the sun and wind. Always wear a wide-brimmed bonnet or hat. And tie it down good. The wind can be fierce. Sun or wind, either one can burn you and leave your skin feeling raw."

"You've managed to stay youthful. What's your secret . . . besides the wide brim?"

Melody laughed. "I guess I just keep telling myself I'm on a grand adventure. But I will say I'm wearyin' of the travel. I'd like to consider settling down to one spot. Granny Taylor says a woman only has so much movin' around the country in her."

"Granny Taylor?"

Melody nodded. "I'll introduce you to her sometime. She goes to our church—that's how we met. Granny's in Texas right now, but she'll be back soon enough. Do you have a church?"

"No, not yet." Marybeth didn't mention the bad time she had with the pastor of her last church. It left her feeling rather shy of returning to a congregation and a pastor's authority.

"We have a wonderful gathering. It's our start at making a Methodist church, and Dr. Scott oversees us. He's a physician and a lay preacher. I'll make sure and give you all the information before Sunday. For now, I need to get home and check on the stew I'm makin'. Still have to get the biscuits in the oven."

Stew and biscuits sounded so good to Marybeth. She hadn't had hot food in what seemed like forever. She could only hope that Edward would have some solution to their situation when he returned. Perhaps he would think to pick up some groceries.

"It was very nice to meet you, Melody, and thank you for the cookies. I hope we'll be good friends."

"You needn't hope because we already are." She grinned in her girlish fashion. "I'll bring Da by to meet you and your husband later this evening." She made her way out of the tent without further ado.

Marybeth stared at the flap of the tent for a moment before going back to check the water again. It was boiling. Only then did she realize she didn't have any tea.

By the time Edward returned to the tent, it was getting dark. Fred had given him a lantern to use. For the life of him, he couldn't remember if Marybeth brought any oil lamps or candles. It was funny that he hadn't even thought of such things when he packed what meager provisions he had.

Along with the lantern, Mrs. Henderson had sent a large, lidded crock with hot roast beef and potatoes, as well as a small flour sack with homemade biscuits.

"Marybeth?" he spoke as he entered the tent.

Inside he found a couple of candles burning and Carrie playing in one of the crates. By the stove, Marybeth seemed to be sorting through her dishware.

"I've brought supper. Mrs. Henderson made a big roast of beef and sent us a hunk along with potatoes and the broth. There are biscuits too."

"Oh, I could cry," Marybeth said, shaking her head. "We have nothing but some of the bread and cheese left over from this morning and a few cookies from a woman I met earlier today. I was starting to wonder how in the world I could be a decent wife and feed my husband, much less myself. And look, you brought a lantern."

"Another gift on loan from the Hendersons." He turned up the light and placed it on the makeshift table by one of the lit candles. He put the food down beside the lantern. "Looks like you've been busy."

"Let's eat, and I can tell you all about it. At least it does seem to stay fairly warm in here." She pointed to Carrie's chair. "Can you put her in there while I dish up the food?"

"Sure." Edward went to where Carrie was now standing, ready for attention. "How are you, little miss?" He picked her up and nuzzled her neck with kisses as he had done before. She squealed with delight at the attention. "Were you a good girl?"

"Yes, I good girl." She nodded, then sobered considerably. "I eat, pease."

"Indeed, you shall." Edward took her to her chair and raised the tray.

Carrie wriggled into place and raised her arms up so that he could pull the tray down around her. With that complete, Edward sat down on one of the crates and waited for Marybeth to bring the food.

"This looks so wonderful," she said, handing him a bowl with a big chunk of meat and several pieces of potato. She dished up smaller pieces of meat for Carrie and mashed some potato and mixed it with broth. She searched the crate that was positioned as her chair and drew out silverware, then replaced the lid and took a seat. "Here you are." She handed Edward a knife and spoon and gave Carrie a child's spoon.

Marybeth dished up her own bowl of food, then looked to Edward. "Would you offer a blessing?"

"Of course." He drew a deep breath and bowed his head. "Father, we thank You for this good food and for the chance to rest and reflect on the day. We ask for Your protection and provisions. Guide us by Your hand. In Jesus's name, amen."

"Amen," Marybeth said, glancing up with a smile.

"Amen!" Carrie exclaimed.

Edward laughed. It was good to be together. He didn't feel nearly so full of despair and sorrow as he had just days ago. Carrie—and even Marybeth—was good like a medicine.

Marybeth opened the sack of biscuits and handed one to Edward. She took up another and sampled it. "Oh, this is so delicious. I don't know when I've enjoyed anything as much as this simple fare," Marybeth said in such a tone of satisfaction that Edward couldn't help but hurry to taste the food. She handed a piece of her biscuit to Carrie.

"It is very good," he agreed. "I feel kind of guilty because I had a hot meal at lunch while you had bread and cheese."

"It just makes this even more appreciated. Maybe we could get some groceries tomorrow, however. We can hardly expect the Hendersons to feed us every night." She gave him a smile and continued. "Did you have a good day? Did Fred tell you what all you'd be doing for your job?"

Edward frowned. Fred had educated him the best he could and informed Edward that he and Fred would be working together—evenings. That would leave Marybeth and Carrie alone, and it wasn't something Edward was looking forward to telling his wife.

"He did," Edward replied and popped a piece of biscuit into his mouth before adding anything else.

"While you were gone, I met the sweetest young lady. Well, she's slightly older than me, so I guess I shouldn't call her that, but she seems so much younger than me. Anyway, her name is Melody Doyle, and her father, Clancy, works for the railroad. They live in the tent next to ours and said they'd come by tonight so she could introduce her father."

Edward nodded and ate a few bites of the roast to put off

the news he knew he would have to share. Maybe they could get through the entire meal before he had to tell her.

"She brought us some sugar cookies, so you can have that for dessert. Now, tell me everything about your job."

Edward knew there was nothing to be done but come right out with the truth. "Fred and I will work at night. The evening and early morning hours. We'll start about four in the afternoon and work until four or so in the morning."

He could see by the way Marybeth's eyes widened that the news was a surprise. Edward wished he could follow up with something encouraging, but there was nothing, and he knew the first thing that would come to her mind.

"What . . . how . . . so Carrie and I will be alone all night?"

"I don't much like it myself, but Fred assured me you'd be fine. They have a regular patrol that comes through on the east side. The mayor and other important city figures live over this way, and they pay for a group of private guards to watch over the area. No one even dares to venture over to this part of town because they know it'll spell trouble. I wouldn't have agreed to the job if Fred hadn't assured me."

"I see." She went back to focusing on the food. "I suppose we'll be all right, then."

"I know it's not a perfect arrangement, and I'll feel much better when we have a real house instead of a tent."

Marybeth didn't look up as she cut into her piece of roast beef. "Yes, I will too."

Edward couldn't begin to push aside the guilt he felt. "I'll tell him no and go to work for the railroad, if you prefer. They're hiring men to stay here in Cheyenne and work. I could do that."

At this Marybeth raised her head and met his gaze. He saw no condemnation in her eyes. She shook her head slowly.

"You came for a reason, and that was to be a lawman. Fred no doubt trusts you and needs you, and I want you to honor your word to him. God will watch over Carrie and me. I was just taken by surprise. That's all."

Edward nodded. "I was too."

She smiled at him. "I suppose we should remind ourselves that there are bound to be a great many more surprises for us. We'll just take each thing as it comes. I believe in you, Edward . . . and in the decision we made."

"And you don't think we've cursed ourselves for the way we handled things?"

A moment of hesitation left her pondering that very question. She shook her head. "No. Not really. Do you?"

"I do not." He breathed the first easy breath he'd had since learning about his hours. "God will see us through this. I still believe it was His plan for us to come here."

"I do as well, and I'm not going to be afraid. I'm going to trust in God."

"I trust God!" Carrie said, pushing her empty plate toward Edward. "More, pease."

"And this is my da, Clancy Doyle," Melody introduced.

The Doyles had come calling just as she'd promised, and Marybeth couldn't help but like the older man. "I'm pleased to meet you, Mr. Doyle."

"As am I," Edward replied.

"Now, there'll be none of that," he said in his Irish brogue. "I'll not be Mr. Doyle to anyone. Call me Clancy."

"I'm Edward, and this is Marybeth," Edward countered. "And the little one there is Carrie."

"Ah, ya've a wee daughter. A greater blessin' can't be had.

Oh, a son is a fine thing, but a daughter is somethin' special." The man's eyes seemed to twinkle in the dim light.

"I'm glad to meet you both and better know my neighbors," Edward said. "I wish I could invite you to sit for a while and enjoy the evening, but as you can see, we don't have much in the way of furniture."

"It's not a problem. I can't be stayin' long. The mornin' comes too early as it is. We just wanted to let ya know we're here if ya should need us."

"That is a comfort and an answer to prayer," Edward admitted.

"Ah, so yar a prayin' man. Good, good. I am meself, and it does me heart good to know ya are as well."

Marybeth relaxed a bit, knowing Melody and her father would be just steps away. "Edward will be working the evenings and nights patrolling the town, so he's right: you are an answer to prayer."

Clancy smiled. "We'll not let harm be comin' yar way, me girl. The meanest scallywag in town knows better than to bring trouble around me doorstep." He looked to Edward. "I'll be keepin' an eye out for yar family along with me own."

"Thank you. I'll do the same for you," Edward promised.

Marybeth noted the older man's build. He had large, firm hands and broad shoulders, but otherwise looked lean and able. No doubt he was well-muscled from working for the railroad and enduring regular fights, as Melody had mentioned.

"We'll be gettin' along just fine, me boy. Have no fear. Between me and yarself and the good Lord, we'll have no trouble at all."

"Oh, and, Marybeth, I'm going shopping in the morning. If you and Carrie want to join me and some others, that would be fine. Or I would be happy to pick up some things for you if you'd rather."

"Another answer to prayer." Marybeth had wondered what they were going to do for food. "If you don't mind, I'll make a list and give you the money to shop for me. What time should I have it ready?"

"Nine is early enough. I have other chores to see to first." Melody headed for the tent flaps. "I'll see you in the morning."

9

The next couple of days were devoted to learning his job as deputy. Edward found it a bit overwhelming. Evansville was a settled place and, compared to Cheyenne, had relatively little crime. Cheyenne, it seemed, had something happening every minute of the day.

There were the difficulties with con men trying to rob people of their last cent, soiled doves selling themselves and often stealing what they could on the side, and men who just seemed born to fight.

Fred showed him how he managed certain situations, telling Edward that often it would be up to him to judge the situation and decide not only on the crime but also the punishment. For lesser offenses, Fred usually wrote his own style of ticket. He would fine the person fighting or the one who damaged property, for example, and give them a piece of paper stating how much they were to pay and by what date. He would sign and make the offender sign, giving each of them a copy and record of the offense.

Edward didn't like the idea of having to do that. It seemed simpler to just haul the man in, but as Fred pointed out, most men would rather pay the fine than be marched out several miles to Fort Russell in order to serve time. There, the men would be put to work building barracks and other buildings. Fred said the army was working at double speed to get all their soldiers housed indoors before the blizzards started up. Besides, Cheyenne needed the money in order to provide amenities to the community, and so far, jail fines and license fees were about the only way they were getting money in their coffers.

Hearing a commotion, Fred motioned Edward to follow him into Lucky Bill's Saloon and Bordello. This area of town was often called the hog ranch, a gathering of seedy establishments particularly designed to free soldiers and railroad workers from their weekly pay. It was the worst of "Chicago," Fred had explained. It was here that the meanest of men drank and fought and the most corrupt of women did the same.

Overhead was an arrangement of lanterns that hung just low enough to shed light on the gambling tables, but high enough that no one could reach them and pull them down to throw. There were roughly crafted plank-board tables where men stood to play the roulette wheel or blackjack and other tables where poker was the focal game. Poorly made stools were all that passed for chairs—if a man had the luxury of one at all. Most stood.

"I've never seen anything like this place. Whoever heard of standing to play cards?"

"The chairs always go first in the fights," Fred said as they worked their way over to what seemed the source of the problem. "Can't get them fixed or replaced fast enough."

"What's going on here?" Fred asked, pushing two men aside. At the center of the confrontation were the Garlow brothers. Hank had just put his fist into another man's face. Edward could see that they were, as Fred had told him, the bottom of the barrel.

"You stay out of it, lawman. We're settlin' things just fine without your interference," Hank said, still holding his victim by the collar. Emory had his man pinned against a tent pole.

"Hank, you know I can't let you go on beating this man. Let him go and tell me what happened."

Hank looked at his brother, and for a minute Edward worried they were going to come after him and Fred. Instead, the twosome dropped their holds on the men and came to face Fred. Edward kept his hand on the butt of his revolver. He often found that when dealing with particularly difficult men, this was usually enough to dissuade careless action.

"They cheated us," Hank declared. "Dealt off the bottom."

"I saw it too," Emory said in support of his brother.

"No one was cheating you," another man chimed in. Several other men agreed with him.

"Well, it seems to me you've done all you could to convince him that such action was not in his best interest," Fred replied.

Edward assessed the man Hank had been beating. His eyes were already swelling, and his nose appeared to be broken. Blood covered the front of his shirt. It seemed to be coming from the man's nose.

"I ain't finished with him," Hank said, crossing his arms.

Fred took a step forward. "I say you are. You can either agree or come with me down to the jail."

Hank's eyes were cold and unfeeling. Men like Hank didn't always see the benefit in letting a thing go.

Hank's gaze bore into Fred's. The two men seemed momentarily frozen in time. Edward glanced around just to make sure no one was going to cause trouble. It was a lawman's job to have eyes in the back of his head and have complete surveillance of the entire room.

After what seemed far too long, Hank finally shrugged. "He wasn't worth the effort anyway."

Fred nodded. "I figured not. Now, I don't want to have any more trouble from the two of you. Understand? If I must break up another fight between you and someone else, you're gonna spend a day out at the army post." He motioned to the holstered gun on Hank's hip. "Go check your guns and stay out of trouble."

Edward relaxed his hand and backed up a pace for Fred to turn. The man had always been good at putting down fights and disagreements between his men. Edward could only hope that Hank would take his words to heart.

He did not.

Fred had no sooner turned to go than Hank picked up an empty bottle and went after him. Edward delivered a hard punch to the man's back, throwing Hank off-balance. He crashed into one of the few tables where the men were seated and landed on top of their game. They were not happy and tossed Hank aside and onto the floor. Two of the bigger men got to their feet and stared down at Hank, just daring him to rise and cause problems.

Fred shook his head. "Hank Garlow, you don't know when to stop. Guess you can spend the night at the jail and help the army out tomorrow."

Edward took hold of Hank as he got to his feet. The man wasn't happy to be manhandled, but he had the wisdom to cooperate.

After settling him in at the jail, Fred and Edward once again walked the town's streets. They headed downtown this time. The better saloons and gambling halls were here. The problems were less to deal with because this was the area of town where the city planners might enjoy a game of cards or a few drinks. Often the vigilante members could be found imbibing and discussing the problems of the day.

Appearing here was enough to keep things under control most evenings, Fred had told Edward the day before. But from time to time, there was the occasional mishap. Once while enjoying himself at a game of blackjack, a certain Mr. Smith was confronted by Mrs. Smith, who held a large boning knife. She accused her husband of having stolen her milk-and-egg money. With the knife ominously tucked under his chin, the man pleaded his innocence for several minutes. With each denial, the woman dug the knife into his flesh. Finally, the man had enough and confessed that he had done exactly as she thought. Instead of dropping the knife, however, she plunged it into his neck. One could never tell how the folks of Cheyenne were going to respond. Thankfully, the man lived, and the couple reconciled and moved to Denver.

It was stories like that which left Edward unsure he'd done the right thing in coming to Cheyenne, especially where it concerned Marybeth and Carrie. He worried about them sleeping alone each night and had no idea of what would happen when the snow came with any regularity.

"You've been awfully quiet this evening," Fred said as they left one establishment and entered another.

A piano player offered a soothing classical piece that Edward had heard somewhere before. The man was hardly more than a boy, but he played with such expertise that it was easy to see why he'd been hired.

"That's Jake Landry's son Mark. He's nineteen and has played like that since he was a little guy. 'Naturally gifted,' his piano teacher declared. She could play him a tune and he'd pick it right up without any trouble at all."

Edward noted the young man. "Never heard of such a thing."

"Nobody here had either. Not that he's been here long. His folks came in October from Denver. Jake planned to build on the west side, figuring he'd make more money. Then there was a ruckus at one of the local establishments over there, and they burned it to the ground. Took three infantry companies marching in and taking charge to quell the mob that rose up afterward. Landry decided a more respectable part of town would probably serve him better.

"As you can see, the place isn't bad. They have dinner in the back room, so Landry situated the bar up front along with an area to dance. Wouldn't surprise me to see him clean up the place even more and get rid of the bar and dance floor. They make good money serving dinner each night, and most of the decent folks in town will make their way here. Since it's in a location on the edge of respectability, I figure it will do well with most of the town in time."

They stepped out of the place and started back down the street. For a little while neither said anything, but finally Edward felt he owed Fred an explanation.

"I'm worried about Marybeth and Carrie. I don't like them being alone at night. Maybe if they were stayin' in a regular house, it wouldn't be so bad, but leavin' them in that tent just worries my mind."

"I can respect that. Cheyenne's a big change for anyone, and you've seen just how bad things can get in this place. Tell me this, how much money do you have left?"

"We've got a fair sum, and I'm adding to it with my salary. We're doing all right. Marybeth has a house back in Indiana that my brother-in-law is gonna sell for her. When we get that money squared away, I figure we'll have enough to build."

"Well, in the meantime, I could make a suggestion. It just came to me and is a way you could help me as well as yourself."

"What's that?"

"I'm putting in a shed in my backyard. It'll be about fifteen by twenty. I have the frame up but had to stop due to a lack of funds. If you have the money to help me finish it off, I'll let you live there rent free until you can get your own house built. You can fix it up any way you see fit. We'll find a stove and put that in there, and you can use our outhouse, which will be close by. There's a pump in the backyard that will be even closer and a clothesline."

"I'd probably spend more in rent during the next few months than what it would take to finish the place off for you. Are you sure you want to do that?"

"I worry for them too, and you'll be a whole lot more use to me if your mind isn't stewin' over their safety. I figured to build the place for myself to do my woodworking and such, so it's not like I wouldn't have a stove in there anyway. We'll just make it a small cookstove instead of a heating stove. That way you can have all the comforts of home."

"When do you think we could get around to finishing it?" Edward was encouraged by the idea and didn't want to waste any time. Not only would the shed provide better shelter, but it would be on the same grounds as Henderson's house, and that would be safer than the tent.

"If you have the money, we can get started tomorrow. We both have the day off. No reason you and the missus can't come by and see what's going on. You and I can take the wagon and get some building supplies out at the sawmill. I have plenty of nails."

"That sounds great." He knew his tone betrayed his excitement. "I think this will be a great surprise for Marybeth."

⤙⤚

Marybeth lay awake listening to every sound . . . every footstep. Despite what Fred had said, there was plenty of activity in the area, and half of that was folks using the bathroom facilities. The nights seemed endless, and she couldn't keep from fearing what might happen. There was only a tied flap between her and anyone who might want to enter the tent and cause trouble.

The ground was hard, and she rolled to her side, desperate to ease the ache in her hips. There had been mention of Fred loaning them some old cots, but so far no one had delivered on that idea. She pulled her knees up and hugged them close. What time was it, anyway? Edward had the only timepiece, and she was sure he'd taken it with him as he usually did.

Carrie seemed unconcerned with Marybeth's worry. She slept peacefully, clutching her doll. The temperatures were dropping, but Carrie seemed quite comfortable—hard ground and all. Melody had come by earlier in the day to say that her father had said it was going to snow in the next day or two. He'd read the signs in the clouds and felt it in his bones. Figured it would be a bad storm.

It was hard to imagine what she would do. She and Carrie would probably be alone, and so far, Marybeth hadn't found anything she could put around the tent to help buffer the wind. Maybe tomorrow she'd ask Melody for ideas.

She yawned and closed her eyes. The Bible verse from Psalms came to mind again. *"What time I am afraid, I will trust in thee."* It offered her comfort, and she murmured it over and over, feeling a sense of calm wash over her.

God was in control. She didn't need to be afraid. Stretching back out, Marybeth relaxed and let herself drift off to sleep.

When Edward showed up later that morning, Marybeth shot up from her pallet. The rifle was hanging overhead. Edward had made a place for it there to keep Carrie from getting her hands on it.

"Is that you, Edward?" she whispered in the dark.

"It's me." She heard him strike a match. The glow illuminated his face as he lit a candle. "Sorry if I scared you."

"That's all right. I haven't been able to sleep much tonight anyway." She tightened her robe sash. Sleeping fully clothed had been a necessity, and the robe added one more layer to fend off the cold.

"Was there trouble?" Edward asked.

"No, just my fretting." She left Carrie sleeping and moved to the table. "Are you hungry?"

"No, I ate late. Why don't you sit, and I'll tell you an idea Fred and I had tonight. It might afford you some comfort."

Marybeth did as he suggested and waited for Edward to join her. He took off his holster and gun and hung it up on a peg near the top of the tent pole.

"Fred is building a shed behind his house. Kind of a workshop. It's going to be about five feet wider and ten feet longer than this place. He suggested we spend the money we would be using for rent and help him get the place finished instead. Then he'd let us live there until we could build our own house on that lot we're being given by the city."

"We'd be in a building?" Marybeth questioned. "Beside their house?"

"In back of it but yes. Fred said we could decorate it however we wanted, and he'd put in a cookstove rather than a heat stove. That way we could have our own meals and such."

"That would be wonderful." She didn't want to get her hopes up too much.

"It wouldn't be like having a real house, but we can't build until George sells your property. Fred said he wouldn't charge us rent because we would have helped him finish off the place. There's a pump at the back door of his house and a privy just a ways from where the building would be. Clotheslines too. And you'd have his wife and children as company."

"It sounds too good to be true. When will it be built?"

"If you're in agreement with us using the last of our savings to do this, he said we could come over later this morning and see what's what. He and I can go get supplies and get started today."

"I haven't even had a chance to meet Mrs. Henderson. What if she doesn't go for this idea?"

"I asked Fred if he thought she would have a problem with it, but he assured me she'd love the company. She hates it here. Hates being away from her family back east. You'd be good company for her."

"I'd love to be company for her. It gets lonely here."

He looked at her oddly for a moment. "I'm sorry. I didn't know. I never really thought about you being lonely."

She forced a smile. The last thing she wanted was to worry him. "It's not that bad. I think it just seems compounded by you being gone all evening and then most of the night. I have too much time to think, especially after Carrie falls asleep. I try to go to sleep when she does because I know she'll wake up early and want to play and eat."

Marybeth shrugged and lowered her gaze to the table. "But I can't stop thinking about what would happen to us if you got killed out there. It's pretty scary to consider. I can't go back home. There's no home there, and I'd just be in the same predicament as I was before."

"That's not true. Inga would take you and Carrie in. My family would provide for you because you're family now. I promise. They're good like that."

"I know they're good people, but I wouldn't want to be a burden on them. Besides, I'd still have to figure a way to get back there. I can't imagine making that trip alone."

"Well then don't. You don't have to make that trip at all. Nothing's going to happen to me."

She wanted to believe that. "I'm praying for you, and I know God is watching over you. I don't mean to fret, so just pay me no attention. I shouldn't have said anything."

"That's not my thinkin' at all, Marybeth. If you're concerned about something, I want to know. I want us to talk about it. I can give you that much. In fact, there's a lot I can give you. I do care about you. I love you and Carrie. Maybe not in the way you deserve, but you're both very precious to me."

Marybeth felt the sense of loneliness return. She knew he cared. She knew he'd be there to watch over them, but for some reason it didn't satisfy her the way she wished it would. She wouldn't say anything, however. She had agreed to this marriage. She'd known it would be in name only. She knew Edward's conditions for their union, and she had agreed to them. Let it not be said that she would break her word and cause problems just because her heart felt overwhelmed by that sense of void.

"I think the shed sounds really nice."

Edward nodded. "I think so too. It will see us through the winter months, and come spring, we'll build us a real home."

"A real home." Marybeth swallowed the lump in her throat. Would she ever have a real home?

10

"Mrs. Henderson, I'm so pleased to meet you," Mary-beth said.

The petite woman gave her a smile and shifted her two-year-old son from one hip to the other. "I'm very pleased to meet you. Please call me Eve."

"I will, and you call me Marybeth." She turned and looked at the framework of the workshop Fred had planned. "What do you think of this venture?"

"I love the idea. You have no idea how much. I think we could benefit each other greatly."

Marybeth turned back to face Eve. "I thought the same. I've been most uncomfortable living in a tent."

"We lived that way for a month in the summer, and I told Fred we absolutely had to have a house. Fortunately"—she lowered her voice—"we had the money needed to build. My father arranged for supplies and men to come to Cheyenne and help Fred build this wonderful home we now have."

Glancing over at the white-washed two-story wooden house, Marybeth could only dream a similar place might one day be theirs.

"My father chided Fred about bringing us out here to the 'ends of the earth.'" She shook her head. "I wanted so much to go back home to Indiana when Father left. This is not the kind of place I hoped to raise my boys."

"Perhaps in time it will be better," Marybeth replied. She saw Edward and Fred were approaching. "Did you fellas figure it all out?"

"We did. Why don't we go inside and out of the cold?" Fred suggested. "I'm sure Eve has some coffee on the stove."

"I do, and water for tea if you'd rather have that, Marybeth."

"That would be wonderful." She turned to where Carrie was playing with Samuel. "Carrie, let's go inside."

"Wanna play," Carrie called back.

"You can play inside where it's warmer. Now come on."

"You too, Samuel. Inside right now," Fred commanded. The boy immediately got to his feet and headed to the house. Carrie ran after him.

"So are you ladies in agreement regarding this transaction?" Fred asked.

Marybeth looked to Eve, and both women nodded. "The sooner it's done, the better as far as I'm concerned," Eve replied.

"Good. Then Edward and I will go get the supplies needed. I'll also see if I can wrangle a couple of guys to come and help. A lot of folks owe me favors," Fred said, opening the back door to his house. "We ought to be able to have this up and ready in a week or so."

Marybeth marveled at the amount of work the men got done that day. She and Eve had visited inside, after Eve gave her a tour of the house. It was a charming place, and Eve had made it quite homey with furniture she'd managed to buy locally. She said it would have to do until spring, when they planned to ship out some of the things they'd left in Indiana. It made Marybeth think that perhaps she should have asked George to put some of her furniture in storage so they could ship it out in the spring.

By evening, the outside walls and roof were complete. It hadn't been shingled, but Edward assured her that would be done soon enough. Every day the next week, Fred and Edward took a couple of hours before their shift to work on the place. Sometimes another man or two joined them, but mostly it was just the two of them now that the walls were in place.

The biggest concern was the cookstove. New ones cost far too much money and would take quite a while to have shipped. Fred thought he knew someone he could talk to about getting a used one, but most of the stoves in Cheyenne were hard-won prizes that nobody wanted to part with.

Marybeth was almost to the point where she would have found a way to make a campfire for heat in the shed. Didn't the native people of the plains put campfires in their teepees? She knew she had heard or read about that somewhere. The shed still had dirt for floors. Maybe she should suggest that.

Life in a tent got harder as the temperatures continued to drop. Then the snowstorm came. It was over a week later than Melody's father predicted, but it was a bad one, and the only thing Marybeth could do was pray.

Carrie came and crawled up on her lap as the wind howled. She put her hands over her ears, and Marybeth did her best to offer comfort.

"It's just the wind, baby. It won't be like this forever." At least she hoped it wouldn't be. So far there had been plenty of wind since their arrival in Cheyenne, and Marybeth wasn't exactly sure it ever died down.

"Wanna go play with boys," Carrie announced.

"We can't go outside. It's snowing too hard. It's called a blizzard."

"Izard."

"Close enough." Marybeth hugged her sister close.

Thankfully, Edward had replenished their coal supplies just before the storm hit. They would keep warm enough, so long as the tent didn't blow away. Marybeth was grateful that the owner of the tent had put in the extra stakes to hold it in place. Melody had assured her that they'd not had winds so bad that any of the tents were uprooted, but there was always a first time for things. At least that's the way Marybeth saw it. She had nightmares about the tent picking up off the ground, and the wind whisking all their meager belongings across the vast landscape.

By eight o'clock that evening, Marybeth knew she should encourage Carrie to go to bed. The wind was still wreaking havoc outside, however, and the poor girl was more frightened than ever. Marybeth started singing hymns that she could remember, and that seemed to help. Carrie tried to sing along as well.

The familiar words of comfort began to ease her tensions. Finally, Marybeth got the Bible out and motioned Carrie to their pallet. Marybeth brought the lantern and positioned it safely away from the bed, atop the crate.

She opened to the Psalms, her favorite place to go when worries overwhelmed. Psalm Ninety-One was an all-time favorite in time of storms.

"'He that dwelleth in the secret place of the most High shall abide under the shadow of the Almighty. I will say of the LORD, He is my refuge and my fortress: my God; in him will I trust.'"

"I trust God," Carrie added in a sleepy tone, then yawned.

"Yes." Marybeth smiled and bent to kiss Carrie's forehead. "I trust God."

Carrie smiled and clutched her doll close. She closed her eyes, and Marybeth continued to read. "'Surely he shall deliver thee from the snare of the fowler, and from the noisome pestilence. He shall cover thee with his feathers, and under his wings shalt thou trust: his truth shall be thy shield and buckler. Thou shalt not be afraid for the terror by night; nor for the arrow that flieth by day. . . .'" Marybeth let the words fade away.

God had always comforted with the Bible. He was always there and would always see her through. She had only to keep near Him—to look to Him for her shelter and protection.

Why was it so hard to remember that? She found herself fretting about Edward and his job. She worried about being left alone with Carrie. They had made friends of the Hendersons and Doyles, but they could only help so much. People weren't where her faith should rest. That was the truth of it, and Marybeth needed to remember that without allowing herself to fall into despair.

A heavy gust shook the walls of the tent, drawing her attention. She watched for a moment, then glanced at her sister to see if she was afraid. But Carrie's eyes remained closed. She was falling asleep or already there. She wasn't afraid. She trusted Marybeth to take care of her, and she trusted God. Marybeth wondered if Carrie understood those words and what they meant.

Did she herself understand them? What did it really mean to trust God? If she still fretted and worried about things, did she really trust? She wanted to give up all her worries and fears and trust God for everything. There was certainly nothing she could do in and of herself.

I'm trying so hard, Lord. I want to trust You completely. I want to give You every worry I have and know that You have already provided for each need. She smoothed back Carrie's hair from her face and pulled her covers up around her head. *I want to trust You like this child trusts me . . . and You.*

Marybeth got up and took the lantern to the table. She placed the Bible there as well and smiled. It was going to be all right. She just had to remember that, even when things around her looked bad. She needed to trust God the most at those times and remember His faithfulness.

She slipped out of her shoes and blew out the lantern. Let the wind howl. She would go to bed and pray for as long as she had the ability to stay awake. She would pray for all those she knew and loved. Especially Edward. He had to be out in this storm, patrolling. Hopefully evil men would give up their practice and stay in their homes to avoid the snow.

Edward felt as if he were frozen to the bone. He couldn't feel his feet anymore, and that gave him grave concern. It reminded him of times during the war. The early years when the regiment had escorted prisoners to St. Louis. The Twenty-Fifth Regiment had been assigned to that area shortly after their formation. Edward easily remembered the freakish ice storm and desperate drop in temperatures as they marched the Confederate men. He had thought they all might freeze to death. But just as fast as it came on, the temperatures warmed the next day, and the sun came out to melt any remaining ice. He wished the sun would come out here.

It had been three days of this brutal storm. Snowdrifts were everywhere, and the winds were relentless. The temperatures were so low that even animals were brought inside, if possible. He couldn't help but wonder how Marybeth and Carrie were faring. This night had been the worst of it. Old-timers from elsewhere told Edward that meant the storm would soon play itself out and come to an end. He prayed that might be so.

The bad weather had done little to calm bad tempers or even keep men at home. Most were more at home in the bawdy and gambling houses anyway. They came there to keep from losing their minds to the constant moan of the winds. Fred said it had a way of making people go crazy, and Edward had seen more than one man lose his composure and start a senseless fight.

Now as he headed home, Edward could only pray that the storm would dissipate and calm would return. Well, whatever calm could be had in Cheyenne.

There wasn't even a hint of light by which to find his way home, and all at once Edward realized that he wasn't sure where he was. He couldn't even make out the houses or whether he was keeping to the poorly graded roadway. He squinted in the darkness against the icy winds and tried to get his bearings. Why hadn't he paid better attention? People died in weather like this.

He caught sight of a light in the window of a house not far from the street. It was a small house, single story. It looked like the kind on the far northern edge of the city. But what direction was he heading? He hadn't meant to come north. He wanted to go east.

A gust of wind rose up with such force that it nearly drove Edward to the ground. As it was, he stumbled backward several paces and reached out aimlessly for something to grab hold of. There was nothing.

He pulled his coat up higher and snugged his hat down as much as he could. Bending forward he pushed toward the house light he'd seen. Glancing up, however, he realized it was gone. There was nothing.

The cold wind stole his breath, and the icy snow coated his face, nearly freezing his open eyes. This was not at all what he had bargained for. He pressed on, hoping that he might see or hear something familiar.

God, I need You to show me the way. I fear I'm lost and . . . dead if You don't intercede.

Marybeth woke with a start. She thought she'd heard something. Had Edward come home? She sat up and glanced around her. It was still dark, but the wind had calmed. It was eerily still and left her feeling a sense of dread. She got up and felt her way along the crate to where she'd left her shoes. She slipped them on, then lit the lantern. She could only guess at the hour.

She added coal to the stove and built up the fire with a few pieces of kindling. Holding her hands out, she felt the warmth of the flame and prayed it would ignite the coal. She thought about looking outside but decided against it. If she moved the blanket she'd placed at the edge of the flaps and opened them, it would let in far too much cold air. Better she just wait it out. Hopefully Edward would be home soon.

It wasn't long before the room warmed sufficiently. Marybeth turned up the lamp a bit, not all that worried the light would wake Carrie. The child was usually a deep sleeper. She checked the pail of water that was kept by the stove. Thankfully, it hadn't frozen.

Marybeth dipped out water into one of her larger pots and placed it on the stove. When it was heated, she'd have water for the oatmeal she planned to make for breakfast, as well as cleaning up afterward and maybe even tea. She was grateful Edward had thought to buy groceries before the storm hit. It was hard to imagine not being able to get out to a store just blocks away. The storm had been unlike anything Marybeth had ever experienced, and she wondered if this was just the first of many to come.

She was about to sit down when she heard something outside. It sounded like someone dragging something. Maybe one of the men was trying to clear a path. She waited to see if the sound continued. It lasted another few minutes and then stopped. She sighed. There was no telling what it had been.

Finally, the water began to boil, and Marybeth dipped some out and put it in the kettle. She took a small amount of tea and added it to the water, then placed it on the stove. After a few steeping minutes, she took a towel and grabbed the kettle off and placed it on the table. Next, she took up the strainer and a cup, but before she could pour the tea, she heard the unmistakable sound of someone at the flaps.

She hurried to pull back the blanket. "Edward? Is that you?"

He didn't answer, and for a moment Marybeth wondered if she should get the rifle. Something stopped her from it, however, and instead she hurried to untie the flaps. At first, she didn't recognize the icy man standing in the opening of the tent. She looked him up and down, and as he reached out for her, he was barely able to speak.

"Marybeth."

It came out like a gasp. Marybeth took hold of his arm and pulled him inside the tent. She hurried to redo the ties on the flaps and block out the frigid air.

"Come sit by the fire." She hurried around him and drew up the crate he used as a chair.

She reached for his hat and took it from his head. Snow rained down around them. She hadn't thought to try to brush it off before bringing him in. Glancing at him now, she saw his clothes were getting snow all over the rug. It didn't matter. She could hardly force him to disrobe outside.

"Edward, we need to get you out of those wet clothes." She opened the little oven door to spread additional warmth. She began unbuttoning his coat, worried at the color of his face. It was pale gray. Edward sat so stiff, she feared he'd frozen.

The tea. She stopped trying to unbutton the coat and went for the strainer and cup. She would start him thawing from the inside out. She poured the tea and came back to where he sat.

"Here, I need you to drink this tea. It will help warm you up." She took hold of his right hand. "Can you hold the cup?"

He grunted and took it in hand. Raising it to his lips, he couldn't seem to hold it still. It wobbled and spilled a bit, but finally he bent to take in some of the liquid.

Marybeth whispered a prayer of thanks. She decided to forget the coat for a moment and started on his boots. It took some doing, but she managed to take them off, as well as the wet socks. His feet felt like blocks of ice.

"We've got to get your feet warmed up." She rubbed them for several minutes. "Keep drinking the tea." Edward did as he was told, still not saying much of anything.

Marybeth knew using hot water on frozen feet was not the way to go. She remembered once when she'd been quite young that her father had endured something like what Edward must have gone through. Mother had taken water no warmer than room temperature to bathe his feet. Marybeth went to the half-empty bucket. This would have to do.

She brought it to where Edward sat, then went to retrieve a towel. "I'm going to wash your feet and hopefully thaw them out. It will probably hurt." Her father had howled in pain as Mother did what she could to warm him up.

"Go ahead," he managed to say. Marybeth took this as a good sign and went to work.

If there was pain, Edward made no outward sign. Perhaps he remembered Carrie was sleeping or maybe he just didn't want to scare Marybeth. She worked for a long time, tenderly wiping his feet with the water. As she felt the flesh warm a bit, she prayed that he wouldn't suffer frostbite.

Convinced she had done what she could for his feet, she helped him out of his coat. Thankfully, the shirt underneath was dry. She hung the coat on a peg, then went to where he kept his clothes and got a dry pair of woolen socks. She put the bucket of water aside and lay several towels down to absorb any dampness. The last thing she wanted to do was put warm, dry socks on his feet and have him place them in melted snow.

That was when she noticed that his pants still had snow caked on them. "Edward, you have to take off your pants. I'll get you another pair, but there's nothing I can do about affording you privacy. If you stand up, I'll help you slip them down, and then you can sit again." She knew he didn't have much strength left.

She helped him to his feet and waited as he fumbled with the buckle of his holster. She took it from him and hung the holster and gun up on the peg. She could barely reach it and nearly lost her footing. Righting herself, she took hold of the crate rather than grab the tent pole. The last thing she needed was to knock that loose and bring down their shelter.

Edward was reseated with his pants around his knees by the time Marybeth returned with his dry pants. She pulled off his wet trousers and felt his long johns. They were surprisingly dry. Marybeth worked the dry pants onto him. She felt no sense of embarrassment or hesitation. Her husband was freezing, and it was her job to help him warm up.

Without warning, the shivering began. He nearly dropped the empty teacup. Marybeth took it and put it aside. Edward shook so hard that Marybeth had to struggle to finish getting his pants on him. She helped him stand and the shaking worsened.

"I'm so sorry, Edward." She continued to work until she had him redressed, socks included. "Come on. We need to get you to bed and warm you."

She led him to his pallet, and as he struggled to lie down, she grabbed up her blankets and joined him. "You need my body warmth," she said as he looked at her oddly. "If you don't get warm . . . you may die."

That seemed to sober him, and he gave a hint of a nod. Marybeth carefully placed the covers over him and snuggled in under their warmth. She pulled Edward into her arms as she might have done for Carrie. It felt like the most natural thing in the world, even though Marybeth had never held a man in this fashion.

How odd that it should take a snowstorm and threat of freezing limbs to put them in each other's arms. Something stirred inside her. She knew she cared deeply for Edward. She always had. At least ever since Janey announced that she had plans to marry him.

But Janey wasn't her concern anymore, and the feelings welling up inside Marybeth weren't those of compassion for her best friend's husband. She pushed down her emotions and did her best to focus on Edward's trembling. She couldn't allow herself to fall in love with this man. Edward had made it clear this was a marriage of convenience only. Unfortunately, Marybeth knew her feelings were going beyond that boundary.

11

The moment Edward woke up, he felt the strange sensation of someone near. He opened his eyes and found himself in Marybeth's arms with Carrie snuggled down between them. What was going on? He tried to remember what had happened.

It came to him in a flash. He'd gotten lost in the storm the night before. Fred had sent him home early, but he'd lost his way. He didn't even remember finding their tent.

Little by little memories of Marybeth's tender care came to mind. She had been awake and ready when he'd stumbled against the flaps of the tent. His hands had refused to work at the ties. Edward remembered the desperation of the moment. He hadn't even been sure he was at the right tent.

He closed his eyes and listened to sounds around him. For the most part, there was little to be heard but the rhythmic breathing of Marybeth and Carrie. It seemed the whole world was silent.

Edward remembered mornings when he and Janey had slept in. There was always something so intimate about those times. They would inevitably end up in each other's arms sharing tender romantic moments. Of course, this was completely different. He was married to Marybeth, but they weren't intimate. Her arms around him were only there to aid in keeping him alive.

Carrie woke up first. She sat straight up and wiped her eyes several times before looking at Edward with a silly grin. "You seep."

He wasn't sure if she was declaring what had happened or ordering him back to bed. He grinned and reached out to tickle her. She giggled and bounced away from him, rolling over onto Marybeth.

"Quiet, Carrie," Marybeth half whispered, half moaned. She opened her eyes.

"Morning," Edward said, hoping the situation wouldn't startle her too much.

Marybeth glanced over and smiled. She'd never looked quite so pretty. For a moment, Edward lost his thoughts in the reflection of her dark blue eyes.

"The storm has stopped," she said matter-of-factly. She closed her eyes again, then without warning sat up, pulling her arm from under Edward's head. "How are you feeling?" The relaxed look in her eyes was gone. It was as if all at once she realized their situation.

She struggled to her feet, and Carrie followed suit. Gone was the warmth and the welcome intimacy of the moment. Edward stretched and sat up. "I think I feel just fine, thanks to your quick thinking and care."

"I was so worried. You were nearly frozen to death. You could hardly speak or move," Marybeth said, going to the stove. "I'll be glad when we get moved over to the Hendersons' place."

"Yeah, me too." He watched her go about her duties. She

had a methodical way of arranging her tasks. Marybeth was all about making order out of chaos.

"What time is it?"

Edward shook his head. "I have no idea. My watch is in my jacket pocket."

Marybeth looked around the room and found the discarded piece. She checked the pockets and produced the watch. She opened it carefully and shook her head. "It must have frozen. This can't be the time."

"What does it say?"

"It's nearly noon." Marybeth held the timepiece to her ear. "It's ticking just fine. Oh, goodness. Do you really suppose we've slept that long? That certainly isn't like Carrie."

The toddler danced in a circle on her pallet and paid them little attention. She was her happy self with no idea of the dangers that had passed in the night.

"After days of blizzard, we were worn out. It's probably all for the best. I feel pretty good, if I do say so. You're a good nurse, Marybeth." Their eyes met, and Edward couldn't help but offer her a smile.

Her cheeks flushed slightly, and she looked away. "I was going to make oatmeal for breakfast, but since it's nearly noon, I should probably warm up the stew I made. I'll warm some bread too. It shouldn't take long. I'm sure you're hungry."

"I eat," Carrie declared. "Wanna eat, pease."

Marybeth seemed to relax a bit. She laughed and pointed to Carrie's feet. "Get your boots on, and I'll button them."

As promised, it wasn't all that long before Marybeth had lunch on the table and Carrie's boots buttoned up. Edward offered grace, and Marybeth dished up bowls of stew from the pot on the stove.

"How did you manage to get lost last night?" Marybeth asked as she brought the last bowl to the table.

"The better question is, How did I manage to get home? I have no idea how I found this place. Had to be the good Lord's leading." Edward took a piece of bread and soaked it in the stew's gravy.

"I'm thankful He was watching over you."

"Me too. Fred had just told me about stories he'd heard of people wandering off in storms like the one we had, never to be seen again. I thought it kind of strange, but I don't anymore. There's nothing out here to guide a person home. No streetlamps or road markings. Not that you could see them in that snow. I've never seen a blizzard quite like that."

"Me neither."

"Sure sorry for the bother last night."

Marybeth shook her head. "No bother at all. I was just worried you might have frozen your feet or hands. Do your toes and fingers feel all right?"

"Right as rain."

They avoided the topic of Marybeth helping him undress and get in bed. Avoided talking about sleeping with him in her arms. Edward decided they both knew what had happened, and it didn't need to complicate matters now.

"I'm more determined than ever to get us moved over to Fred's place," Edward said as he finished up his stew. He got up and went to the stove to refill his bowl. "If I can secure a stove today, we could move."

"Melody told me stoves are hard to come by. She said the jail spent twenty-five dollars apiece on the two that are there."

"Yeah, and we don't have that much to spend. Say, do you want any more of this stew?"

"No, go ahead and finish it," Marybeth said as she gave Carrie another small piece of bread. The child was in a world all her own, working hard to keep her spoon from losing its contents.

Edward dumped the rest of the stew into his bowl and set the pot aside. "Fred told me there was going to be a sale today—if the storm was over. A man was hanged for murder, and when that happens, they sell off the man's stuff to pay for the expense of his burial. He had a cookstove, so I figured to try and bid on it."

"I have a few dollars, if you need them," Marybeth replied.

"No, save it for buying groceries. I have enough. The supplies to finish Fred's building were expensive, but I've been very careful with my pay and can use that too." He rejoined Marybeth at the table. "I'll check it out as soon as I finish eating."

Marybeth met his gaze, and Edward couldn't help but reach out and touch her hand.

"Thank you for saving my life. I think I probably would have died outside the tent if you hadn't heard me and helped me in. I had just about given up."

She squeezed his fingers. "We're a team now. I intend to be a good wife to you, Edward. You saved me and Carrie. I owe you my life, because without the two of you, I don't think I could have gone on."

Edward gave a nod, but he wasn't in any hurry to let go of her hand. It was strange the way a whir of emotions left him feeling off center. She really was the most remarkable of women. She wasn't easily frightened and could fend for herself when necessary. Janey had always spoken of Marybeth as being so smart and capable. She had always wanted to be more like her friend, though Edward had assured her she was just perfect the way she was. But in Cheyenne, it was a blessing to have a woman like Marybeth.

⁓

Marybeth tidied up around the tent after Edward left. She had a lot of dirty clothes that needed washing, but the idea of trying to heat up water and scrub clothes in the small space was hard to consider. Still, it would have to be done. Edward made sure she had plenty of water, so there really wasn't any good excuse to avoid it.

"Hello!" Melody called from outside.

"Come in." Marybeth breathed a sigh of relief at the excuse to further distance herself from laundry.

Melody entered the tent wearing a hooded wool cloak. She held a basket of something in her arms and quickly extended it to Marybeth.

"I baked cookies yesterday during the storm. Seemed like there was nothing else to do. Da slept most of the day, since the railroad wasn't going to even attempt to work on construction."

"I thought your father was a rail builder." Marybeth took the basket and put it on the table.

"He is, but in the winter when they stop working on the line, the men who stick around take on any job that's available. A lot of them leave the area and never come back. Sometimes I wish Da would get that notion." She took a seat without Marybeth even needing to suggest it.

Carrie popped up from the crate and grinned. "I want cookies."

"In a little bit," Marybeth said. "You keep playing while I talk to Melody."

The little girl frowned and seemed on the verge of complaint, but she surprised Marybeth and went back to her play. Marybeth took a seat at the table.

"Edward's looking for a stove to buy, and once that's installed at the Hendersons', we can move."

"I'm sure it'll be nicer to be in a real building. Although I haven't really minded the tent. Da keeps me supplied with plenty of coal and wood. He's ingenious in the way he's rigged things up to protect us from the wind. We're always warm and secure. I don't need much room for anything else."

"There isn't enough room for doing the laundry indoors. I suppose in the summer it's not as much trouble."

"Da pays to have it done in the winter. Not that I couldn't manage, but he knows it's hard to take care of in the winter. It's like a Christmas gift to me."

"Christmas will be here before we know it. And Carrie's birthday. She was born on the thirtieth of December."

"And she'll be two this year?"

Marybeth nodded. "She's growing fast."

"Before you know it, you'll have another baby, and then caring for one will seem like a dream."

Her words took Marybeth by surprise, but she covered it by popping up and reaching for the tea kettle. "Would you like some tea?"

Melody shook her head. "No, that's not necessary. I just wanted to stop by and visit for a minute, then I'm heading off to deliver more cookies."

Marybeth took her seat again. "Edward nearly lost his way in the snowstorm last night. When he finally found the tent, he was half frozen to death."

"A lot of folks get lost and die out here. Not just in the snows either. There's so little to mark the way. Some try to follow Crow Creek, but that doesn't always bode well. There were several times last summer they had to rally the army to go out and search for some poor lost soul."

"I can't even imagine. Coming here on the train, we saw stretch after stretch of nothing but prairie and endless horizons."

"I remember it well." Melody glanced around. "Are you going to need help packing? I can carve out the time to do that if you need. My winter days are mostly spent cooking and reading, what with Da having the laundry done. They even do the mending. Once I get things cleaned up in the morning and manage whatever food we need, I don't have too much to do. Now, wet spring and hot summer days are a whole different story. But come spring, we'll be movin' on once again, so that will be work enough just seein' to that."

"I don't envy you." Moving every few months didn't sound like any fun at all. Just imagining the packing and unpacking was enough to weary a soul.

"It's not an easy life, to be sure, but it's mine. So just let me know, and I'll come help you."

Marybeth smiled. "That would be wonderful. We don't have much, but obviously it will all need to be repacked."

"If the Hendersons have a wagon, I wouldn't bother to pack the rugs. We can roll those and just load them on the wagon."

"I hadn't thought of that, but Edward did say that Fred would come and pick up the crates, so I'll keep that in mind. That will help a lot. I won't need to clean them so thoroughly if they aren't going to be loaded in the crates."

Melody got to her feet. "Well, just be givin' me a shout, and I'll come a-runnin', as Da would say." She laughed and headed for the flaps. "I'll miss you being next door, but you won't be that far away."

"No, not really. I'll expect you to stop by often. With or without cookies."

After Melody had gone, Marybeth thought about the move. She hoped—prayed—it would be within the next few days. The Henderson house was closer to town proper, and being in a wooden structure where she could actually lock a door would give her great relief. Of course, she and Carrie would still spend their nights alone.

She looked again at the pile of clothes. Maybe she could ask Edward about sending it to the laundry. She laughed to herself. That would be the day. She wasn't going to shirk her wifely responsibilities and ask someone else to wash her clothes.

"Well, Miss Carrie, I suppose it's time I just get busy."

Carrie was standing at the edge of the crate and began to clap her hands. "Get busy."

Two hours later, it was dark again, and Edward hadn't come home. The day had passed so quickly that Marybeth hadn't even thought about what to cook for their dinner. She usually made plenty so that she'd have enough for lunch the next day. She looked through the things she had to work with. In winter, the tent families kept a box outside the flaps with perishable items. Unfortunately, the current cold snap froze everything hard.

There was still a hunk of ham left, and Marybeth knew she had beans. Ham and beans were a good solution. She could make up a big pot and bake some corn bread as well. It would last them a couple of days, and even Carrie ate that without protest.

She brought the food in, then secured the flaps for the night. She'd had Carrie to the outhouse only a half hour earlier, so they were ready to be inside until morning.

The few things Marybeth had managed to get washed hung from a rope that Edward had secured from one tent pole to the other. Melody had told Marybeth that this was how a lot of folks dried their clothes. They also used the lines outside even in the cold. The clothes would often freeze but dried all the same. Later Marybeth would heat up the irons and finish the process, but first things first.

She thought again about the night before and Edward getting lost. She silently thanked God for watching over him. The fear of what she and Carrie would have done if he'd died crept into the forefront of her thoughts once again. No matter how hard she tried not to fret, she found it nearly impossible to let it go.

It dawned on her that she'd not been to any church services or prayer meetings since leaving Indiana. She and Edward had read the Bible together and prayed over their meals, but it wasn't the same. Melody had talked about the church where she and her father went. It wasn't so much a church as a few people who met together at city hall and listened to Dr. Scott preach. Melody said he was a good speaker and seemed to know the Bible very well.

Marybeth missed gathering with other Christians. Even when there were troubles like the kind Pastor Orton had brought about, Marybeth knew that the fellowship was something her soul craved. Not to mention the importance of hearing the Bible taught. She would speak to Edward and see if they couldn't start going to church on Sundays. It would cut into Edward's sleep, but maybe he missed it as much as she did.

By the time the beans were cooked, it was late. She had forgotten how long it would take to ready them and had fixed ham-and-cheese sandwiches for their supper while the beans continued to boil. Carrie had long since fallen asleep, and Marybeth took that time to heat up the irons and create a makeshift ironing board on the crate they used as a table. Oh, how she had taken for granted the comforts of home. Back in Indiana she had had a lovely ironing board and clothesline. There had been cupboards with plenty of space for all of her pans and dishes.

Memories of home and days when her mother had been alive came back to cheer her. Marybeth had loved working in the garden with her mother. Mama had a way of telling stories and teaching Marybeth about the cultivation of food all at the same time. It was more fun than work, even on hot, humid days when Marybeth would have loved to go swimming instead of labor in the dirt.

After Mama had died and Papa remarried, Marybeth had enjoyed learning things from Carrie's mother, Sarah. She'd been with them such a short time. Just a year. But Marybeth considered her a friend. They had both been so excited when it was announced that Sarah was expecting a baby. Marybeth had never looked forward to anything as much as she did the birth of her sister. But the delivery had been hard, and two hours after holding her infant daughter, Sarah slipped away from them. The doctor said she bled to death. A year later, they lost Janey. Childbirth had taken the life of both women—good friends that Marybeth had thought would be around forever.

The memories of saying good-bye to each still haunted Marybeth. Both had known they were dying. Sarah had made Marybeth promise she would be a mother to Carrie. Janey had asked Marybeth to watch over Edward.

Tears came to Marybeth as she let the memories fade. How different she had thought her life would be. Before her stepmother died, she had dreamed of marrying and living in a house near Edward and Janey. They would help each other, and their children would grow up together. They would attend church on Sundays and perhaps share Sunday meals. Sadly, that never happened.

But she had kept her promises. She had been a mother to Carrie and had watched over Edward. And she would go on with those tasks for as long as God gave her breath. It was her duty and pleasure. She was glad that she had them both and wasn't going to allow the devil to rob her of her joy. Even if life hadn't turned out the way she had hoped and dreamed, she would do her best and be thankful for what she had.

12

This is so much more than I'd imagined," Marybeth said, looking around her new home.

The workshop Fred planned was twenty by fifteen, but with some leftover lumber, he and Edward had added a little room off the kitchen area for bathing and laundry. They'd even managed to build some floor-to-ceiling shelves for storage. In the kitchen, they had put up counters where eventually Fred would do woodworking. For now, they served very well for food preparation and clean-up. They'd even nailed a couple of Fred's old crates to the wall to act as cupboards.

Eve had come up with a small table, as well as a couple of cots they had used when they first arrived.

"They aren't much," she had apologized, "but much better than sleeping on the floor."

And there was a floor! Not just hard-packed dirt. Most sheds didn't have that kind of luxury, but Fred said he'd always planned to have a floor, and so they did.

Edward and Fred had secured the stove at the sale of the dead man's things. It was a little bigger than the one in the tent but not by much. Still, once the men had it set up and safely vented, it warmed the entire room in a very short time. It was going to be perfect.

"I'm sorry there's no window just yet," Fred said. "I ordered a small one, but they said it might take a while to get it. Once it comes, we'll put it in over here, where I'll work." He pointed to the counter area where they'd framed a spot for a window. Edward had nailed a board over the open space from the outside to keep things warm inside.

Marybeth wasn't about to complain. "There weren't any windows in the tent either. This is just fine by me, Fred. You and Eve were more than generous. I'm excited about our new home."

"Sorry it's too cold to paint. The place would look completely different if you had a coat of paint on the walls," Eve Henderson said as she arrived.

"Again, it's just perfect. It's so much better than what we had." Marybeth had such a sense of peace. Where the tent never felt like home, this was already making her feel happy and relaxed.

"It won't be quite so hard to find, eh, Ed?" Fred said, laughing.

Marybeth had never heard anyone called Edward by the shortened version of his name. She didn't think it suited him. He was Edward, and that's all she saw him as. Not Ed or Eddie or Teddie. Just Edward.

"I've given serious thought to running a rope from the house to the jail," Edward said, laughing. "I doubt the freight wagons would appreciate it, but at least I'd find my way without trouble."

They all chuckled at that, but Marybeth knew they all took quite seriously the problem that could easily happen again.

When she, Carrie, and Melody walked over following the wagon with their things, Marybeth couldn't help but see how easy it had been for Edward to lose his way. Once you left the center of town, things got a little confusing, and on the outer edges of town, it was really bad. There were no street signs or landmarks, just wide-open spaces.

Eve turned to go. "It's nearly time for the menfolk to go to work. Why don't you all come up to the house and have a bite to eat? You didn't stop for lunch, so I know you must be hungry. The children are waiting and ready to eat." She and Melody had been watching over Carrie and the Henderson boys while the rest of them worked to get the shed in order.

"That suits me just fine," Fred replied and offered Eve his arm. "Let me escort you, milady." She smiled and took hold of him to make her trudge through the snow a little easier.

Edward reached out for Marybeth's hand. "It's kind of slick, so let me steady you."

Marybeth didn't argue. She took hold of his arm, and they followed the Hendersons toward the two-story white house. It was such a lovely house, and Marybeth was glad for any excuse to revisit the well-appointed rooms and to have a hot meal.

"Melody told me that you and Fred attend church with her," Marybeth said they as stepped into the house. "Do you suppose we'd be welcome to come?" She hadn't mentioned to Edward that she was going to ask about church. She hoped he wouldn't be against the idea.

"We'd love to have you," Eve replied, carefully wiping her boots. "We don't have a lot of people yet, but we're hoping we can keep gaining numbers and get a good amount of money set aside over time to build our own church."

"It'd be good to have you and your family, Edward," Fred

said. "I don't know why I didn't think to invite you since we have Sunday off. We meet at seven in the evening. There's a Sunday school class at two in the afternoon. Dr. Scott has the help of Reverend Allen. He's another lay minister, and he seems quite knowledgeable."

"Sounds good to me." Edward looked at Marybeth. "I've been thinking about finding a church for us."

"There are others who are gathering in homes and store-fronts. People know the need for God's Word out here. Sometimes just living this close to hell makes people more aware of their need for heaven," Fred said. "No matter what, we Cheyenneites know God is the answer for our community to better itself. Only with God-fearing people in positions of authority can we hope to clean up the west side and see this city mature into something great."

"Better be careful, Fred," Edward said with a hint of amuse-ment in his tone. "You're sounding more and more like a politician. Before you know it, they'll have you running for some office."

Fred chuckled. "They've already asked me a few times."

"What do you mean we have to go back to work for the railroad?" Emory asked his older brother. "I ain't of a mind to go back."

"I don't care. We're out of money, and our gambling isn't paying off the way we need it to." Hank Garlow looked at his brother and shook his head. "And you eat more than three men. I can't afford to feed you."

"Still ain't no reason to force a man to go back to work." Emory did up the buttons on his shirt.

"And that's another thing. You need a bath. You smell

worse than a barrel of dead rats. And that shirt hasn't seen a good washing in months."

"It's winter. Going down to the creek for a bath is out of the question, and you know it, so why give me a bad time about it? Can't afford one of them fancy bathhouses or a laundry to wash my clothes. Besides, you ain't exactly smellin' of roses yourself."

Hank threw an empty whiskey bottle at his brother. Emory barely ducked in time to keep from being hit on the side of the head. The bottle sailed over him and shattered against the wall.

"Now, who's gonna clean that up?" Emory asked. "You're so worried about cleanliness. You do it."

"I'm heading out. Gonna find me a game and something to eat." Hank stood and started putting on his coat.

"I thought you said we were out of money."

"We are. You ever know me to let that put an end to my fun?" He headed for the door and grabbed his felt hat from a peg at the door. "You comin'?"

Emory nodded and hurried to take up his coat. "Maybe we can rob some drunk. It's late enough there ought to be a few that have crawled into a bottle by now."

"My thoughts exactly. We'll find someone down on their luck—but not too down. Maybe we should start in town and work our way west."

Emory followed Hank out the door. They went about four blocks in silence without seeing a soul. The cold made Hank feel mean. He didn't have the patience to deal with Emory and his nonsense. If he started in whining about having to work, Hank was going to lay him out.

They spied their victim as they worked their way down Seventeenth Street. This town boasted drinkers around the clock, and finding people drunk this early wasn't at all unusual. Hank always used this to his benefit. Most of the sober souls were busy hurrying home or seeking supper. They paid little attention to the scum of their society. Especially when they knew they'd be joining them in a few short hours.

Hank and Emory followed the staggering man without his noticing for two blocks before maneuvering him behind one of the hotels, where they hit him over the head and easily relieved him of what money he had. They left him unconscious but alive and hurried away in the growing shadows of dusk.

"It's enough to get us started in a game and maybe get us something to eat," Hank said as they headed to the west side.

"And a drink or two?" Emory asked.

"Yeah. A drink or two would suit me just fine." Hank glanced back over his shoulder. He was always worried about someone coming after them. The law in this town was getting stronger every day, and new rules and regulations were constantly being approved. It wasn't at all what Hank liked to see, but it was the way of things, and he knew there was no escaping it.

The wind picked up and blew a sudden gust. Hank grabbed his hat just before it flew off his head. "Come on, Emory. Pick up your feet. I'm tired of being out in the cold."

Edward was grateful to have the move behind him. The tent had never been satisfactory. There had been so little room, and now with double the space, he figured they would be content until they could arrange for their own home come spring.

The biggest trouble now was the men and women who had too much time on their hands. The gamblers and prostitutes were happy to keep the railroad workers busy. With Christmas nearly upon them, the temperatures remained cold, and people were agitated and anxious. It snowed twice that week, and with the wind, it made for blizzard conditions, forcing people to remain inside. This meant more fighting. Barroom fights broke out nightly and often with severe results. Edward hoped and prayed this wasn't going to be the way of things until spring. Surely these people could learn to get along with each other.

"Are you ready?" Marybeth asked, adjusting her bonnet.

Edward glanced up and nodded. "I am. You?"

"Yes, I finally have Carrie dressed and ready to go. Cleaning her up after supper took a little longer than I expected."

Carrie came running and jumped into Edward's arms. "We go now."

He chuckled. "Yes, we go now."

He carried the little girl all the way to city hall, where they were supposed to meet for the seven o'clock church service. Despite the darkness, Carrie pointed out different things along the way and asked about them. She was especially concerned about a couple of dogs chasing each other.

Once inside, Edward and Marybeth were quickly introduced by Melody to Dr. Scott and some of the other congregants.

"Pleased to meet you and glad to have you join us. Find a seat, and we'll get started shortly."

Edward led them to a roughly made bench positioned at the back of the room. They had no sooner taken a seat when Fred and Eve entered with their boys. Eve gave Marybeth a wave, then said something to Fred. Edward found himself grateful for his former commander and his family. They had made this transition so much easier. Having their friendship meant the world to him.

"If everyone would take a seat, we have a couple of announcements," Dr. Scott proclaimed. Everyone found a place to sit, and the room quieted.

Dr. Scott stood at the front of the room. "I want to welcome all of you who are new to our congregation. You might find it a little strange to hold services at seven in the evening on Sunday, but it was a combination of issues that brought us to this decision. When we have a place of our own, we will hold regular Sunday morning services. The more you tithe, the sooner we'll be able to break ground, so keep that in mind."

He chuckled and pulled out a piece of paper from his pocket. "The ladies are planning a church fair for the Saturday before Christmas—that's next Saturday. This will be a grand sale of baked goods and sewing items to raise money for a new church. I have permission for us to hold the sale here at city hall, so we won't have to worry about finding another location. The plan is to start at nine in the morning and run it until everything is sold. I'll have the door unlocked by eight o'clock, as Mrs. Scott assures me you'll be able to get everything set up in an hour. Men, make sure you're here to support your ladies in getting tables up. We'll be making them from scrap, so bring your hammers and any extra nails you might have on hand.

"Ladies, I want to encourage you to make lots of baked goods. This town is full of men who miss their wives and mamas and will buy up just about anything sweet you put together. Men, after you assist your ladies, please stick around to welcome the folks coming in. Invite them to church services, and let them know we plan to hold a revival in January.

"Lastly, Christmas Day services are available to us here.

City hall won't be open to the public, so we'll gather for a brief celebration at ten o'clock in the morning. Now please join me in prayer as we open our services."

Edward found that he immensely enjoyed Dr. Scott's teachings. The man had a very personable way about him—probably his years of being a physician. He commented more than once that he and Rev. Allen were only temporarily filling the pulpit because they felt God had called them for such a time as this. His entire sermon was centered on the topic of answering God's call. It gave Edward a renewed sense of purpose and calm. He'd felt called to come to Cheyenne, and in doing so, he had been compelled to help Marybeth and Carrie, as well. Even if their marriage was only one of convenience, they were committed as a family to seek God. Surely He would bless them in that.

The cold night air caused Carrie to seek Edward out as soon as they exited the building. She reached out to him from Marybeth's arms and once he held her, Carrie buried her face into the lining of Edward's coat collar.

"Poor baby," Marybeth said, pulling the hood of her cloak up over her bonnet. "She's not used to being out in such cold weather."

"I don't think any of us were ready for the cold temperatures here, but we'll do what we must do. Are you going to make some baked goods for the sale?"

"I thought I would. My mama used to make a plum cake that was quite delicious. I could make that and sell slices of the cake. Melody gave me some plums she'd canned last summer. They'd be perfect for the cake."

"How would you make it so you could sell the slices?"

"Hmm, that is a good question. Perhaps it would be better if I just made little hand pies. I could still use the plums."

"That sounds perfect. I know I can't be much help to you, but let me know if there's anything I can do."

"Well, we'll need some things from the store. I have a list made up of the regular things we need. I'll just add to it. Maybe Eve or Melody would be willing to watch Carrie, and I could go with you."

"Things are pretty unstable right now. I'd rather you wait at home and let me do the shopping. I'm happy to get anything that you need."

"That's fine, Edward. I would rather avoid conflict, and God knows you're in enough danger every day."

They walked a bit further before Edward added, "All I ask is that I get first dibs on the pies."

She laughed. "I wouldn't be much of a wife if I didn't see to it that my husband got to try them first."

Edward spoke without thinking. "You're a very good wife, Marybeth. The best, in fact."

13

Edward's words stayed with Marybeth for a long time after that evening. She couldn't help but find her affection for him growing. He was so thoughtful. Every day after he got up, he brought her two buckets of water. Before he left for his shift at the jail, he brought her two more. He was always considerate of their needs too. He made sure there was a barrel to burn the trash and took care of that chore most of the time so she didn't have to. He was also so good with Carrie. She loved him very much and freely called him Papa.

Life was much better at the Hendersons' than it had been in the tent. It seemed everyone was more relaxed and content. Melody stopped by often, and many times Eve volunteered to watch Carrie so that Marybeth and Melody could work on one of their projects for the sale. Sometimes she invited them to come to the house, where they all worked together. It was such great fellowship for Marybeth, who had been absent good friends since Janey's and Sarah's deaths.

The twenty-first of December was the day of the sale, and Marybeth had no trouble whatsoever in selling her pies, bread, and cookies. None of the ladies had to work very hard at all to sell their baked goods and sewing projects, and Dr. Scott declared that several hundred dollars had been made. And all well before noon.

Before she knew it, Christmas was upon them, and Marybeth was excited to present the gifts she'd been working on. Since the blizzard, Marybeth had been determined to see to it that Edward and Carrie had better coats to wear. She squirreled away money after their arrival in Cheyenne for emergencies and decided this was a critical need. After speaking to Eve, they arranged to have Fred pick up fabric for the coats at Armstrongs'. Enough, in fact, to make both coats from the same fabric. She figured that would amuse Carrie. Marybeth had worked every day on the creations after Edward went to work, and now she had them ready to present for Christmas.

"Who's ready for presents?" Edward asked, coming inside. It had been snowing that morning, and he was sprinkled with flakes all over his head and shoulders.

Marybeth gave it no thought and went to him with a dish towel and wiped the snow away. "I see it's still coming down."

"It is. I remember when I was a boy, snow on Christmas seemed magical." He smiled and looked at Carrie, who sat in her chair playing with her doll. "Who wants a Christmas present?" he asked, moving to where she sat. He pulled off his coat and casually draped it over the top of the child. Carrie giggled, and when Edward pulled it away, she squealed with delight. "I'll take that as a yes." He set his coat aside and looked at Marybeth. "How about you?"

"Me? What about me?"

"Are you ready for your Christmas present?"

Marybeth was surprised by this. "Are you ready for yours?"

Edward laughed. "Didn't know I had one coming, but sure. I'm always ready for presents."

They started with Carrie. Edward completely surprised Marybeth by presenting Carrie with a set of alphabet blocks. Each block was cut from a square of sanded wood that was painted with a letter of the alphabet on each side. It would be a most helpful tool in teaching Carrie how to read.

"Oh, Edward, what a perfect gift." Marybeth picked up one of the blocks. "Wherever did you get them?"

"Fred made them. He makes all sorts of wood toys and tools. He's especially good at making ax and sledge handles. Right now, he uses one of the spare bedrooms, but once we move out, he'll have all this space to really expand."

"These are quite beautiful, as well as useful. I can see why he wanted to build this place as a workshop." She put the block down. "I have a present for you too, Miss Carrie."

Marybeth went to her suitcase and opened it up. She lifted out the dark navy coat and held it up for Carrie to see. "Look here. You have a new coat."

Carrie looked up but wasn't all that interested. Marybeth laughed. Why should she be? A coat was nowhere near as much fun as a set of blocks. She put the coat aside.

"I guess I can't compete with blocks."

"She'll appreciate it when she has to walk to church."

Marybeth went back to the trunk. "Oh, I don't mind at all. She's a baby and has a right to enjoy her toys. Hopefully, my next endeavor will be met with more approval." She lifted another item from the suitcase and brought it to Edward.

He took the folded material and shook it out. His eyes widened. "A coat for me? Marybeth, this looks perfect." He quickly tried it on for size. "It fits like it was made for me."

"Because it was. I wanted to make sure you had a new coat since your old one seemed so thin."

"This will be much better suited to the cold. Thank you!" He grinned and shook his head. "You continue to amaze me."

"Thank you . . . I think." She went to the crate where she usually sat and picked up her teacup. The contents were cold, but she didn't care. She sipped the last of the cinnamon tea and smiled to see her family so content.

"I guess it's time for your present," Edward said, heading for the back laundry room.

Marybeth frowned. What could he have back there? She hadn't even expected him to get her anything.

He returned shortly carrying a rocking chair. She gasped, unable to contain her surprise. When had he managed to hide that there?

She jumped to her feet as he placed the rocker near Carrie. "Now you have a proper chair."

"Oh, Edward, it's too wonderful." She approached it in awe and ran her fingers along the beautifully curved arm of the chair.

"Are you gonna try it out?"

With only a bit of hesitation, she sat down and felt the chair sway back. She smiled and began to rock in earnest. It was perfect.

"Edward, this is such a wonderful gift. I could never have imagined it. Oh, to have a real chair!" She closed her eyes and rocked back and forth without speaking. It was almost like being home. No. This was home, and it finally was starting to feel that way.

"Do you like it?"

She opened her eyes and jumped up. Without thought to

what she was doing, she went to him and hugged him close. "I don't just like it—I love it. I have never had a better gift."

She lifted her face to his and felt her heart skip a beat. He was smiling and gazing down at her with such a look of tenderness . . . and dare she say love? Without warning, he lowered his face and let his lips claim hers. Her first grown-up kiss. A kiss unlike any she had known. And from a man with whom she was falling in love.

Marybeth wrapped her arms around his neck and sighed. But just as quickly as the kiss had started, Edward put an end to it. He pushed Marybeth away and muttered something under his breath. He stormed from the room without another word, leaving Marybeth staring after him with mouth agape. What had happened?

She went to the still-open door and gazed out after him. Where would he go? It was Christmas, and they were due to go to church in two hours.

"Please come back," she whispered. "Please."

I kissed her. What a fool. I actually kissed her.

Edward muttered to himself and kicked at the snow like an adolescent who'd just been reprimanded by his father.

Why had he let it happen? No. Why had he *made* it happen? He was to blame, pure and simple. She had embraced him, that much was true. But he was the one who wanted to kiss her. He'd looked down and seen the joy in her expression over a chair. A stupid rocking chair. A standard comfort of life that shouldn't have mattered so much. But it did. She had given up everything to come west with him. The impact was really starting to bother him.

Edward had taken her from the home she'd shared with

her mother and father and brought her to the wilds of the Dakota Territory. To this hell-on-wheels town, as so many referenced it. The poor woman couldn't even go shopping without an armed escort.

"You're a fool, Vogel. A pure and simple fool."

And now he'd kissed her, and she'd returned the kiss. He'd given her a promise of something he could never fulfill. He'd given her false hopes of a husband who could love her as a wife deserved to be loved.

He glanced around the neighborhood. It was Christmas morning, for pity's sake. People were celebrating the joy of Jesus come to earth. And he'd kissed Marybeth Kruger. Marybeth Vogel. His wife.

"Now what? What do I do now?"

He drew a deep breath and headed back to the house. He'd apologize. He'd explain it was the joy of the moment. Seeing her happy. Feeling happy himself. She'd understand. Marybeth was that way.

Carrie was still playing with her blocks when Edward walked in. Marybeth was putting dishes away.

"I'm sorry for my actions. I shouldn't have kissed you. It wasn't right."

Marybeth looked up at him as if nothing had happened. She smiled. "We all get caught up in the moment when things are going well. We should probably get our things together and get ready for church."

Edward studied her for a moment, then nodded. He went to where he had his things and took up his Bible. She wasn't upset with him. That was a relief. He wouldn't have been able to stand it if she'd cried or felt uncared for because of his words. That would have troubled him more than he could say.

He glanced at her from across the room and frowned. But why wasn't she upset?

⌒

Marybeth hated herself for not being honest with Edward. She knew it was her fault for letting the kiss happen. She'd gone and lost control and hugged him. It was only natural that they should kiss. Wasn't it?

She helped Carrie into her coat, then did up the buttons.

"Pretty," Carrie said, touching each cloth-covered button. "Tanks."

"Oh, darling girl, you're welcome. Merry Christmas." Marybeth pulled her close and kissed Carrie's forehead.

Carrie surprised her by wrapping her arms around Marybeth's neck. "Wuv you."

"I love you too." Marybeth felt tears come to her eyes. They weren't because of Carrie, however. "You're so sweet." She hugged Carrie and put her face against the little girl's neck, hoping she could get control of her emotions before Edward saw.

"You my mama," Carrie said, and this time Marybeth gasped and pulled back.

"What did you say?"

"Mama." Carrie patted her cheek. "My mama."

Marybeth had never really worked with Carrie to call her anything in particular. Pa had always called her darlin' girl or my gal. Marybeth's name was rarely used. Now Carrie had decided for herself to call Marybeth Mama. No doubt she'd heard the boys calling Eve Mama. It made perfect sense.

"Well, this solves a lot of issues, doesn't it?" she said, sniffing back her tears. "Yes, I am your mama. And someday you'll hear the entire story and know the complicated truth of our relationship, but for now, I'm just Mama."

"*My* mama," Carrie stressed.

Marybeth laughed and wiped at her eyes. "You've given me the best Christmas present ever." She kissed Carrie again, then went for her bonnet.

"I guess we're Papa and Mama now," Edward said, his tone soft . . . tender.

Marybeth didn't look at him as she tied her bonnet on. "Yes, that's what we are. I'm glad she made the decision for me on what she should call me." She glanced up and met his gaze. "Now I know my place."

She said it more for herself but knew Edward would take it as affirmation for what he'd said. She smiled and reached for her cloak. Carrie had redeemed the day, and Marybeth wasn't going to let Edward's actions and comments cause her pain. She had made an agreement with him. It wasn't his fault that her feelings had gotten out of control. Marybeth was determined not to cause trouble for their arrangement. She needed him. Carrie needed him.

I can do this. I can live without love.

"We want you to come over for Christmas dinner," Eve told Marybeth after the church service. "Fred and I want to show you our appreciation."

"We're the ones who should be showing you appreciation. We are so much better off than we were before. You have blessed us by letting us live in the workshop until spring. I can't imagine anything more giving and loving. You two are really precious people."

Eve hugged her and then stood back. "I needed a friend,

Marybeth. Another woman with a child and household to keep. Someone who could understand the woes of life out here. Someone who knew what we'd left behind in Indiana. And someone who loved God more than anything."

"I do love Him," Marybeth replied. "He's all that's getting me through some days." She didn't bother to add that this was one of those days.

Edward and Fred soon joined them. "Did Eve invite you to Christmas dinner?" Fred asked.

"She did." Marybeth looked to Edward. "Is that all right with you?"

"Sure. I'm always happy when someone wants to cook for me, and Fred assures me that Eve has made quite a few desserts. You know my sweet tooth."

Marybeth smiled. She did. In fact, she knew almost everything about Edward Vogel.

"It's settled, then. Let's go to our house and break bread," Fred said, smiling.

Just then, the boys and Carrie came running. The boys threw themselves against Eve, laughing.

"My mama," Samuel said, looking at Carrie. "Not yours."

Carrie was unconcerned. She wrapped her arms around Marybeth's legs and hugged her tightly. "My mama."

Marybeth would have lost her balance, but Edward took hold of her arm and steadied her. They exchanged a look and began to laugh.

"Well, at least we know where that came from," Edward said, reaching down to lift Carrie in his arms.

She put her cheek against his and wrapped her little arms around his neck. "My papa," she proclaimed.

"Well, there you have it," Fred said, laughing. "She's put her claim on you both. There's no getting out of it now."

14

Carrie turned two on the thirtieth of December. It was hard to believe she was growing so fast. Already it seemed she had taken a huge leap in her talking skills. Marybeth credited it to playing with the Henderson boys. Back in Indiana, the only time Marybeth had let Carrie play with other children much was when she'd left her with the next-door neighbor. Those times were few and far between, however, and Mrs. Parker's children were usually in school.

Marybeth made Carrie a cake, and Edward presented her with a little wooden bed that he and Fred had made. Marybeth was impressed with the quality despite Edward's declaration that it had been made with scrap lumber.

"I think it's wonderful that you helped to make this," Marybeth declared as she looked the bed over.

"I'm glad you and Eve were able to make the little mattress for it," Edward replied.

Carrie climbed into the bed and back out several times. Laughing, she gave it a pat. "Tanks for my bed."

"You are quite welcome." Edward lifted her up and took her to her chair. "Now it's time to celebrate with cake."

"Cake, pease," Carrie called out from her feeding chair, getting more and more excited. "Cake! Cake!"

Marybeth turned back to the little girl. "I suppose cake is more exciting than a bed." She sliced a small piece and presented it to Carrie. "Happy birthday, sweetheart."

"Tanks." Carrie grabbed the piece with her hands, not even bothering to try to eat it with a fork.

Marybeth couldn't help but laugh at her antics. Sometimes a gal just had to do what a gal had to do. Carrie devoured the piece and pounded the top of the wooden tray. "I like cake."

Both Edward and Marybeth laughed at that. Edward reached over and gave her a quick kiss on the cheek despite the frosting that remained. "So do I."

"More pease."

"Just a little bit." Marybeth sliced another small piece and gave it to Carrie.

"This is mighty good cake, Marybeth." Edward was nearly finished with his first piece, and Marybeth knew he'd want a second. She sliced him another large piece and brought it to him. He didn't hesitate to take it.

"I'm going to have to eat fast and get down to the jail. Time's getting away from me." He went to work on the cake and followed it with a big swig of coffee. "Now, that's the way to finish a meal. Cake and hot coffee. We ought to have that every day."

Marybeth laughed. "It was hard enough just to get this cake made. Having cake everyday would be a little difficult."

Their life had been surprisingly peaceful and pleasant since the Christmas morning disaster. Marybeth had gone out of her way to be of good cheer. She loved making the shed a home, and she was determined to give Edward nothing to regret.

It didn't stop her from thinking about him almost constantly, however. She couldn't help but wonder exactly when her feelings for him started to deepen, but they had, and she was clearly in love with her husband. The only problem was, he couldn't return that love. She had prayed about it, asking God to show them what to do. She and Carrie had a good life . . . well, at least a decent life. Marybeth didn't want anything to interfere with that or cause Edward to regret taking them on.

"I'll be heading out," Edward said, getting his holster and gun from atop one of the crates that they used for a cupboard.

"Gun," Carrie said, pointing her tiny index finger. "No, no, no."

Marybeth might have laughed at the little girl's serious expression and waggled finger, but she didn't dare. She and Edward were working hard to teach Carrie the dangers of even touching the weapon.

"Very good, Carrie. The gun is a big no. You mustn't ever touch it. It will give you bad ouchies." Marybeth started to clean up the tray. Cake crumbs and frosting were everywhere it seemed.

Edward came to Carrie after he strapped on his gun. "You're a good girl, Carrie." This time he avoided her sticky face and kissed the top of her head.

Marybeth watched him with a tenderness that made her heart ache. "Be careful tonight. I'll be praying for you."

"I'll be careful." Edward ran his hand through the little girl's silky blond hair. "You've got cake and frosting in your hair, missy." He glanced up at Marybeth. "Looks like she's gonna need a good cleaning."

"I had it planned. Water is already heating." Marybeth used her damp rag to wipe a big smear of frosting from Carrie's dress. "By the time I finish with her, I'll need a bath."

"Be nice if we could get a tub. I'll keep my eyes open for

something of use to us in that department." He took up his hat and headed for the door. "Oh, I'm meeting Dr. Scott in the morning. We're gonna talk about the upcoming revival, so I'll be late coming home."

"I'm so excited about our revival. Dr. Scott's wife seems to think there will be a great many folks converted if we can just get them to attend."

"The Spirit of God will guide folks. We just need to extend the invitation and our friendship. I remember my pa sayin' that folks need a Savior, but they also need a friend." He smiled. "Pa also said we need to be careful and not try to be both."

"Out here they do need both. I can't imagine getting through the days and nights without the comfort of Jesus. It must be a terrible loneliness to be without God. It's hard enough with Him."

Edward frowned. "Are you havin' a rough time of it, Marybeth?"

She hadn't meant to say anything to cause him to question their arrangement. "No. There are days that are harder than others, but since we came to the shed here . . . well, things are much better. I didn't mean to suggest they weren't. It's just that this is a difficult part of the country. There are dangers everywhere, and that won't go away anytime soon."

"Come spring it will change a lot. Fred said it's almost an overnight difference when the train moves on down the tracks. Most of the heathens, as he calls them, pack up fast and move on down the line. It's not called 'Hell on Wheels' for no reason."

"It would be nice if all the bad and negative could leave with them. I'm not fool enough to believe that, though. Even back in Indiana we had our bad folks and difficult days. Still, to have most of the west side load up and go . . . well, I think that will benefit us more than anything. And hopefully we'll hear something by then from George about my house. I think I'll borrow some paper and write him a letter. I can let him and Inga know how we're doing. After sending them that first letter, we've really been poor correspondents."

"True enough. Well, include my love in it and tell Inga I'll try to write to her soon. Give her my love and tell her to keep praying for us."

Without further comment, Edward left. Marybeth paused in her work and heaved a heavy sigh. Another evening alone. Another day gone by.

"Want down pease."

Marybeth shook off her feelings of gloom. "First, we have to wash you up." She grabbed the porcelain bowl she used for such things. There was already room temperature water in the buckets, and with the hot water from the stove, it made a nice warm bath.

"All right. Let's get you washed up properly." Marybeth undid the buttons of Carrie's little dress and slipped it down. "Goodness, how did you get cake and frosting under your collar?"

Marybeth soon had her undressed and kept Carrie in her trayed chair to contain her. It was far easier this way. Oh, for the days when she'd had a proper bathtub.

Carrie wasn't a fan of washing up, but she endured knowing she wouldn't be let down until the bathing was finished. Marybeth hurried the process, knowing Carrie would soon get cranky. As a final measure, Marybeth rubbed a washcloth over Carrie's head, just in case there was some hidden frosting lurking.

Carrie looked up at Marybeth for inspection and gave her a big toothy smile. "I clean." She held up her hands and splayed out her fingers.

"Indeed, you are." Marybeth wiped the tray down before lifting it up so that Carrie could jump off the seat. She was such a daredevil and loved this part of the ritual.

"All right, little miss, we need to get you dressed. And then you're going to need to play with your blocks while I start washing clothes. Can you be a good girl and stay away from the stove?"

"It hot, and I don't touch," she said, shaking her head in a most serious manner.

Marybeth smiled and gave her sister a nod. "That's right. You don't ever touch. It's hot."

"Ouchie."

"Yes." Marybeth put Carrie in a clean dress, noting that it didn't fit quite as loosely as it once did. She was growing up. That was for sure. The thought was bittersweet. She was such a darling baby, probably the only one Marybeth would ever have.

She bit her lip as tears came to her eyes. When Mama had died, Marybeth had pledged herself to taking care of her father. When he'd married Sarah, Marybeth gave some consideration to a life of her own—of courtship and marriage. She hoped to marry and live close to Janey and Edward. But then Sarah and Janey died, changing everything.

With the two-year-old dressed, Marybeth led her to where her blocks were waiting. "I love you, baby. You are precious to me." She knelt down by Carrie and hugged her close.

"My mama," Carrie said, patting Marybeth's face ever so gently. "I wuv you."

Sunday, January 5, 1868, was a grand day in the life of Cheyenne. The newly built school was dedicated, and throngs of people turned out despite the temperatures dropping to minus twenty-three degrees. Edward insisted that Marybeth and Carrie stay home. It was much too cold for Carrie, who had taken sick. It appeared to be nothing more than sniffles, but he didn't want it turning into something worse. He promised Marybeth he'd give her all the details later.

The school had been built on Nineteenth Street and measured twenty-four by forty. The three-man school committee had deemed that plenty big for the town's first school. Money had been raised by Cheyenne's citizens, and in November the ground had been broken to build despite the onset of winter weather. Now here they were with the better half of Cheyenne standing in the frigid weather to celebrate one more step toward civilized living.

The crowd was ushered into the school, and shortly thereafter, Dr. Scott quieted them so that he could open in prayer.

Afterward, Dr. George H. Russell addressed the crowd. "We've hired a principal and headmaster, Mr. Arnold, and I want to welcome him and his wife, who will also help with teaching since we have over one hundred students signed up for classes."

The crowd gasped at the number as the couple came forward. Edward couldn't help but wonder how one man or even one man and woman could manage one hundred children ranging in age from six to sixteen.

"Mr. and Mrs. Arnold, we are very glad to have you join us in Cheyenne. We know that you will do a fine job." The couple smiled and took seats with the other speakers for the celebration.

"We are proud of our townsfolk for raising funds to build this fine school, although expenses did exceed the amount we raised. We must remember that education is critical for our children, however. We may be, nay, we will be called upon to dig deeper in our pockets to finance this institution, but it is necessary if Cheyenne is to become the great city that everyone believes it can be."

After Dr. Russell concluded his thoughts, twenty-five-year-old William W. Corlett addressed the crowd. Corlett, a lawyer now teamed up to create a law firm with another city father, J. R. Whitehead, was enthusiastic about Cheyenne's growth and development. Edward knew the man from the newly formed court system. Corlett was a knowledgeable man who felt compelled to bring law and order to the town. He spoke to the Cheyenneites about their responsibility to civilize this area and drive the battle forward to becoming their own territory and then a state, with Cheyenne as the capital city. Cheers went up all around, and soon Rev. Allen closed the celebration in benediction.

Edward kept his eyes open for any signs of trouble despite it being his night off. Thankfully, the people seemed completely devoted to a happy spirit rather than an argumentative one.

Dr. Scott made his way to where Edward stood and shook his hand. "Good to see you, Edward. I don't suppose it will be all that long until that little girl of yours will be joining the scholars here."

"She just celebrated her second birthday last week, so it will be a few years."

"By then you'll no doubt have a few more to add to the number."

Edward looked away lest the doctor see the truth in his eyes. There wouldn't be any more children in the Vogel family.

"Dr. Scott," another man said, coming to join them.

"Reverend Cook, it's good to see you again. Do you know Edward Vogel? He's one of our city deputies."

Edward gave the man a nod. "It's a pleasure to meet you."

"Reverend Cook is heading up the Episcopal church."

"There's not much to show for it yet," the older man declared, "but I am determined to see it through. In fact, with over one hundred children already flooding into this school, I'm of a mind to write to my bishop and suggest we form a parish school."

"I suppose first there ought to be an actual church," Dr. Scott said, looking at the man with a smile.

"Yes, I agree. First must come the church, but I'm certain we can do something to help further education in this place as well."

Edward listened to the two men discuss the merits of schools run by the church for several minutes, then excused himself and made his way out. Marybeth would be excited to hear all the news, especially since Dr. Scott had cancelled church services in order to celebrate the new school. They'd all be glad when they could boast a church of their own and hold regular services in the morning.

Of course, there weren't any churches in Cheyenne that were set up in buildings of their own. Saloons and brothels got built first. Churches only went up when civilized people came to town, and while there were more and more of those coming every day, churches were still just a dream. Folks would have to go on meeting in buildings set aside for other purposes, at times when it wouldn't interfere with those purposes.

It would all come in time, he reminded himself. They just celebrated the first school, and there was already talk of changing out the tent hospital for a two-story building. Cheyenne hadn't even been a town for all that long. They would have to be patient. The railroad and its needs held precedence. The rest would follow.

15

"hanks for inviting us over," Marybeth said a few nights later as Eve ushered her and Carrie into the house. "I'm glad you weren't worried about Carrie's cold. It gives me a sense of relief to know that someone as experienced with children as you are isn't concerned."

"If it were something worse, I think we'd see signs of that. She just seems to have a congested head—nothing more. The boys have it too, so I thought maybe you'd enjoy just talking and letting the children play together. I know I could use a friend."

Marybeth nodded. "It does get lonely at times." She forced a smile.

The petite woman returned a smile that didn't quite reach her eyes. "Boys, take Carrie to your room and play."

"Come on," Samuel said, reaching for Carrie's hand. "We can build something."

"Build something," Carrie echoed. David followed them like a faithful puppy.

"David will follow Samuel anywhere. He's completely devoted to his big brother." Eve pointed to a large overstuffed chair by the fireplace. "Please sit. I'll get us some tea."

Marybeth took a seat, admiring the upholstery on the chair. She ran her hand over the armrest and settled back. It was easily the most comfortable chair in which she'd ever sat.

Eve returned after a few moments, bringing a tray with tea and a few shortbread cookies. She poured the tea and handed Marybeth a cup and saucer.

"Smells good." Marybeth breathed deep of the aroma.

"It's a special oolong tea from China. My mother found it on a trip to San Francisco, and we've tried to keep some on hand ever since." She took her seat and poured another cup. "When Fred and I moved here, she sent some with me. It hasn't been easy to get, but the railroad will change all of that. Hopefully, it will bring down the price as well. Although"— she gave a little shrug—"my folks can afford it."

Marybeth sampled the brew. It was exquisite. A slight woody fragrance with a hint of sweetness.

"I'm a poor hostess. I forgot to ask if you wanted sugar or cream."

"Neither. I usually drink my tea plain. This is very good."

"Help yourself to the cookies. They are another indulgence of mine. My mother always had them at her teas. Our cook would make dozens and dozens. These I made myself. When I learned we were moving here, I had the cook show me how to make them. It isn't hard at all."

"I have a recipe for shortbread. It's very simple. Just three ingredients."

Eve glanced at the fire. "Mine is that way too. So simple." She sighed. "I miss having tea with my mother. She always held such wonderful teas." This time her smile was more genuine. She turned to Marybeth. "What about your mother? What did she think of you coming here?"

"My mother died when I was thirteen. If she were around,

I think she'd be worried for me. The dangers out here are enough to make any mother worry."

"I know. I fear constantly for the boys. Fred said I don't need to be afraid. He says the Indians would never attack the city and that the army is strong enough to repel them if they did. But the army is miles away, and we live on the edge of town. And not only that, there are the outlaws that roam free in Cheyenne. They're a worrisome bunch, to be sure."

"I agree. Edward says things will change once the railroad moves on west."

"Fred says the same thing, but I worry that won't be the case." She sipped her tea. "Especially now."

"Why especially now?" Marybeth asked. She could hear Carrie babbling to the boys about something, then came a squeal of laughter. Oh, to be so young and carefree.

"We're going to have another baby," Eve replied.

The statement drew Marybeth's immediate attention. "Oh, goodness. Congratulations. You must be so excited."

"Actually no. I'm afraid. We had the boys back east. We had everything we could hope for or need. Here . . . well, you know for yourself it's limited."

"Yes, I suppose it is, but there are doctors if something goes wrong. I'm sure there are midwives too. I assisted my stepmother when she gave birth to . . ." Marybeth hadn't been going to say anything about Carrie being her sister. She shrugged. "I can understand your worries, however."

"You'll be up against it yourself soon enough. No doubt you and Edward will be having another baby."

Marybeth didn't want to lie to this woman. She'd just made friends. She supposed it couldn't hurt to tell her the truth. After all, Edward had told Fred.

"My marriage isn't what it seems and neither is Carrie.

She's my sister. Her mother died giving her life. We're raising her as our own daughter, but we'll tell her the truth one day."

"Oh my, I never would have suspected. I mean, she calls you Mama and acts like the boys do with me."

"I'm the only mother she's known, so I suppose that comes naturally. She wasn't really calling me much of anything until she started playing with your boys. She's talking more about everything since meeting up with them."

"They do seem to have fun together." Eve gazed again at the fire. "It's not the life I would have given them, but Fred seems to think they'll be just fine."

"I'm sure they will. The town is settling down more every day, and everyone seems to think that once the railroad moves west, the troublesome folk will go with it."

"I can attest to the fact that they do seem eager to follow it," Eve replied. "And have done so since this line started in Omaha."

"I suppose they see railroad men with plenty of money and nothing to spend it on. It makes sense that they would do whatever it takes to get their share of that money."

"I suppose so." Eve leaned back and met Marybeth's gaze. "You said your marriage wasn't what it seemed. What did you mean?"

"Edward and I are married only in name. He was my best friend's husband, and he loved her so dearly he swore he'd never love another. We married because some folks back in Indiana wanted to take Carrie away from me after my pa died. They rightfully pointed out that I had no way to make a living, and my father hadn't left us with all that much. I was so afraid they would take her, but Edward came up with the perfect solution."

"I don't think I could live in a loveless marriage."

"Edward loves me in his own way, and I love him. We were good friends. Still are. It just seemed the most amicable way to resolve several problems. Your husband wrote to Edward about needing family men to settle Cheyenne, and he figured marriage to me would afford him that status. We served a purpose to help each other."

"Still, it's got to be difficult. Every girl dreams of finding the right man to spend her life with," Eve said, shaking her head. "A soul can't live without love."

"I'm not without love, as I said. Edward cares deeply for Carrie and me. He just doesn't love me as a husband does a wife." Marybeth found herself wishing she'd said nothing. Now that they were discussing it, she wasn't really sure why it seemed important to tell Eve the truth. "I would appreciate it if you kept it to yourself. I really don't want everyone to know."

"Of course not."

"Fred knows. Edward felt he had to tell him the truth when we arrived, so I suppose if you need to discuss the matter you could talk to him."

"There's no need for discussion. You are Mrs. Vogel, and Carrie is your daughter. No one needs to think otherwise." She smiled. "More tea?"

"Yes, please." Marybeth let go a long breath. She didn't know Eve all that well, but she felt confident her secret was safe. "And I believe I'll try your shortbread."

Edward made the rounds around town, checking locked doors and speaking to one person or another as he filled his time. He was now known to most of the business owners, as well as many of the low-life characters whom he found necessary to deal with.

On an average night, Edward interrupted at least a couple dozen fights, or what he and Fred had come to call "personal disagreements." These consisted of gaming issues, as well as barroom complaints and problems with the ladies of the evening. Usually, fines were issued if there was a big enough complaint, but mostly they just did what they could to keep the peace and separate the people involved.

Edward had learned quickly that in a place like Cheyenne, the rules he'd followed back home wouldn't work. These were people who were used to calling the shots—living life in a loose manner of disregard. They held little value for human life. Fred said it was impossible to teach them such a thing. Their ways were set by the wrongs done them in their youth. Only God would be able to take those hearts of stone and give them flesh. However, they still had to abide by some rules, and the only thing they really understood was money and the lack thereof. Threaten their funding, and they were less likely to cause problems.

Edward made his way back to where he'd started at Lucky Bill's. So far things were pretty normal as he made his way inside. He gave Bill a nod and made his way to the bar.

"Any problems, Bill?"

The older, well-muscled man put a cup of coffee in front of Edward. "Things have been pretty quiet. There were a couple of disagreements earlier, but I calmed them down quick enough."

"Thanks for the coffee. Temperatures are dropping again. I suppose we'll get more snow."

"Probably. No one seems to know all that much about this place, so it's anyone's guess."

"You're cheating. I saw you deal that card off the bottom!" The accusation immediately drew Edward and Bill's attention.

Edward searched for the source of trouble and found the accused and accuser facing off about ten feet away at one of the plank-board tables. The man being confronted was the same card dealer Hank Garlow had beaten up some time back. The man doing the confronting was none other than Hank himself. His brother stood against the wall about five feet away.

"I wasn't cheating," the man told Garlow. He pushed back his coat to reveal a pistol.

"I saw you. You were dealing them off the bottom just like last time, and I ain't gonna tolerate being cheated by a lowlife like you," Hank countered. He copied the man's movements and revealed his own gun. "Now give me back the money you stole from me."

"I didn't steal anything, Hank. And if you don't clear out, I'll cut you down where you stand." He turned slightly toward Emory as the younger man eased his coat behind his gun. "And you stay out of this unless you want to be next."

"Stay out of it, Emory. I don't need your help to handle a snake like him." Hank's gaze never left the man.

Edward moved across the room to stand beside the dealer. "That's enough, boys. Probably better end this game. Find another way of amusing yourselves. And you all know that your guns were supposed to be checked. City ordinance doesn't allow for carrying firearms in city limits." Edward knew few of the west-enders followed through on the rules, but he wanted it out there just for the record.

"He owes me money," Hank declared. "I want it now."

"You'll get it," the man replied, pulling his gun.

Hank was much too fast. He shot at the man and hit him in the chest. It didn't deter the dealer from raising his gun to fire.

Everything happened at once. Edward knocked the gun

from the man's hand as Hank Garlow fired a second round. Hank's bullet hit him in the side, sending pain throughout Edward's body. It felt as if someone had just plowed into him, knocking him to the ground. A final blast from what must have been Hank's gun sounded one more time, but there was nothing Edward could do.

The card dealer fell to the ground beside him. It was evident the man was dead. A bullet hole oozed blood from just above his lifeless eyes. Bill told someone to go for the doctor, then threatened to shoot Hank if he didn't put his gun away.

Edward reached down to touch his side and drew up his hand. It was covered in blood. The sight of his own blood made him feel a bit woozy. Fighting it off, Edward struggled to sit up, but someone pushed him back down.

"Steady there, Deputy." The man turned away. "Someone help me get him up on the table."

A couple of men came and lifted Edward and put him on one of the plank-board tables that only moments before had held cards and chips. Edward did what he could to assess his situation. He was breathing just fine and could feel his heart pounding away. The wound couldn't be all that bad.

"He's losing a lot of blood," Bill said. "Pilson, go get me a bunch of bar towels." Bill looked down at Edward. "You're bleeding bad, Deputy. Hold still, and I'll do what I can."

Edward felt waves of dizziness mingled with pain. He didn't want to lose consciousness, but it seemed that was the way things were going.

"Marybeth," he whispered. Someone needed to tell her what had happened. He looked at Bill through fading vision. "Marybeth."

Hank sat back down and collected money from the table. Emory joined him and picked up the bottle of whiskey one of the men had abandoned.

"You killed another one, Hank. What's that now? Twelve?"

"Something like that," Hank said, chuckling. "But you all saw, he drew on me, and it was a fair fight."

"But you shot the deputy," someone said from the crowd.

"Yeah, but he was just in the way. I didn't shoot him on purpose. You all saw that too."

Fred Henderson appeared just then. He rushed to his now unconscious deputy. Following behind him came men that Hank knew only too well: members of the vigilante committee.

"What happened?" Fred asked Bill.

"Card game got out of hand. Garlow accused the dealer of cheating. Dealer pulled a gun on him," Bill replied. "Edward tried to break it up but got in the way of one of Hank's bullets."

"It was an accident," Hank declared loud enough for everyone to hear. "I had no problem with the deputy."

Fred looked at him hard, then glanced back at Bill. "Is that the way of it?"

"Yeah, the fight was self-defense, and Edward just got in the way. He's bleeding bad. We sent for the doc. The dealer is dead." Everyone around them agreed.

Henderson nodded, and the vigilantes seemed satisfied. Someone gave the order to collect the card dealer, while another asked if anyone knew him. Folks gathered around to tell what they could.

Hank looked at Emory and shrugged. "Wanna go somewhere else?"

"Yeah, this place is a mess."

Fred stepped in front of Hank. "You seem to cause an awful lot of trouble around here."

"Ain't me, lawman. You heard them. It was self-defense. The man was cheating."

"I heard what they said, but you always seem to find yourself at the center of these things. Maybe you should consider movin' on. Maybe head back to Julesburg or Omaha."

Hank lifted his chin a bit and puffed out his chest. "Ain't going nowhere. I have a job with the railroad, and they're here so that means I am as well." He didn't take his gaze off the man. He knew from having run into Fred and Edward before that they were friends. The last thing he needed was the man going for revenge. "Now, if you'll excuse me. Emory and I were just leaving. Got some other plans."

"Don't you even care to know if he lives or dies?" the lawman asked.

Hank shook his head. "Not in particular. I had no grudge against him. He got in the way, and that's all there was to it. If he dies, he dies."

"Never met anyone as coldhearted as you, Garlow."

His comment rather confused Hank. Why should he care about the deputy? Why should it seem strange to anyone that he didn't?

"I'm gonna take that as a compliment," Hank finally replied. "Come on, Emory. Let's go find some supper."

16

Marybeth was just about to gather Carrie and head back to the shed when Fred burst into the house, out of breath. He glanced at his wife and then saw Marybeth.

"There's been trouble, and you need to come with me right now." He barely paused for breath. "Eve, I need you to keep Carrie for her. Edward's been shot."

"Of course. You go ahead, Marybeth. Carrie can stay with us tonight. She'll be fine."

Marybeth barely heard her words. Edward had been shot. She jumped to her feet. "Take me to him."

Fred nodded. "Get your coat."

Marybeth moved to the front door, where Eve had hung her cloak over the back of a chair. Carrie's was there as well. She saw Fred go to Eve and whisper something. The action caused a shiver to go up her spine. What was he telling her? Was Edward really dead instead of just injured? Had Fred told her that he was shot to prepare her for the next blow?

She felt frozen in place holding her wrap and watching Fred kiss his wife goodbye. Fred came to her quickly and, without words, took the cloak and helped her on with it. Marybeth went through the motions but hardly knew what she was doing.

Oh, God, please help Edward. Don't let him die.

Fred put his arm around her and pushed her toward the door. "Let's go."

Marybeth had to quicken her pace to keep step with Fred. "Where . . . where is he?"

"Dr. Scott's place."

A bitter cold gust of air blew at them from the west. Marybeth didn't even attempt to hide her face. "What happened?"

"Hank Garlow had a shootout with a card dealer. Ed got caught up in the middle of it. Hank shot him in the side, but he didn't intend to. He killed the dealer."

"Oh, goodness."

She let Fred halfway pull her along the streets until they were in town. When Fred momentarily slowed his steps, Marybeth drew away from him and stopped.

"Is he dead, Fred?" She could hardly make out Fred's features, so there was no way to read his expression.

"It's not good. He was losing a lot of blood. An army assistant surgeon just happened to be nearby, and he jumped in immediately to help. We brought him to Dr. Scott's, and that's really all I know since I left to come get you."

Marybeth nodded and started walking again. "Let's hurry."

She wasn't sorry she'd asked the question. She'd always been able to deal with the truth better than someone telling her a lie to shield her from pain. It'd been that way when Pa had died. She knew when they'd come to her doorstep with the news that it wasn't good. But rather than just tell her, they tried to ease her into the truth of what had happened.

"Just tell me if he's dead," she had demanded, *"and then you can fill me in on what happened."*

The folks who had gathered to give her the bad news looked momentarily stunned, but they nodded and confirmed her suspicions. Her father had died instantly. The truth was something of a punch in the gut, but Marybeth preferred getting it straightaway rather than playing at the issue.

Now she was facing another life-and-death situation with Edward. Her worst fears were revealed, laid open for all to see.

God, please give me strength to deal with this and please keep Edward alive.

They arrived at Dr. Scott's. It was well lit, no doubt due to the circumstances. Fred didn't bother to knock but opened the door and made his way inside with Marybeth.

The temperature within was a sharp contrast to that outside. The welcome warmth helped Marybeth focus. She glanced around. The front room was void of people, but there was plenty of noise coming from the next room.

Fred stopped and gazed in with Marybeth close on his heels. Inside the exam room, Edward was stretched out on his back. Two men, Dr. Scott and another, who Marybeth presumed was the army surgeon, were working over him. Mrs. Scott was busy handing them whatever they asked for. There was blood on the doctors. Blood on the table. So much blood.

Marybeth wanted to offer her own help but knew there was little she could do. She prayed that God would give the men insight so that they would know what to do to keep Edward from dying.

Suddenly, it was all too much. She looked behind her and saw a chair. Making her way to it, she sank down feeling the strength go out of her legs. Her biggest fear had come true.

What was she going to do? How could she go on without Edward?

She remembered that he had said Inga and George would take her and Carrie in. Maybe if George hadn't sold the house she and Carrie could just return there. No, that wouldn't work. Pastor Orton was sure to show up with the judge and demand she give over Carrie. Nothing on that aspect would have changed. It would merely have been delayed.

Oh, God, please don't let Edward die. I need him so much. I know that may seem selfish, but it's the truth of the matter. Carrie and I need him.

Fred came and sat beside her. "I'm sorry this happened. Sorry as I can be. Garlow may not have meant to shoot Edward, but he's not one to care about his deeds so long as they serve his purpose."

"I feared something like this happening. Edward told me not to worry, but I did just the same."

"I'm sorry. It's all my fault that he's even here in Cheyenne."

Fred sounded so saddened that Marybeth felt the need to comfort him. "Edward wanted this life. He wanted to come west even before losing Janey. They talked all the time about going west and settling in Denver. It could have been there as easily as here. It's not your fault at all."

"I always enjoyed working with Ed. He was strong and capable and followed orders well. I never knew a young man more faithful and loyal."

"He is that," Marybeth agreed, wishing Fred wouldn't talk about Edward in the past tense. "When he believes in a thing or a person, he never gives up on them. He has the greatest admiration for you, Fred. I was always hearing about Major Henderson and his great exploits."

Fred smiled. "We had a great many exploits to be sure.

When I thought of men I'd like to have at my side in this town, Ed was the first name that came to mind."

She still didn't like the shortened name but tolerated it for Fred's sake. "I know Edward felt complimented by your request for him to come. That had to mean a lot since he thought so highly of you."

Dr. Scott appeared in the open doorway. His apron was smeared with blood. It was all Marybeth could focus on.

"I think we finally got the bleeding stopped. The next forty-eight hours will tell us everything. If he doesn't take an infection, he should be able to get beyond this. He's strong and young."

Marybeth let tears come to her eyes. "Thank God." She sniffed. "When can I see him?"

"Let us get him settled in a bed," Dr. Scott replied. "We have a room we use for patients. Fred, if you'll help us get him moved, that would be much appreciated."

"Certainly." He followed the doctor, leaving Marybeth alone.

Closing her eyes, Marybeth prayed for Edward, as well as herself. She'd never had to deal with something like this. Attending to the sick was one thing, but the wounded was entirely different. She had never been able to stomach wounds very well.

"Are you all right, my dear?"

Marybeth looked up. It was Mrs. Scott who posed the question. "I'm just a bit overwhelmed."

"That's understandable," Mrs. Scott replied. "These are trying times, to be sure. Still, you must remember that God is on the side of right. Edward is a good man who loves God, and God will look after His own."

"Yes, but sometimes God calls His own home." Marybeth

shook her head. "I don't want Him to do that. Not yet." Tears came to her eyes. "I love him so much."

"Of course you do." Mrs. Scott gave her a sympathetic smile. "He's your own dear husband."

Marybeth buried her face in her hands. No one understood. She had fallen in love with her husband against his wishes. And now he might be dying. The thought of losing him was too much.

"There, there, dear. Don't take on so. He's in good hands."

Marybeth fought to control her tears. "I'm sure . . . I'm sure . . . he is." She wiped her eyes on her sleeve. "I'm sorry for falling to pieces."

"Don't be. It's only natural when you care about someone. In a few minutes I'll take you to his side. We have two cots in the room, so you can stay with him if you like."

"Thank you. I'd like to do that. I don't want him to be alone, and I feel like I need to be with him."

The older woman smiled. "Of course you do. Now sit here, and I'll go check and see if they're ready for you to come back."

Marybeth nodded and eased back against the chair. Why was this so hard? Why couldn't she be strong and silent, without shedding tears and making a scene?

But I've never felt this way about anyone before. The very thought of him in pain causes me pain. If he were to die, I know a part of myself would die as well. Is this how it is when you fall in love?

Marybeth had only ever thought of the good things related to falling in love. And in honesty she'd given those thoughts little consideration. She had, after all, promised to take care of her father and baby sister. Falling in love would only be possible if the man in question was devoted to helping her with her obligations. Edward had agreed to those things, but he'd also made it clear that he wanted nothing of intimacy in their relationship. It altered everything and forced Marybeth to put aside thoughts of romance and falling in love.

"You can come back now, Marybeth," Mrs. Scott said upon returning.

Marybeth got to her feet and followed the older woman through the examination room into another room. She looked neither left nor right as they passed by the place where they'd worked on Edward. Marybeth knew she would probably have difficulty with the blood. Edward's blood.

The room was lit with a single oil lamp on a stand by the door. The narrow bed where Edward now rested was made up with sheets, a pillow, and blankets. He looked for all purposes to be sleeping and nothing more.

Fred brought a wooden chair for Marybeth to sit on and placed it by Edward's bed. She looked at him and nodded her thanks. Speaking, however, was impossible with the lump that had formed in her throat.

She sat down beside the cot and took hold of Edward's hand. It was cold and lifeless. She rubbed his hand with hers.

"I'll be back to check on him from time to time," Dr. Scott said. "When you tire, just feel free to stretch out on the cot. Mrs. Scott has already left blankets for you."

Marybeth nodded. Her gaze never left Edward's face. He was so pale. She supposed that was due to the loss of blood. She heard the others slip away, but they left the door open. No doubt to get to Edward quickly should she call out.

She drew his hand to her cheek. "You . . . you have to get better. You . . . can't . . ." She couldn't say the word *die*. It might make it happen.

Prayer was her only hope. Marybeth knew that was a

powerful gift God gave His children. She began to pray as never before, pleading with God on Edward's behalf.

Please hear me, Lord. Please. Edward needs You more than ever. He's injured and has lost a lot of blood. Only You can save him.

She closed her eyes and kissed his fingers. If it was possible to will someone to live, Marybeth was giving it her all.

"Marybeth?"

She looked up to find Melody. "What are you doing here?"

"My father was in the bar when Edward got shot. He was playing cards at another table. He helped the men get Edward here to Dr. Scott, then came to get me in case you needed anything."

"Oh, thank you. Please give him our thanks as well."

"I will. He's talking to Dr. Scott just now. I came back to see if there's anything I can do for you. I'd be happy to watch Carrie. I can take her to our tent or stay with her in your new place."

"Oh, that would be wonderful, Melody. She's with Eve and the boys right now. They've probably already gone to bed. If you would fetch her in the morning and take her to our place, that would be perfect. You can use anything we have to take care of her and make yourself comfortable."

Melody smiled and put her hand on Marybeth's shoulder. "I'll do just that. We'll be praying too. Da said it was pretty bad."

"Yes, he lost a lot of blood." Marybeth refrained from saying anything more. She didn't want to speak her fears aloud for fear of giving them some sort of power.

"Try not to worry. A lot of folks are praying. God will see you through this."

"It's just so hard. I can't lose him."

"You won't." Melody touched her shoulder. "I'm sure he'll recover. I wish I could stay here with you, but I know I'll better serve you taking care of Carrie."

"There's nothing here either of us can do but pray. And we can do that anywhere." Marybeth gave Melody a glance. "Thank you for coming and for helping with Carrie."

"That's what friends do. They bear one another's burdens."

When she'd gone, Marybeth stared down at Edward and forced a smile. She would trust this to God. She had to. She wouldn't let Satan defeat her. No matter what happened, God was the one she would trust. Let His will be done. But, oh, how she prayed that Edward's survival was His will.

Marybeth didn't remember when she had slipped onto the cot. When she woke up, she was covered in several blankets and felt quite rested. She glanced over at Edward. His color was better, but she didn't know if he'd regained consciousness.

She pulled on her boots and fumbled with the buttons. It seemed to take forever without a buttonhook, but she finally managed to secure the lower half of buttons on each boot. She had just transferred from cot to chair when Dr. Scott came in to check on Edward.

"How is he?" she asked.

"Doing well. His heart rate has been strong and regular and his breath more relaxed. The bleeding has stopped just as we hoped. It's all very positive."

"I'm so glad." Marybeth watched as the doctor felt Edward's head.

"He's running a slight fever, but that's typical. The body is fighting, and a low fever is actually a good sign that all is working as it should. We'll keep an eye on it, though. We don't want it to get out of hand."

She'd never heard anyone say a fever was a good thing. "Should I try to cool him down? Maybe wipe him with a cold cloth?"

"Not just yet. Let's watch him carefully. The next hours are critical. If he takes a turn for the worse, the fever will climb, and his breathing will be labored. I'll be back to check on him every hour. Now, what about you? How did you sleep?"

"Quite well. Thank you." Marybeth wasn't at all interested in discussing herself. She reached for Edward's hand and held it fast.

"Mrs. Scott hopes you'll join us for breakfast."

"No, I don't want to leave him, but please tell her thank you."

"You can tell her yourself. I'm sure she'll insist on bringing you something on a tray."

Marybeth shook her head. "I wouldn't want her to go to any trouble on my account. You have both been so good to help Edward."

Dr. Scott smiled. "That's my job, child. You're only going to be trouble to me if you pass out from weakness because you didn't let Mrs. Scott feed you. Cooperate, and that's the best thanks you can give me." He left the room, and Marybeth couldn't help but smile.

"He's a good man, our Dr. Scott," she told Edward. "I think you are in the best hands available to us." She touched Edward's forehead. It was warm, and it worried her even if the doctor said a fever was good. "You must get well, Edward. I need you so much. Please don't die." Those pesky tears came again, and Marybeth didn't even attempt to stop them.

"Don't leave me. I . . . need . . . you." She pressed a kiss on his cheek. "I love you."

"Love . . . you," he whispered in return.

Marybeth straightened and could see Edward was looking at her. "Oh! You're awake. Dr. Scott! Dr. Scott, come quickly." She jumped up and ran to the door. "Dr. Scott!"

"What's all the excitement about?" the older man questioned as he appeared.

"Edward is awake. He's speaking." She didn't bother to tell him what Edward had said. She wasn't even sure what he meant by it.

Dr. Scott smiled and approached Edward's cot. "Well, it's good to see you back amongst the living."

"What . . . happened?"

"You were shot. Hank Garlow was trying to set things right with a cardsharp and accidentally hit you with a bullet."

Edward closed his eyes and shook his head ever so slightly. "I don't remember much."

"You don't have to, son. There were plenty of witnesses." Dr. Scott pressed a wooden tube against his ear and against Edward's chest. He listened for several minutes, then moved the tube to another location on his patient's chest.

"Your lungs sound clear and the heart strong. These are all very good signs." Dr. Scott straightened. "Keep improving like this and we'll have you home before you know it."

The words were music to Marybeth's ears. Still, she could see how very weak Edward was and that he needed to rest. She waited until Dr. Scott was finished examining him before posing a question.

"Should he eat something?"

Dr. Scott gave her a smile. "Mrs. Scott has a famous broth that I helped her create. It has curative properties. I'll have her warm some up, and you can spoon that down him. He doesn't need to eat much, however. He needs to sleep. Rest is best. That's what my mother used to say."

Marybeth nodded and glanced back at her husband. Edward looked as if he'd fallen back asleep. She reached for the covers and pulled them up and over his chest. With the movement, Edward opened his eyes again.

"Do you need something?" Marybeth asked.

"No. You?"

"I just need you to recover. To get completely well. I was afraid I'd lost you."

He gave the hint of a nod. "Almost."

She trembled and pushed down her fears. "Guess God had other plans."

17

Edward had been with the Scotts now for a week, and the doctor wasn't yet talking about his release. He hadn't taken an infection but was very weak from the loss of blood. Marybeth prayed daily for Edward's recovery and did her best to be at his side to relieve Mrs. Scott from having to be his constant nurse.

Melody and Eve had worked out an arrangement for seeing to Carrie. Eve would have her at the house to play with the boys and take an afternoon nap. Then Melody would come by and pick her up and take her to the shed, where they would play until Marybeth got home. Sometimes Melody even made supper, which was quite nice. Always the shed was warm and welcoming, which helped to bolster Marybeth's worried spirits.

Besides her concern over Edward's recovery, Marybeth couldn't imagine what this ordeal was going to cost them. Dr. Scott had said nothing of the bill, but Marybeth felt he was due his wage for saving Edward's life. The assistant army surgeon had said that Edward would surely have died if they'd waited even five minutes more to stop the bleeding. There wasn't any amount of money Marybeth wouldn't pay in gratitude for that miracle. The only problem was that they didn't have much money since Edward wasn't working. Thankfully, Marybeth had come up with a solution that was seeing them through.

Fred walked her to the doctor's each morning, but often Marybeth came home on her own. It just wasn't convenient to wait and find someone who had time to escort her. She knew it was a risk, but one she felt she had to take. It was on one of those walks home that she saw a local laundry requesting a seamstress. Marybeth checked into the job and realized it was something she could easily manage. It didn't pay a lot, but enough so that she could keep food on the table for her and Carrie.

A knock sounded on the door, taking her from her thoughts. She knew it would be Fred. Marybeth had already dropped Carrie off with Eve, and Fred had promised to come get her after he attended to a couple of things.

"Sorry it took so long, Marybeth," Fred said as she opened the door. "You ready?"

"I am." She took up her coin purse and slipped it in her pocket. "Let's go."

They began the walk to town with Fred commenting on Carrie. "I see she's gotten over her cold."

"Yes, I used that syrup that Eve gave me. It helped her so much, and now she's feeling as good as ever."

"I'm glad to hear it. I see you've brought your sewing again."

Marybeth found it was easy to work on the mending while sitting with Edward. If he needed anything she could just set it aside and tend to him. "It's something I can do to keep busy and not just fret over Edward."

"I wish you'd told me sooner about the situation." Fred

shook his head. "I hate thinking of you two staying in that cold shed without coal or wood."

When Fred found out they were low on coal he assured Marybeth that he would provide whatever was needed. And he did. From that day forward, the bin was full, and she didn't have to worry about heating and cooking. Fred and Eve were both so good to check in and see if she or Carrie had needs. Melody and her father were helpful as well. In their short time in Cheyenne, they had made good friends.

"We're doing fine. I was just thinking of how much God has blessed us here in Cheyenne."

"I wish Eve could see it that way. She hates this place. She doesn't say a lot about it because she knows I feel called to be here, but she'd have us packed and on the next train east if I gave her the go-ahead."

"It's a hard country to be sure. I heard someone say that come warm weather we'll have Indians to worry about."

"The army will keep them peaceful. There are really some good folks among the native peoples."

"Some are warring, though, aren't they?"

"At times. I think many of those situations are of our own making. People tend to fight when they feel threatened, and the way the white man is pushing through their lands without regard to their needs is pretty threatening, if you ask me."

"I suppose so. I hadn't really considered it."

They reached Dr. Scott's place and were immediately ushered inside by Mrs. Scott. "Would you like some coffee?" she asked.

Fred shook his head. "No, I need to get home and go to bed. My shift will come around soon enough, and I'll be expected to be awake and alert all night. Ed doing well?"

Mrs. Scott laughed. "Mercy, yes. He's already had his

breakfast. He's got a bit of a recovery ahead of him, but he's doing quite well."

"Good to hear. Please tell him that I'll stop by this evening to see him."

Marybeth turned to Fred. "I'll make sure he knows. Thanks for seeing me here. I appreciate so much all that you and Eve are doing for us."

"My pleasure," Fred replied. "And my pleasure will be even greater when Ed is back on his feet and able to work with me again."

"That won't come for a few weeks," Dr. Scott said, entering the foyer. "He needs to be convinced of that by you, Fred. He's thinking he'll jump up and be back to work next week. I keep trying to explain to him that he must heal."

"I'll make sure he gets it through his head." Fred tipped his hat at the ladies and headed out the door, while Marybeth made her way to Edward's room. He was sitting up, reading the *Daily Leader* newspaper.

"Any good news?" she asked, coming into the room with a smile.

"The railroad is proposing to build a hospital at the corner of Seventeenth and Hill. It will have operating rooms, bathing rooms, wards, and even private rooms."

"Now if they can just convince doctors to come to Cheyenne."

Edward put the paper down. "They will. They'll pay them enough to convince them."

Marybeth settled into the chair she always used and nodded. "I'm sure you're right. The railroad always seems to have plenty of money for what they want."

"They've got over ten thousand men employed along the line and probably half of them are right here in Cheyenne.

And now they're making plans for the rails to connect to Denver. This is going to change everything in the West. We'll never be the same."

"No, I don't suppose so. I just hope we all live through it."

"Before you know it, we'll be all settled and civilized and then look out. We'll rival Denver."

Another week slipped by, and Edward's strength continued to improve. Even Dr. Scott was impressed with his healing.

"This is looking quite good. There's always something to be said for youth. You're also in good shape. I think we'll probably be letting you finish your recuperation at home soon."

"I'll be thankful for that. Not that you and the missus don't host a very nice hospital."

Dr. Scott replaced the bandage on Edward's wound. "We were called to serve and extend the love of Christ. We do our best."

"I wish all men of the cloth would see it that way," Marybeth said as she picked up her sewing.

"Mrs. Scott shared with me that you had a rather bad encounter with your pastor back home."

"Yes, I'm afraid so. Our pastor in Indiana was in everyone's business. He made it his job to know everything about everyone. He said that was his duty because we were his flock. But he also attempted to impose his will on us."

"Perhaps he felt that was how he could best bear the burdens of his congregants. Sometimes we can push too hard and impose ourselves in the lives of others without meaning to do anything more than extend the love of Jesus."

Marybeth considered his words for a moment. "He told us we were cursed for marrying like we did." She hadn't meant to bring that up and quickly moved on. "We both felt it was God's will for us, however."

"The Old Testament talks about people being cursed for their sin, but with Christ as your Savior, He takes all of that on so you don't have to. You aren't cursed if you have Jesus." He went to a porcelain bowl and poured water to wash his hands. "I hope you won't let it sour you on serving God and others," Dr. Scott continued. "He was just one man, and we've all got our faults and sins."

Marybeth had never really considered Pastor Orton that way. For some reason, she always thought of pastors as above sin. "You've helped me to think about the entire matter in a different light."

"I'm glad. We often expect perfection from men of God, but they aren't perfect. No one is. You know, I think when I talked about that at the revival, folks were quite surprised."

Marybeth nodded. "Goodness, that was right after Edward got shot. I nearly forgot. How did the revival go? I wanted to be there, but then all of this happened."

Dr. Scott chuckled. "I can give a good hellfire-and-brimstone sermon when called to. I am quite passionate about saving souls. Can't imagine standing before the Lord and admitting I had the information and ability to tell lost folks about Jesus offering salvation and did nothing. I think about thirty people got saved."

Marybeth smiled as she reattached a sleeve. "I don't know how anyone gets by without the assurance that when they die, they'll be with Jesus."

"A lot of folks don't believe it can be as simple as believing in Him and asking Him into their hearts. They want to make it hard, adding all sorts of other nonsense. Few ever think of the thief on the cross asking Jesus to remember him when He came into His kingdom. Jesus didn't require the man do anything else. He told him he would be with Him that day in paradise. He didn't have to buy a church pew or tithe a certain amount. Didn't have to take communion, memorize Scriptures, or get baptized. He just had to accept Jesus."

"I guess people think that because it is such an important matter that it can't be that simple," Edward said, grimacing as he tried to sit up. "These stitches gonna come out soon?"

"Yes, I'll probably take them out tomorrow. Try to be patient." Dr. Scott finished washing his hands and dried them on a towel.

"Sorry. I do my best, but I'm not used to just lying around."

"Well, you're going to have to promise to do so for at least another week after I send you home. Preferably two. I want to make sure your innards are fully repaired, and that takes time."

Marybeth was glad to hear that Dr. Scott was thinking about releasing Edward. She wouldn't feel at ease until he was home safe. Of course, then she'd be the one having to tend his wound, but given that it had already begun to heal, she figured she could stomach changing the bandage and cleaning the site.

"Well, I have other patients to see," Dr. Scott said, heading for the door. "You can be up for a few hours today. Just remember to get help. I don't want you getting out of bed on your own."

"I won't do it on my own. I promise," Edward said with a grin.

Marybeth focused on her sewing. How would it be when

Edward returned? So far, he'd said nothing about her declaration of love. She was grateful for that. She didn't want her feelings causing him worries. Hopefully he just thought it was the same kind of friendship love they'd mentioned before.

"You look deep in thought," Edward said.

Marybeth glanced up from the shirt momentarily, wondering what she should say. "I guess . . . I was."

"Has it been terribly hard on you?"

She was touched by the tenderness in his tone. "I was terrified that you would die. They told me you'd lost a lot of blood, and then I saw it for myself. Fred didn't seem at all confident that you would make it."

"He should know better. He's seen me wounded before this."

"That's right, you got shot in the war. Tell me about that." She hoped getting his mind on something else would keep him from asking her more about what she was thinking.

"Not a lot to tell. I was wounded in the Siege of Savannah. Shot through the left side. Now I have a scar on each side. Both times I was lucky enough to avoid it hitting the intestines. The doctors told me I would have died if the colon had been hit. Guess God put those bullets right where He wanted them. Bled a lot both times, and field hospitals are little better equipped than what we have here. But I made it through again, and I know it was because of God and the good doctors."

"I'm so sorry you had to go through this. People are evil to try to kill others."

"Hank didn't mean to shoot me. At least not this time. The man's heart is black as sin, however, and I get the feeling it's just a matter of time with him. Fred said the bad ones are all

188

in mean spirits because of the winter months. But it's nearly February and not too long before things will start warming up, and besides that, Fred said Hank and Emory have left town. No one has seen them since the shooting."

"I'm glad to hear that. I wish all the violent ones would just leave."

Edward shrugged. "That would probably take most of the population. And they're the ones keeping the money flowing on the west side of town."

Marybeth didn't want to think about that. There were far too many rowdies in Cheyenne. For all she knew, every shirt she had repaired could very well belong to one of them.

"You're doing an awful lot of sewing these days. Everything all right?" Edward asked.

"Oh, this?" Marybeth hadn't told him about the money situation. She supposed there was no time like the present. "I took on work. Since most of our money went to finishing out Fred's shed, there wasn't much left for food and coal. We're fine now."

Edward frowned. "I never thought to tell you that I have some money in the bank. I've been saving up some of each paycheck. You can go there and get money. I put you on the account even though they tried to dissuade me."

"Why would they dissuade you?"

"They said women on men's accounts just complicate matters and lead to no good, but I assured them you weren't the typical woman." He smiled. "And you aren't. I've been blessed by the way you've been at my side through this."

"Pa never trusted banks much. He said they were full of rules dreamed up to keep you from your money." She shrugged. "With the sewing and Fred providing coal, we've gotten by just fine. It's not like I need to fix hearty meals for you, so Carrie and I mainly eat simple. We can go on doing that until you get to come home, and then I'll worry about adding in meat and vegetables."

"No, don't wait. You two need decent food. I can just imagine you're having oatmeal and a piece of bread. Maybe some cheese. That's not enough. Get some real food. Oh, and don't forget to pay Dr. Scott. We definitely want to see his account properly settled."

She laughed and tied off her thread. "You're mighty bossy for a man who nearly lost his life."

"Maybe that's exactly why I'm bossy. I'm glad to be alive and figure to take charge of my family again."

"I'll be glad for that. Although, we have good friends, Edward. They've been there every step of the way for us. Melody has been good to watch Carrie so I could be here with you. Eve too. The ladies have even sent over the occasional meal, and Fred and Eve have had us to lunch several times. Fred has provided coal, as I mentioned, and he's walked me here so I can be with you. Mr. Doyle has brought wood and even an occasional peppermint stick for Carrie. They're all so dear to care about us. God has blessed us with good people to call friends."

"He has. I know. I wasn't afraid for you and Carrie. As dear as you are to me." He met her gaze. "And you are. More than I figured."

Marybeth nodded. "And you are to me. More than I figured."

"There's something else. I'm not sure exactly how to explain it, but I'm just going to say it. When I told you that I loved you—"

"You don't have to say anything," Marybeth interrupted. "I know you didn't mean anything by it."

"But I did."

She looked at him for a long moment. "I meant it too."

"I know. It doesn't change things. Not really. But I meant the words."

For several long minutes neither one said anything more. What was there to say? Marybeth had made herself clear, just as Edward had. It was hardly appropriate to tell him that she wanted more from him when he was barely past the throes of death.

18

Edward didn't like to admit it, but his feelings for Marybeth had changed. They were growing stronger toward her in the way he'd once felt about Janey. He was starting to think of her first thing every morning when he awoke, and then throughout the day, she'd come to mind at the strangest times. And always . . . always those feelings were ones of tenderness.

He'd only been home for three days now but seeing the way they lived in the small shed instead of a house was starting to rub him the wrong way. Marybeth deserved a home—a house with bedrooms and a proper kitchen. She deserved so much more than he was giving her, and even though it would be another month before the weather would start warming up, he was eager to plan a house.

"So have you heard anything from George and Inga? Father?" he asked as she cleaned up after lunch. She had insisted that he sit in her rocking chair for better support than the old crate he was used to using. He leaned back, grateful for the comfort. "I would have thought we'd have had a letter from them."

"No," Marybeth admitted as she dried the dishes. "Nothing since the brief note they sent after the New Year. I wrote and told them about your being shot and then another letter to let them know you were well on the mend, but I've heard nothing from them."

Edward frowned. "I hope they're doing all right. It's not like Inga. She wrote me all the time when I was in the army."

"They're probably just extra busy, and it has only been a few weeks, not even a month since I wrote them last. I have no idea how slow the mail moves this time of year. And it can't be easy to keep up with the horses and those boys of theirs, as well as your father's needs. Then to try and settle my affairs on top of everything else is just an added inconvenience. I'm sure they'll write when they get time. I'll check at the post office later. Melody and I are supposed to go shopping, and I need to return these mended clothes and get paid."

"Did you go to the bank like I told you to do?" he asked, worried that Marybeth was working much too hard.

"I haven't needed to. There's been more than enough money for the few needs we have. I will though, I promise. I need to buy more meat. We need to get you back on your feet, after all. Dr. Scott said you could benefit from some good beef liver."

Edward's eyes narrowed, and he shook his head. "I don't eat liver. Never have. Pa tried to make me once when I was just four or five. I threw up everywhere, and they never tried that again. I can't even abide the smell."

Marybeth smiled. "What a relief. I can't stand it either. I was wondering how in the world I was going to cook it for you."

He chuckled. "Well, good. Now that that's settled, we can

talk about something more pleasant. I was thinking we could start making plans for the new house."

"I'd like that. It's always fun to dream."

"This is no dream. We're going to get us a house before the weather turns hot. I'm determined."

"We still have to wait for the money, Edward. We can't very well buy supplies on wishes and dreams."

"No, but we can make plans. Once things are settled, we'll be able to get started. We have that nice plot of land the city gave me for signing on as a deputy. It's just a few blocks away. A perfect area for a family. So we might as well be ready. For instance, how many bedrooms do you suppose we should have?"

Marybeth looked away. Edward got the feeling something was wrong. "What is it?"

She shook her head but refused to look back at him. She busied herself instead with arranging the dishes.

"Marybeth, is something wrong?"

For a long moment, she said nothing. Finally, when she turned to face him, Edward could see there were tears in her eyes.

"What is it?"

She shook her head. "I've been wanting to say something—to talk about my . . . feelings for you."

Edward hadn't expected this. He knew he was struggling with his own heart. How could he hope to deal with hers as well? "Go on." He barely whispered the words, knowing this conversation could well cause problems for them both.

"I . . . well, seeing you nearly die was hard on me. I feared the worst, and it did something to me. I realized as I prayed for you and watched and tried to help you . . . that . . ." She heaved a heavy sigh. "Edward, I've lost my heart to you."

He couldn't help but nod. "I know. My feelings for you have changed in that same direction. I feel things for you that I thought I'd only ever feel for Janey."

She seemed almost relieved by this and joined him at the table. "Edward, I know we started this arrangement as . . . well, just that. An arrangement of convenience to help each other, but I've fallen in love with you. I want to be married to you in every way."

He shook his head without thinking. "No, I can't. I won't."

She looked surprised and bit her lower lip. She bowed her head. Edward felt terrible, and all he wanted to do was hold her and assure her that everything would be all right—that he would somehow find an amicable solution. But he had no confidence that he could make that happen.

"I'm sorry. I know I agreed to this arrangement," Marybeth said after several minutes. "I never expected to fall in love. I wasn't looking for that at all. But now that it's happened, I'm completely devoted. I won't ever stop loving you."

Trapped. Like a wounded animal, Edward knew he couldn't just get up and leave. His body was still working to recover, and even if he left . . . where would he go? Still, he didn't want to discuss the matter. Partly he feared hurting Marybeth. And partly he feared giving in to his own desires.

"I do love you, Marybeth. I won't deny that my feelings have changed." He hated that he had to hurt her. "But I won't be a husband to you in an intimate manner. I can't. I can't bear the thought of another wife dying in childbirth."

"Women have babies all the time and live. Janey was a sickly person. All of her life she was far more fragile than me. She caught colds and congestion every winter. She suffered with weak spells and fatigue. You know that very well. I don't have those problems. I'm not like her. I'm stronger."

He knew she was right. Janey had often commented on how she wished she had a constitution like Marybeth's. Marybeth would trudge through the snow to see Janey when she was sick. It never seemed to cause any problems for Marybeth.

"There are people in this world who aren't as strong physically, but Janey was strong in other ways," Marybeth said. "She was smart and considerate. Those were things I cherished about her."

"You're smart and considerate too. Don't think I don't know that. You two share a lot of similar qualities, but you've definitely got your differences as well. You have a better sense of humor. Janey was much too serious at times. She knew it too."

"She did." Marybeth dabbed her face with the edge of her apron. "She used to ask me how she could be more lighthearted. We used to pray together that she'd learn to see the humorous side of things."

"I don't remember her saying anything about that." Edward looked away. He didn't want to talk about Janey. With his growing feelings for Marybeth, he found the memories of his dead wife fading.

"She didn't want you to know," Marybeth replied. "We prayed about a lot of things that way. She wanted to be a good wife to you. I want to be that as well."

Edward couldn't keep from meeting her glance. "You are a good wife. You've endured so much in just the few short months we've been married. I have no complaints, and if not for the fears I have about what might happen, I would . . . I'd make you my wife in . . . every way." His mouth filled with cotton, and his throat went dry.

He saw her cheeks flush red as she looked away. Talking

about the intimacy of marriage, or in their case the lack of, wasn't easy for either of them.

"I'm sorry," she whispered. She cleared her throat and returned her gaze to him. "I should never have brought this up. You started talking about the house, however, and I couldn't help it. How many bedrooms should we have, you asked. I suppose the correct answer should be three. One for Carrie. One for me. One for you."

A knock sounded at the door to the shed. "It's me, Marybeth," Melody's cheerful voice rang out.

Marybeth lifted her chin slightly as Edward had noticed her doing when trying to face a problem head-on. She took her cloak from a peg by the door. "I'll be leaving with Melody. Eve is watching Carrie, as you know. Do you need me to help you back to bed, or would you like to sit for a while?"

"I'll sit."

She nodded, not quite looking him in the eye. And with that she opened the door and greeted Melody.

"I'm ready. I even put on those boy's trousers you gave me because it turned so cold. They are a lot warmer than pettipants." Marybeth took up her basket with the sewing.

"I told you." Melody looked past her to Edward. "How are you feeling today, Edward?"

"Better, thanks."

She nodded and turned to go as Marybeth closed the door behind her. Edward sat staring at that closed door for a long time. What in the world was he going to do? He'd never wanted to hold anyone more than he wanted to hold Marybeth. He wanted to be the one to cheer her and put a smile back on her face. And he sure as all get out didn't want separate bedrooms.

Marybeth did her best not to appear distraught or upset as she pulled on her gloves. She couldn't very well explain the crux of her problem to Melody. She glanced up and saw Eve at the back door to her house. Marybeth waved, and Eve motioned them over.

"Would you please pick me up some peppermint oil? I'm battling morning sickness, and I'm all out. The only thing that ever helps me is peppermint tea."

Marybeth came to the back step. "Of course. Do you need anything else?"

Eve shook her head. "Just the things we talked about earlier. Here's another dollar in case you don't have enough."

Marybeth took the money and slipped it in her pocket. "We'll be back before you know it. I'm just sorry you have to watch Carrie when you don't feel well."

"She's already asleep. The boys too. They were so rambunctious this morning. Made me glad Fred had to work extra hours. But at least he has tonight off. I cherish the nights when he can be here with me. I just never feel quite as safe without him."

Marybeth nodded. She felt safer with Edward at home too. Even an injured Edward was a force to be reckoned with, and she knew he would keep them protected from all harm. She pushed aside their earlier conversation. Somehow, she had to find a way to be content with the bargain she'd made.

"We will be back as soon as possible." Marybeth shifted the basket and smiled. "Try to get some rest while everyone else is sleeping."

She and Melody crossed the yard and headed for the street. Thanks to wagons and carriages, there were sets of ruts to follow rather than having to trudge through the snow. Marybeth put Edward out of her mind and brought up the fact that the church was now meeting at the new school.

"I like it better than meeting at city hall," Melody declared. "It's warmer and a lot more comfortable."

"Dr. Scott says we're getting a good savings set aside to build our own church. He thinks in maybe another year, or two at the most, we'll be able to start."

They talked about what the new church might look like and some of the new congregants, then the conversation turned to the Union Pacific's plans.

"Da says they'll get started clearing more land when they can. They've already graded fifteen miles west of town. He says there are over fifteen hundred men working to cut trees in the foothills. The railroad intends to have over a hundred thousand ties ready before they start laying tracks come April. It causes a slowdown for regular folks to get lumber, but Da says it'll get shipped in from back east."

"Edward is talking about us building our house in the spring," Marybeth said, hoping it was a safe topic. "I suppose we'll have to order the things we'll need."

"You might be able to get them up from Denver. I don't know when that railroad route will be put in place, but in the meantime, there is the freight and stage road. With that and the regular train service, we're doing pretty good for quality and quantity of supplies."

"It does seem like we've been getting better and better selections. I was glad to see milk again last time we went to Armstrongs'."

"Yes, and the *Leader* advertised fresh oysters at Spaid's. Da loves oyster soup. I make it for him whenever the oysters are available." Melody glanced heavenward. "I'm so glad it's a sunny day. Makes me think spring really will come around before long."

Marybeth agreed. She was already weary of the snow and cold. It wasn't that she hadn't lived with it in Indiana, but with this town situated out in the middle of nowhere with few trees and miles of open ground, the winter seemed much crueler. More isolating and deadly. Whenever the wind picked up, Marybeth worried about whether or not they'd have a blizzard.

"Melody Doyle!" a man's voice called out. "Melody!"

Both women looked in the direction of the voice. A man came running toward them. Marybeth tensed until he drew near. He was hardly more than a boy.

"Ya need to come. Your pa got hurt. Ain't all that bad, but he'll need ya to help get him home. He sent me to find ya."

"What happened to him, Zach?"

"Fell off one of the ladders."

Melody looked to Marybeth. "I'm so sorry. I won't be able to help you with the groceries."

"You go ahead. Your father needs you."

"He's probably thrown his back out. I just hope he hasn't broken something."

"Doc said he didn't think he was busted up, but he's hurtin' pretty good," the boy replied.

Melody shook her head. "I hate leaving you to manage for yourself. You shouldn't be alone. Why don't you head home, and we'll try again tomorrow?"

"I'll be fine. It seems quiet around here, and besides, Eve needs that peppermint oil. Most of the rowdies are sleeping it off so they can get all riled up again tonight, and the railroad men are mostly still working. I've got to turn in this sewing and pick up another batch. Then I'll hurry my shopping and get back before much time passes. Go on now, and tell your pa I'll be praying for him."

Melody hurried away with the boy. Both did a quickstep for the first block, then broke into a run. Marybeth whispered a prayer for Mr. Doyle and headed on down the block to Grier's Laundry. Just as she'd known, the exchange didn't take long at all. Next, she made her way to Armstrongs'. It seemed there were more people on the street just in the short time since she'd arrived. Something told her she should probably just turn around and go home, but Eve needed the peppermint oil.

Lord, please keep me in Your care and keep evil from me.

She knew Edward wouldn't like that she hadn't returned home, and she hated to displease him. Still, she kept seeing Eve's pale face. She glanced over her shoulder, then down the street. No one seemed to even notice her.

Stop fretting. She was being her own worst enemy. Marybeth whispered another prayer and headed forward with even greater determination. She was safe in God's care. To think otherwise was to doubt Him, and she wasn't about to do that now. Not when so much was at stake. The future might be questionable where she and Edward were concerned, but she knew that God could work out the details to even that situation.

She thought of her Bible verse that morning. Psalm 118, verse six. She steadied her nerves and whispered it aloud. "'The LORD is on my side; I will not fear: what can man do unto me?'"

Besides break my heart.

No. That verse included Edward. She wasn't going to let him discourage her or send her into more tears. She loved him, and she was his wife. She would honor God and the promises she made, and she would begin to pray like never before that God would somehow bring Edward around to a peace of heart that would allow him to let go of his fears.

"The LORD is on my side; I will not fear: what can man do unto me?"

19

Edward sat in the silence of the shed for a long time. He thought of his conversation with Marybeth and her sorrow over his determination to keep their marriage platonic. He knew he wasn't being fair to her. He should have seen the possibility of her falling in love with him. But he had convinced himself that would never happen. Just as he was convinced that it couldn't happen to him.

Yet it had. He had fallen in love with Marybeth. He pounded his fists on the arms of the rocker. Why hadn't he guarded his heart better?

"I'm a fool. That's what I am."

And now they were both up against it. They needed each other, and they loved each other. They were a true family in every way except for his refusal to be intimate. He wasn't even willing to be open with his affection for her. That would only lead to more desire, and he couldn't allow that.

He rubbed his side. Sitting too long caused it to ache, so he got up carefully and made his way to the cot. He knew he had to rest and clear his mind. He would pray. God had never failed to guide him, and He wouldn't stop now.

He reached for his Bible. "Lord, this one is a mess, and I need some answers."

～

Marybeth entered Armstrongs' and immediately looked for Cynthia Armstrong. She didn't have far to look. The woman was balancing several bolts of cloth and climbing a ladder to put them on a top shelf.

"Good thing you aren't afraid of heights," Marybeth said, coming to stand at the counter.

Cynthia placed the fabric on the shelf. "It is." She stretched to put the final bolt in place.

Marybeth found it a bit unnerving. "Please don't fall."

"Don't worry. I find myself up in the air probably half the day. I'm used to it." She glanced around the store. "Where's Melody?"

"Her father fell from a ladder. I guess that's why it's on my mind. He was hurt and needed to have her help getting home. I decided to come on ahead because Eve is suffering morning sickness and needs peppermint oil for her tea."

Cynthia nodded. "Anything else?"

Marybeth produced a list. "The first line of goods is for her. The second for me."

The older woman reviewed their needs. "I will wrap hers separately. Say, we've got something new. Mrs. Cameron brought it back with her after their trip to Boston. Look here." Cynthia disappeared behind the front counter.

Marybeth followed over to see what the woman was all excited about. It was only a moment before she produced a small box.

"This is Bell's Seasoning. Mrs. Cameron says they had it on their turkey and in the stuffing, and it was unlike anything she'd ever had. It's best with poultry dishes and works for chicken as well as turkey."

"That sounds quite interesting. I've never been one to use much in the way of spices. My pa never cared for anything but salt and pepper. I wonder if Edward would like it."

"Well, you should probably try a box. The supply won't last long once word gets out."

Marybeth nodded. "I'll take one. Hopefully I'll be able to figure out how to use it properly."

"Mrs. Cameron said the cook told her to use half a teaspoon to start. Some people don't like the strong taste of sage. I tried it yesterday on my chicken. Seems like I could have used a bit more. The sage suited us just fine."

"Is it just sage?"

Cynthia shook her head. "No, there are supposed to be six different spices, but no one is sure what they are. You can definitely smell the sage, though. There's no disguising that one."

"No, I don't suppose so."

Marybeth waited patiently while Cynthia grabbed up the rest of her order. After she'd paid, Marybeth put the things in her basket alongside the sewing. "I need to check on my mail and see if Edward's sister has finally written. Do you suppose it will be safe enough to do so?"

Cynthia nodded. "I can walk a ways with you." She pulled off her apron. "Let me tell Joe and get him up front to run the place for a few minutes. He's been unloading inventory all morning and will probably love the break."

"I hate to be a bother."

Cynthia shook her head. "No bother. We ladies need to look out for each other."

Marybeth smiled and waited by the front door. Cynthia

returned, pulling on an old heavy coat. It looked like a man's coat.

She laughed as she approached Marybeth. "You look positively intrigued by my wrap. This was one of Joe's old coats. I often throw it on for a quick trip outside. Believe me, you aren't the first one to be surprised. I get comments all the time."

"It looks like it will do the job, and that's all that really matters."

They made their way down the block and turned. Cynthia headed back to the store while Marybeth went on another block west, pulling her hood forward as the wind picked up. There was no mail waiting for her, unfortunately. More than anything she wanted to hear from Edward's family and know if George had managed to sell her house. Once that was done, they could move forward on their plans. However, thinking about building a house brought up her conversation with Edward. It was painful to imagine that they would live a separate life under one roof.

She made her way back toward the east, glad to leave the town and its activities for the more residential parts of Cheyenne. Reaching Dodge Street, she turned north toward Eighteenth. She had just passed a row of houses when she heard something behind her. It might have been nothing more than the wind, but when a male voice called out, Marybeth walked a little faster. Her heartbeat quickened, and though she wanted to turn around, she knew she didn't dare.

"Wait! Stop!"

She tried to refrain from doing so, but the commands were given with such an air of authority, Marybeth couldn't help herself. She took another step but glanced over her shoulder.

"Please, I need your help."

She stopped and turned. "Dr. Scott?" She pushed back her hood. "What in the world is going on?"

"Marybeth! I need your help. Come with me. Quickly. I have a patient in labor. She's not doing well." Marybeth nodded and followed him into the small house.

Inside the house was rather dark, but Marybeth could make out a sofa and two wooden chairs in the front room. To the left was a kitchen area.

"I need you to help me with the patient first, then come back here and get water on to boil."

Marybeth put her basket down and pulled off her cloak. "I'll do whatever I can."

She followed Dr. Scott into a bedroom off the living area. There was a nice double bed along one wall and a chest on the other. There was a wooden chair seated at the end of the bed, and it was here that a woman sat moaning in pain.

"I've got us some help, Mrs. Martin." Dr. Scott came to where she sat. "This is Marybeth Vogel. She happened to be walking by so it was faster to have her come help us than for me to leave you and get my wife."

The woman glanced up. Her expression was pain-filled and tight. She nodded. Marybeth did likewise and awaited instructions.

"Mrs. Martin's baby is breech, but her waters haven't yet broken. I need to try and turn the baby before they do. I want you to help me position her on the bed and then hold on to her."

Marybeth remembered the same thing had happened to her stepmother. She tried not to think about how that ended.

She followed Dr. Scott's directions to the letter, and only when he was satisfied with the arrangement did he instruct Marybeth to climb up on the bed.

"Take hold of her arms. Mrs. Martin, you must remain strong. This won't be comfortable."

Marybeth watched the doctor as he pressed and pushed on the woman's swollen belly. He would pause and feel the baby, then start again. Unfortunately, whenever he made progress, the baby seemed determined to return to the breech position. Then, without warning, the woman's waters ruptured and spilled out onto the towels the doctor had placed beneath her.

"Well, it looks like this will be a breech birth," Dr. Scott said. He looked to Marybeth. "Go ahead and get that fire built up and put water on."

Marybeth left the room and hurried to comply. She couldn't help but think of her stepmother, Sarah. It had been such a joyous occasion. They had all looked forward to Carrie's birth. It was just too sad to remember the look in Sarah's eyes when she knew she was dying and wouldn't be there for her daughter's life.

"She'll need you, Marybeth. Promise me you'll take care of her. Be a mother to her." Sarah had barely had the strength to cradle Carrie close.

"I will be, I promise," Marybeth had said with tears flooding her eyes.

This gave Sarah great relief. She looked almost angelic as she smiled first at Marybeth and then at her husband. *"You will all do very well together,"* she whispered. She had grimaced and looked again to Marybeth. *"Better take her now."*

Marybeth had lifted her sister from the dying woman's arms. Carrie looked up at Marybeth as if knowing what had been said and what was happening. Marybeth drew her in close and prayed for God to spare her stepmother. But He hadn't.

A loud moan broke into her thoughts, and Marybeth realized Mrs. Martin was crying out. She hurried to get more water on the stove before going to see what else Dr. Scott might need.

He was lighting a second lamp when Marybeth came into the bedroom. He looked at Marybeth and smiled. "Mrs. Martin says her husband should be home soon. He works for the railroad."

Marybeth had lost track of time. She nodded and went to the woman's side. "Do you have more towels?"

The woman nodded. "In the chest off the kitchen."

Marybeth went to retrieve them. She knew it was best to clear away the wet towels. There were four large towels in the chest, and Marybeth took them all. Dr. Scott helped her to remove the wet ones and replace them with the dry ones.

"When her husband gets here, I'll have him fetch Mrs. Scott and then take you home. I know they must be worried about you."

Marybeth hadn't really considered it but knew he was right. She'd gone to town with Melody, and they would have expected her to return before now. She whispered a prayer that they wouldn't worry too much, then whispered another that Mrs. Martin could be safely delivered of her baby. And all the while she thought of Edward's fears of having another child and facing just such a situation.

Where is she?

Edward paced the floor of the shed, unable to find peace. He had slept and woke up to Eve knocking on their door. She had come to ask if Marybeth had made it home yet. It had been hours, and still there was no sign of her. When Fred got home, he went to check and see if maybe they'd gone to Melody's tent. Melody related what had happened with her father and that Marybeth had gone on to town alone. That was when everyone started to fear the worst.

"I'll go look for her," Fred said after telling Edward what he knew. "You stay here in case she gets back."

But Edward feared she'd never get back. She'd been upset when she'd gone. Probably wasn't paying any attention to what was going on around her. She hadn't used good judgment and had gone on into town without anyone else at her side.

This was all his fault. He'd hurt her. She had shared her heart, and he had been a cad. He'd refused her love, even though his own for her burned just as bright.

Please, Lord, bring her home safe and unharmed.

He was grateful that Eve had offered to keep Carrie at the house. The boys would keep her entertained, she assured. Edward had only been able to nod in agreement. Now the time was slipping away, and it was dark outside, and there was still no sign of Marybeth.

He'd been such a fool to bring her out here. To marry her. He had been so sure he'd never feel anything more than friendship for her but, watching her day in and day out—seeing her care for him so tenderly after he'd been shot—it had changed him. Changed them both.

And yet, they'd both prayed about marrying. They'd both felt it was the solution they needed for each to be happy. Maybe they'd rushed the situation. Maybe it was nothing more than their own fears and desires that had assured them this was the right answer. Now they were married and neither believed in divorce. They would have to make a go of it for the duration of their lives.

Unless . . .

A thought came to mind. Edward knew they could get an annulment. They hadn't consummated the marriage. An annulment would free them up to go their separate ways. But he didn't want to go his separate way. And Marybeth had no one else in the world. She and Carrie would be alone again, and no doubt someone would come along like Pastor Orton had and take advantage of them.

Marybeth and Carrie would face immediate danger. As much as Edward hated himself for what he'd done by falling in love again, he'd hate himself even more if he caused the person he loved most in the world to be injured more than he'd already hurt her.

Pausing in his pacing, Edward looked at his pocket watch. It was nearly six. She'd been gone for almost five hours. He imagined someone like the Garlow boys finding her. The thoughts running through his head were tormenting and ugly. She'd have no way to protect herself. She carried no weapons.

"I have to go look for her. I can't stay here any longer."

He went to the cot and sat down to pull on his boots. And that's when he heard the sound of wheels outside. The sound of people talking filtered into the shed. Forgetting his injured side, Edward jumped up and all but ran for the door. He threw it open to see Fred helping Marybeth down from a buggy.

"Congratulations again, Tim. I hope that son of yours grows fat and strong," Fred said, holding a lantern high. "We'll be praying for Julia to recover quickly."

"Thanks again, Mrs. Vogel. Appreciate what you did for my missus."

Marybeth gave a wave and turned for the shed. She caught

sight of Edward and stopped. Fred didn't give either one time to speak.

"Well, here she is. Dr. Scott grabbed her off the street to help him with Julia Martin's breech delivery. There wasn't any chance to send back word. I found Tim and her coming this way and hitched a ride with them."

"Sorry I caused everyone so much worry. Fred, these are the things Eve wanted me to pick up for her. Could you take them and bring Carrie home?" She handed him a wrapped package.

"It's suppertime. Eve told me before I headed out to look for you that she wanted us all to eat together this evening. I'm sure she's gonna want to hear all about what happened. I'll take these things on over, and you can take some time to change your clothes and let poor Edward know what you went through."

"That sounds good, Fred. We'll be over in ten or fifteen minutes, if that's all right with Edward." She didn't wait for him to respond but moved past him and into the shed without so much as a look.

Edward looked at Fred. "Nothing bad happened?"

"No, she's all right. God was looking out for her." He gave Edward a smile. "Come on over soon. I don't know about you, but I'm starving."

Edward watched him walk across the yard. Fred started whistling about halfway across. It was an old marching song they used to hear all the time during the war. It used to cheer them on, but it did very little for Edward at the moment.

He came into the shed and closed the door. Thankfully, Marybeth was changing behind a curtain she'd strung between where their cots were placed.

"Are you all right?"

"I am. Dr. Scott needed help. I was headed home when he stopped me. The baby was breech, and it was an emergency. I had no way to get word back to you. We thought Mrs. Martin's husband would be home shortly and I could leave, but he didn't show up. I'm sorry if it worried you."

She stepped out from behind the curtain, tucking a clean blouse into a dark navy skirt. Her hair was a mess and her cheeks quite flushed, but she'd never looked more beautiful. Unable to stop himself, Edward pulled her into his arms and kissed her.

All the pent-up desire he'd denied himself surfaced. He deepened the kiss, feeling her response as she put her arms around his neck. How in the world could they go back to just being friends? How could he live with her day after day and not make their marriage as intimate as any other?

But just as that thought rose up, another followed: the image of Janey being laid out in her wedding dress. The boy wrapped in a white blanket and placed in her arms.

Edward pushed Marybeth away and growled as he turned to leave. He couldn't do this to her—to himself.

"I'm sending you to Indiana to live with Inga and George. You and Carrie will be safe there."

20

I f Edward had slapped her across the face, Marybeth couldn't have been any more shocked. She looked at him for several seconds, then lost control of her temper.

"You aren't sending me anywhere. I'm married to you, and we have a child to raise—together! I'm sick and tired of all this fear guiding and directing the choices we've made. We married in fear, and we remain celibate in fear. We worry about things that have happened and worry even more about those that haven't yet come to be."

She was glad for the look of surprise on his face and shook her index finger at him. "You're shocked that I'm speaking to you like this? Well, good. You need to recognize that I am capable of standing up for what I believe. I might have married you for the wrong reasons, but I'm going to stay with you for the right ones."

"Marybeth, calm down. I know this is hard for you to understand, but you must see reason. This place is much too dangerous. I had no idea how it would be, and it was a failure on my part to bring you and Carrie here. I should have come ahead and checked things out. If I had, I never would have—"

"Married me?" she said, still angry. "Is that what you want to say? That's unfortunate for you. Because we are married, and I do not believe in divorce."

"I wasn't talking about a divorce, Marybeth. But maybe ... well, we could live separate or annul the marriage. I think even God would understand."

"Well, I don't think much of you doing the thinking for God. The Bible says He hates divorce. We made a pledge to each other, and the justice even said, 'What God has joined together, let no man put asunder.' No man. Not you or anyone else. You're stuck with me, no matter how much you hate the idea."

"I don't hate the idea," Edward admitted. "Not at all. I love you, Marybeth. I do. I love you more than I thought was even possible. I want you ... in every way."

"Then stop talking about sending me away. If I went back to Indiana with Carrie, I'd probably find Pastor Orton on my doorstep once again. I'd have to fight to keep her, as he will likely convince the entire community of my being cursed."

"George could settle the matter. He could arrange things so that you wouldn't have to worry about it."

"And how would he do that if you annul our marriage or divorce me?" She put her hands on her hips. Why couldn't he see how ridiculous this entire matter was? "If I'm not under your direct protection, if I'm a single woman, no one is going to allow me to keep my sister. And who could blame them? I won't have money unless I work a job, and then who will take care of her?"

"Inga could. Besides, you'll have the money from the sale of the house."

"And why would I remain with Inga and George if I'd no

longer be married to you?" She arched her brows and looked at him as if to dare him to find a proper answer.

Smartly, he said nothing.

"I am not Inga and George's responsibility, Edward. I'm not going back to Indiana. In fact, if you annul our marriage or divorce me, I will take Carrie and disappear, and you'll never know where we go or how we end up. You'll have that on your conscience, and I'll do nothing to ease your worry."

"Marybeth, I'm sorry. I don't want to hurt you or Carrie. I love you both."

"You have a funny way of showing it. I sat by your side after you nearly died. I take care of you and nurse you back to health, and sending me away is your idea of loving me?"

"You know that's not true. I was afraid tonight. Really afraid. I know what people like the Garlow brothers are capable of, and this town is full of men like them. You don't understand the vile ugliness that's out there. I couldn't live with myself if you became a part of it."

"Then take care of Carrie and me. Keep us safe with you. Watch over our coming and going, but don't send us away." She drew a deep breath and steadied her nerves. "We're your family now. If you don't want to have an intimate marriage, then fine. I cannot make you give up your fears. However, we both know they didn't come from God. The Bible says that God didn't give us a spirit of fear." She shook her head. "We can't live in fear, Edward. It will suck the life right out of us."

"I don't want to live in fear. I don't want that for you or Carrie. That's why I think you should go back to Indiana. I know Inga and my father would welcome you with open arms."

"You're the only one I want welcoming me with open arms," Marybeth said. She picked up her discarded cloak and pulled it around her. "I'm not leaving Cheyenne." And with that, she walked out the door.

She didn't bother to close the door or look back. She knew Edward was watching her. She could feel his gaze on her all the way across the dark yard to the Hendersons' back door.

I have to calm down, or everyone will demand to know what's going on.

The last thing she wanted was to have to explain that her husband wanted to send her away—to annul their marriage or have them live separately.

She clutched her cloak all the tighter and forced a deep breath of the cold air.

Lord, help me to be at peace. I don't want to upset Carrie, and she always senses when I'm in a bad way. Please help me to let go of my anger, and my hurt.

And it did hurt. Edward's rejection hurt more than any other loss she'd known. It didn't matter that his rejection wasn't personally directed toward her. He obviously felt passion for her. No, his rejection was born completely out of the memory of burying his first wife. The fear of losing Marybeth in childbirth was the force that held Edward Vogel at bay.

Pray for him.

She could almost hear her father saying those very words. Marybeth remembered once when she'd been angry with a young man in their neighborhood. He was a bully, and he had pushed her down and ruined her favorite dress. And all because Marybeth refused to give him her apple.

She had come home in tears, demanding Papa go and teach him a lesson. Instead, her father asked if she had prayed for him. He had taken her up on his lap and opened the Bible to Matthew chapter five.

"'Ye have heard that it hath been said, Thou shalt love thy

neighbor, and hate thine enemy. But I say unto you, Love your enemies, bless them that curse you, do good to them that hate you, and pray for them which despitefully use you, and persecute you; That ye may be the children of your Father which is in heaven,'" he read to her.

Of course, Edward wasn't her enemy. He didn't curse her or hate her. He hadn't really spitefully used her or persecuted her. He loved her, but that love was making him afraid.

Pray for him.

She could pray for him. She should pray for him. What wife didn't pray for her husband?

Marybeth knocked on the back door, then let herself in. They were expecting her and had told her before that when she was expected she didn't need to knock. She took a deep breath and forced herself to relax. She would not bring strife to this precious family. They had done nothing but love her and protect her. She hung her cloak on a hook by the door and prayed for peace.

Squaring her shoulders, she stepped into the kitchen, where Eve was working over the stove. "How can I help?" Marybeth asked.

Eve immediately dropped what she was doing and embraced Marybeth.

"I'm so glad you're all right. I was frantic. I felt so bad that you had gone on my account, and when I learned that Melody had to leave you in town to help her father, well, it sent me into a fret."

Marybeth felt sorry for the poor woman. Here she was suffering nausea from being with child and had a brood to care for, and Marybeth added unnecessary worry to her already heavy burden.

"I'm so sorry. I never meant to worry anyone. I just thought

I would quickly take care of things and get back home. And I wouldn't have been gone long at all had Dr. Scott not seen me and commanded my help."

Eve released her and nodded. "I know you didn't mean to worry anyone. I'm just so glad that you're all right." She reached up and smoothed back Marybeth's errant hair. "When no one could find you for hours . . . well, it was almost more than any of us could bear. Poor Edward was beside himself."

"Yes, I know. But I'm here safe and sound. I'm just sorry that it came at such a price to your comfort. Please forgive me."

Eve shook her head. "There's nothing to forgive." She glanced behind Marybeth. "Where's Edward?"

"I'm sure he'll be here soon." Marybeth glanced around the kitchen. "How can I help you?"

"There's nothing left. I was just stirring the potatoes and carrots. I just took the baked ham out to the table. Let me help you. You're all windblown." She reached up and pulled a few of Marybeth's hairpins, then artfully arranged her hair more securely. "There. Go take a seat. Carrie and the boys are in there with Fred."

"Thank you for the help. If you're sure, then I'll go." Marybeth kept looking for something that was yet undone. "You have the bread and butter there as well?"

"It's all there. I'll bring these vegetables, and that will be the last of it. Now scoot. This is my kitchen, after all."

Marybeth laughed. "Yes, ma'am, and a perfect kitchen it is. I hope to have one half as nice."

Eve looked around at the white cabinets. "You will, Marybeth. I know you'll one day have a house just like this one."

"I hope so. I love it here. It's filled with beauty and well-planned rooms . . . and love. This house is just full to the brim with love."

A knock sounded at the back door, and Edward let himself in. He stood for a moment, looking as though he had no idea what to do.

"Come in from the cold, Edward. We're ready to eat. I was just shooing Marybeth out of here. Come get your lovely wife and take her to the table."

Marybeth stiffened and, for a moment, thought to refuse anything to do with him, then her good senses took over. There was nothing positive to be gained by bringing their troubles into this house.

"I'm starved," she said, smiling at Edward. "And I'm betting you are too."

He didn't seem to know quite how to respond at first, but finally he nodded. "I am." He smiled at Eve. "Smells mighty good in here."

"Well, let's stop just smelling and get to eating. Go on now. I'll be right there."

Marybeth smiled at him as though nothing was amiss. Edward wasn't at all expecting that. He figured she'd probably busted into the house and had a good cry in Eve's arms. He fully expected to be lit into by the older woman, just as his ma might have done years ago.

But instead, he found the ladies in good spirits, and Marybeth completely at peace. He moved toward her and offered her his arm. To his surprise, she took it and smiled again.

He escorted her from the kitchen into the dining room, where Fred and the children were already sitting at the table. He had managed to put a block of wood under each child and tied them to the chair with dish towels so that they couldn't jump down or fall.

"Looks like you have this lot secured," Edward said, nodding at the children.

"You have to know how to secure your area," Fred replied. "This works best with the children since we don't have one of those fancy tray chairs that you have for Carrie."

"I've definitely been glad that we brought it with us to Cheyenne," Marybeth replied before Edward could say a word. "Pa always had keen insight about inventions and such. When he first saw that chair, he told me he had no doubts about its usefulness."

"Sounds like a smart man."

Edward nodded. "He was, and he was a good mentor to me. My own pa looked to him for advice and once told me I was fortunate to have such a man in my men of wise counsel."

"Well, I told Eve that as soon as I had time to come over and study that chair, I was going to make us a couple. I think it would be a whole sight easier than tying the children to chairs."

"Here we are," Eve said, bringing a large bowl to the table. "Our potatoes and carrots are finally cooked through."

Fred jumped up and took the bowl from her and placed it on the table. By the time he'd finished with that, Eve was already seated, so he offered grace.

Edward closed his eyes but didn't really focus on Fred's words. The argument he'd had with Marybeth remained as an obstacle between him and God. He was sorry to have hurt her but had no idea how they could go on with things as they were.

"I tell you Tim Martin is prouder than a peacock with that new son of his. The man's grin all but lit up the way home. We probably could have gotten by without my lantern."

"Julia was pleased as well," Marybeth added. "This being their first, she had wanted a boy to carry on her husband's name. It had been most important to both of them."

"It's a good thing to have sons," Fred said, putting a slice of ham on Samuel's plate and cut it into several pieces. He added another larger slice to his own plate and cutting several smaller pieces from it for David. The two-year-old was quite excited at the prospect and gave a little bounce in his seat.

"Gonna eat," he said over and over as his father delivered the ham to his plate.

"He's definitely looking forward to this," Eve said, passing the potatoes and carrots to Edward. "He loves ham. It's probably his favorite food. At least right now. Earlier this summer I could scarcely get him to eat anything but oatmeal."

"Carrie just loves most everything," Marybeth said, preparing food for Carrie's plate. "She takes great pleasure in feeding herself, so the contents never seem quite so important."

"I hope we have a girl this time around," Eve said, buttering a slice of bread. "I rather enjoy Carrie's approach to playtime. She's so much quieter and far gentler than the boys. I think she's been a good influence on them. I only hope they haven't made her too rowdy."

"Not at all. She loves to play with them. She enjoys other children more than I realized. Her first two years she didn't have a lot of playmates. The neighbors had children, but they were older and in school. Then in the summer they were busy with chores. Carrie only had me to entertain her, and I kept her busy with helping me around the house."

"She is quite the little worker. I caught her trying to sweep with my large broom the other day," Eve said, laughing.

Marybeth nodded. "Pa made her a little broom so that she could help me. I left it behind in Indiana, but it wouldn't be so hard to make her another one. I suppose I should check into doing that."

"It's good to train them up early."

The conversation went on, but Edward paid it very little attention. He was still uncertain how to fix things with his wife. His *wife*. He couldn't just send her away because things were hard. He remembered Pa telling him something to that effect just before he married Janey.

"You can't just get rid of them when their actions or words don't suit you, Edward. Don't take a wife if you aren't ready and willing to work with her to figure out difficult issues. It won't always be sunshine and roses. There will be storms."

But he and Marybeth were good together. They didn't argue or bicker over anything, save this one thing. Why couldn't he just give it over to God? Why couldn't he let go of his fear and make them both happy?

"Did you hear me, Ed?"

He looked up and met Fred's gaze. "Sorry. I'm just a little tired. This is my first real outing, you know." He was glad there was an excuse for his rude behavior. The last thing he needed was for his thoughts to become the topic of their dinner conversation.

Fred looked at him and frowned. "I had forgotten. How are you feeling? If you get too tired, I can help you home and then bring the food to you."

"No. No, I'm fine." But he wasn't.

The events of the day had left him to realize just how far he was from trusting God and how close he was to losing all that he cared about.

I don't know what to do, Lord. I'm sorry for my doubts and fears, but I just don't know what to do. I love Marybeth. I want her as my wife. I want to show her all the love and respect she deserves. I don't want to send her away.

He thought of her threat to take Carrie and disappear if he tried to annul their marriage. He almost smiled at her feistiness. She would do it. It would make them miserable, but she would do it. Then he'd spend his time trying to find her and figure out what they should do next. And then they'd be right back to where they started.

Something had to change. He knew that much. The trouble was, it seemed that he was the something that needed to change.

21

Hank Garlow hated working for the railroad or any other organization that held their employees in tight constraint. There were always rules to follow. Supposedly, it was for the safety of the individuals and preservation of the equipment, but Hank wearied of being told what to do and when to do it.

With each drop in temperature and new blizzard, he gave serious consideration to them moving south. He'd heard that the Atchison, Topeka, and Santa Fe Railroad was adding to its line. They planned to run rails through the southern part of Kansas. It had to be warmer there than here.

Emory had suggested they get out of railroad work altogether, but it paid well and regularly. It also set up the perfect situation of men with extra money to spend or be robbed of. Gambling was popular with the men, and Hank and Emory were very good with cards.

But always there were the rules and regulations, and Hank despised them. He and Emory had laid low after killing the card dealer. It was a clear case of self-defense, but the man had friends, and Hank knew one or two of them would be hot-headed enough to come gunning for him and Emory. He'd even convinced Emory to leave town for a couple of weeks. But they'd run out of money, and the only thing left to them was their free pass on the Union Pacific, and that led them back to Cheyenne and the rules.

The wind outside their railroad-provided room kicked up again. It blew a steady breeze, chilling Hank to the bone. The room wasn't at all well insulated. These were part of the buildings that were torn down and taken along the rail as the operation moved west. They were nothing more than cheap board frames with camp stoves that barely kept a man from freezing to death. It was little wonder that a lot of the men opted for boardinghouses with their more permanent structures.

"The *Leader* is advertising a new bathhouse on Thomas Street," Emory said, lowering the paper to look at his brother. "They offer copper tubs to soak in and all the hot water you want. I think that's how I want to spend my afternoon." He grinned and folded the paper. "You ought to come with me."

The idea of soaking in a tub and warming his bones did sound good to Hank. A long hot bath followed by a big steak meal and then a night of cards and perhaps some female entertainment sounded even better.

"I suppose I could go for that." Hank got up from the small table where he and Emory had spent most of the afternoon. "Then we can eat and go to Lucky Bill's. I heard the railroad brought in a new bunch of recruits to cut timber. We could probably make ourselves a little money at cards."

"Or a lot of money would be even better." Emory pulled out his revolver to make sure it was loaded. "I'm ready if you are."

Hank gave his own gun a once-over. A fella couldn't be

too careful. He knew they'd be expected to check their guns, but Hank never did. He just wore his coat over his holster. People knew better than to bother him. Besides, most of the men hid a weapon on their body somewhere. Hank not only had his gun but also kept a large knife in his boot just in case.

"You think we'll run into trouble?" Emory asked.

Hank shrugged and grinned. "If we're lucky."

"It's been so good to have you back to work," Fred said, putting aside a stack of newspapers. "The nights always seem to go by faster with you around. And now that we have someone to stay in the jail while we check things out, I feel a lot better too."

"I hope we're able to keep the extra men around once the railroad heads west."

"I think we will do all right. More people are coming here every day. Good people but a bigger population, nevertheless. We'll need those deputies, and I think the founding fathers understand that. After all, they're the ones who are hoping to reach about ten thousand people by 1880."

"That's a lot of folks. Seems like hoping we'd have that by 1900 would be more realistic," Edward replied. Not that he really cared either way. He still wasn't sure what to do about Marybeth and Carrie. He'd even considered giving his notice and taking them south to Denver. Fred would be disappointed, however, and Edward really wanted to be of use to the man who'd been such an amazing leader in the war.

Edward pulled on his coat. The coat Marybeth had made him for Christmas. Every time he did up the buttons, he couldn't help but think of her. They were hardly speaking. She was kind and kept the house and meals, but now Marybeth focused her time on laundry, sewing, and Carrie. She had even taken to doing her work in the little washroom they'd built off the kitchen. She had a place set up for Carrie to play with her blocks or dolls and an area for her sewing. She would go there with Carrie when they first got up each morning so as to let Edward sleep as undisturbed as possible. A couple of times, he had watched her even though she thought he was asleep. She and Carrie would take a cold breakfast with them and disappear into the room where she could work on mending clothes or washing them. Sometimes she'd put on a roast to cook or a ham. The succulent aroma would often wake Edward in the afternoon. He'd get up, and Marybeth would prepare things for them to share a meal before he went to work.

Edward both dreaded and enjoyed their late lunch together. He would usually read from the Bible at Marybeth's request as she set the food out. Then they'd pray and eat. Before his announcement that he wanted to send her and Carrie to his sister, they had wonderful conversations about a variety of topics. Sometimes Edward would tell her about things that had happened during his time at work. Sometimes Marybeth would share things from her day. Now there was mostly silence, except for Carrie's babbling.

"I suppose you're gonna be moping again this evening," Fred said as they exited the jail.

"Can I ask you something?" Edward posed, ignoring Fred's comment.

"Of course."

Edward shoved his hands in his pockets. Even though it was March, the temperatures were still quite cold at night.

"Did you know Cheyenne and the other towns along the rail would be so bad when you decided to bring Eve and the boys with you?"

"I figured it would be rough, but the alternative wasn't acceptable. I wasn't going to live without my family."

"Even though their safety is put in question every minute of every day?"

Fred looked at Edward and shook his head. "Is this still about when Marybeth didn't get home because she was helping Dr. Scott?"

"I was terrified for her. I was sick to my stomach thinkin' that someone might have taken her. I told her I wanted her to go stay with my sister until I could figure out what to do."

"Something tells me there's more to this than that. Why don't you just explain to me what's going on?"

Fred had always been good at telling when a soldier was lying to him. He seemed to have a sixth sense about such things. Still, how could Edward talk to another man about his marriage? That was way too personal, wasn't it?

But Edward's father wasn't around to talk to, and he did need advice. Before coming to Cheyenne he might have even talked to a pastor, but Dr. Scott was the reason Marybeth had been late to get home. Edward knew he would feel the doctor was to blame for them having problems. Of course, Edward knew that wasn't the case. He was the only reason they were having problems.

"When Janey and the boy died, I vowed I'd never marry again because I didn't want to risk losing another wife in childbirth. I thought I'd be safe with Marybeth. We loved each other as friends and cared deeply about each other, but there was nothing romantic. I didn't feel like there ever would be because I was so guarded with my heart."

"But there are romantic feelings now. Aren't there?"

Edward felt almost like a chastised child. "Yes, sir." He barely muttered the words.

"Don't call me sir. I'm your friend, Ed. We're like brothers. I can see that your feelings for Marybeth have changed. What's wrong, doesn't she reciprocate?"

"Oh, she does. She definitely feels it, same as me. We neither one expected to fall in love, but we have."

"That seems like really good news," Fred said, pausing to try the door to the jewelry shop. It held fast, and he moved on. "Now you can have a complete marriage. It seems more like a blessing than a problem."

"The problem is that I . . . I can't let that happen. I can't make Marybeth my wife. She might conceive, and then we'd be back to facing the possibility of her dying."

"Just listen to yourself. You sure don't sound like that young sergeant who used to volunteer to take the worst of the missions during the war. That man wasn't afraid of anything."

"That man hadn't watched his wife suffer and struggle to give birth only to die. It wasn't hard to risk my own life, but I can't risk Marybeth's."

Fred said nothing and kept walking and trying door handles. When they crossed into the more questionable part of town, Edward saw him undo the buttons on his coat. This would allow easier access to his pistol.

"Well, don't you have any advice?"

"Would you take it if I did? Seems to me you've pretty well made up your mind. What difference will my words make?"

"I don't know," Edward replied, his frustration evident in his tone. "I just thought maybe you'd be able to tell me what to do."

"And you'd actually do it?" Fred chuckled. "Then my advice is go home and love your wife. You'll be a lot happier if the two of you stop fighting your feelings and be the couple God obviously brought you together to be."

"Fred, you aren't hearing me."

"I heard you loud and clear. You're afraid."

Edward couldn't deny that. "I keep seein' Janey writhing in pain. Keep hearing her cries and then the silence."

"Losin' a wife and son has to be the worst thing a man could go through. I've no doubt I'd be torn into pieces over it. Still, life is full of risk and death. You think Eve doesn't worry every time I strap on this holster and go to work? You think she doesn't fret over the boys and the possibility of them catching some disease that could kill them? You think I'm not worried about her givin' birth to this next baby? But I can't let fear take charge. Life wouldn't be worth livin' if I did."

"But most of those things can't be prevented. A man's gotta work. Every job has its dangers. Diseases are everywhere, so a person is gonna get sick at one time or another. You can't keep those things from happening. But I can stop Marybeth from dying in childbirth. We simply won't have children."

"I suppose I could quit my job. Hide my boys. Have nothing more to do with Eve. I could certainly lessen the chances of them dyin' by taking them out of this place. But I've a feeling the next place would have just as many risks. Ed, we can't keep life from happenin', and we sure can't stop death. But fear is somethin' we can put an end to—if we choose to. There are an awful lot of verses in the Bible that talk about fear and bein' afraid. I was just talking to the boys about that the other day. Psalm Fifty-Six for instance."

Edward remembered Marybeth teaching Carrie to memorize verse three in that chapter. "'What time I am afraid, I will trust in thee.'"

Fred smiled. "Exactly. Do you remember the verse after that one?"

"No, I can't say I do."

They started walking again, and Fred chuckled. "Well, it fits pretty well for this situation. It says, 'In God I will praise his word, in God I have put my trust; I will not fear what flesh can do unto me.' You're fearing what flesh can do. Try focusin' on what God can do."

"But God took Janey. He could have saved her."

"He could have. No doubt about that."

"He should have saved her and not me. I faced death and lived, but I should have died. A case of mistaken identity sent me to the hospital in Washington. If that hadn't happened, I would have died. There was a price to pay."

"You think Janey died because you cheated death? You think God isn't in charge of life and death—that somehow you thwarted His plans for you, so He took your wife and son? I want you to really think about that for a minute."

Ed knew he was right and blew out a heavy breath. "I guess it was easier to think that than believe God took Janey and the boy as a part of His plan."

"God allows a lot that we don't understand, and you're still angry with Him for that. You've decided He's not earned your trust back, so you're gonna manage things your own way, but I don't see that's workin' out too well for you."

Edward considered his words. Was that what this was about? Had he taken offense with God for not saving Janey? Was he angry at God?

A spark deep within seemed to erupt into a flame. He was. He was angry at God. Angry that God hadn't saved Janey and the boy. Only God had the power to give life and take it, so the entire responsibility rested with Him, and He had ignored Edward's heart in the matter.

Or had He?

Thoughts of dark nights when Edward's sorrow had been too great to bear came to mind. He remembered quite well those moments and the comfort that God gave. And what about those times when danger was threatening, and Edward had prayed for help, and God had provided it in some of the most unlikely ways? No, God hadn't forgotten nor ignored him.

"I'm sorry if that was hard to hear." Fred paused again and touched Edward's arm. "You can't live in fear, Ed. Bad things will happen. Good things too. But if you let the bad things be the ones you dwell on, then it's like the good never counted for anything. Janey and your son are gone, but Marybeth and Carrie are right here. They love you and need you. You have to decide here and now if you're gonna love them. You're gonna have to make up your mind if you're gonna trust God or forsake Him. There's no halfway, Ed."

Marybeth looked Carrie over for any speck of dirt or hair out of place. They were headed to church with the Hendersons, and Melody had promised to introduce Marybeth to her mentor, Granny Taylor. For months now Marybeth had heard about this precious older woman who was full of sage advice and sound wisdom. Maybe she'd have some answers for Marybeth regarding Edward, although that would require telling Granny about her problems.

But for now, that seemed like a possible solution to Marybeth. She didn't want to talk to Eve, who was only a few weeks from giving birth. At least that was Dr. Scott's surmisal. Marybeth was going over to the Henderson house more and more to watch the children while Eve took a nap or caught up on her own sewing for the baby. It made Eve feel better knowing that Marybeth was at least somewhat familiar with childbirth and that if she went into labor, she'd have someone there to help until Dr. Scott arrived.

"Come on, Carrie. We'll be late if we don't get a move on." She took up the child's bonnet and secured it to her head. She tied it on, then looked to see where she'd put her own wrap. It was lying across the back of the rocking chair.

"Papa come?" Carrie asked.

"No, Papa is doing extra work." *To avoid us,* Marybeth nearly added. She bit her tongue to keep from commenting further.

For the last couple of weeks, Edward had taken to working during his days off. He had given only a brief explanation that he had agreed to take on some extra hours to set aside more money for the future, so he wouldn't be around for church on Sundays. Marybeth had said nothing disagreeable about it but certainly thought plenty. He was doing this on purpose to avoid her, and it irritated her to no end.

However, just as she knew she was right, Marybeth prayed for him. She prayed pretty much day and night, pleading with God to change Edward's heart. Begging God to allow Edward to see that life without love wasn't much of a life at all. Of course, love could exist without intimacy. She knew that, but they were young and in love. . . . Well, they had been in love. They had been good friends. Yet now, their anger and fears were quickly robbing them of those feelings.

Outside, she heard Fred loading his family into their wagon. Marybeth hurried to fasten her cloak, then took Carrie by the hand. "Ready?"

"Ready," Carrie said with great enthusiasm. She loved going to church because there were so many other children there, and it was something different. Something that took them out of the confines of the shed or the Hendersons' house. Marybeth had to admit she looked forward to it herself.

"Good evening, all." Marybeth lifted Carrie into the back of the wagon, where the boys waited with blankets snugged around them. Samuel opened one end to admit Carrie.

Once Carrie was settled, Marybeth climbed up with Fred's help and sat close by. Eve had tried to talk her into sitting with them on the seat, but there really wasn't room. Marybeth told her she preferred to remain in the back in case the children needed something.

They drove to the new school, and the children waved and called out at the sight of their playmates.

Fred parked the wagon and came to help each of them down. Marybeth was glad the trip was a short one. She was more than ready to be inside where it was warm. March days hadn't been so bad, but once the sun went down the nights were still quite chilly—even cold.

Melody found Marybeth almost immediately. She was such a petite young lady that she hardly looked much older than a child herself, even if she was Marybeth's senior by five years. Marybeth admired the way she arranged her hair and clothes. She wasn't trying to attract attention, but in her simplicity and beauty, Melody did just that. Marybeth couldn't help but note the men who watched her from afar.

"Granny Taylor is back from Texas and anxious to meet you. I wrote and told her all about you and Edward and, of course, Miss Carrie." She lifted the two-year-old in her arms. "And how are you today, Miss Carrie?"

"I cold." Carrie gave a shiver and burrowed closer to Melody's wool coat.

"I am too. Let's get inside and get warm."

"I was thinking the same thing," Marybeth said, following Melody into the schoolhouse.

Almost immediately, Marybeth found herself introduced to a white-haired woman. "I'm pleased to meet you, Mrs. Taylor."

"Call me Granny. Everyone does. And I'm quite pleased to meet you. Melody wrote to me telling me all about you."

Marybeth had no idea that she'd been the topic of Melody's correspondences, but she was happy to finally meet the woman her friend so admired. "I hope you left your Texas family in better condition. Melody said they suffered all sorts of problems."

"Oh, they did, but things are much better now. Thank you for asking."

"I told Granny that as soon as she's settled, we need to get together and have a long talk. I just know you'll find a friend in her like I did."

"I wouldn't have it any other way." She smiled at Marybeth and her wrinkled face seemed to smooth and brighten. Granny looked absolutely joy-filled. She exhaled rather loudly. "I'm just so glad to be home."

"This is home?" Marybeth asked. "I would have thought Texas was more home, what with your family there."

"Home is where I decide it is, and for me, it's anywhere that old man is." She nodded toward the man Marybeth knew to be Mr. Taylor. He had remained in Cheyenne when Granny went south to help their family. "My life is never the same without Jed at my side."

Marybeth felt a pang of discomfort and looked away. She felt that way about Edward, and he hadn't been at her side for some time now. With him feeling the way he did, he might as well have been a million miles away. Would he ever come back?

It was getting harder and harder to focus on the sermon when Edward's absence was so obviously apparent. Marybeth got tired of explaining why he wasn't there. Most folks understood, knowing that they were living in a shed on the Hendersons' property. Folks figured their young family was doing what it could to raise money in order to build a house in the spring. And they were, so it wasn't wrong that Marybeth let them think that was all the separation was about.

But Eve knew something wasn't right. Melody did as well, although Marybeth knew neither would say a word. Still, it was there every day and night like an immovable wall that would never be gone.

When church was concluded, Marybeth allowed Carrie to go play for a bit with her friends. There was no sense forcing the child to ignore them just because Marybeth didn't feel like talking to anyone.

Eve came to her side and hooked her arm through Marybeth's. "You aren't fooling me. I know you're miserable."

"Do you think everyone else knows it too?"

"No, you wear it well. You seem perfectly content, and your smile is sincere. But I can see in your eyes that you're hurting."

"Maybe I should take Carrie and leave Cheyenne. Edward is so unhappy that he stays away as much as possible. That's not a good life for either of us, and it's certainly not good for Carrie. She doesn't understand why he's gone so much. She was just getting used to having him for a father."

"He'll come around. I know he will. He knows what God has called him to do. He knows that, as a married man, he has responsibilities that go beyond providing financially." Eve smiled. "Fred says he's got a stubborn streak a mile wide, but that when he gets his head and heart straightened out, he'll do the right thing."

"So long as he doesn't do it merely out of obligation."

"Sometimes we do a thing out of obligation, and in time, we learn to take joy in it." She caught sight of Mrs. Scott. "I need to speak with her. I'll be back in a few minutes."

"That's all right. Take your time, Eve. You shouldn't be rushing around anyway." Marybeth watched her friend walk away. She was getting slower and more meticulous in her steps as the baby grew.

"It won't be long now," Fred said, coming alongside Marybeth.

"No, and it will be such a joy to welcome another baby into the world. I do hope you get a daughter."

"I do too, but you know I'll take whatever the good Lord gives us and be grateful. The boys are my pride and joy to be sure, and having another son won't hurt my feelings at all."

Marybeth glanced up and found Fred watching her intently. She had no idea what all Edward might have told him. It wasn't appropriate for her to even ask, so she wouldn't. However, she saw compassion in Fred's gaze and felt comforted by the knowledge that he understood.

"Don't give up on him," he said in a low voice. "Edward is wrestling with God just as sure as Jacob did. He's spent the last year refusing to deal with the truth of the matter."

"What truth is that?" Marybeth asked.

"That a loving God can take away the people you love the most and still be loving. Edward never took his broken heart to God for fixin' after Janey died. He took it to God to leave and never retrieve. He didn't want to ever feel anything for anyone. Now he does, and he realizes that God is calling him to reconciliation."

"With me," she said and sighed.

"No. With God."

22

Edward took time for a meal around one in the morning. The Star Dance Hall and Saloon was known for having food readily available all night long, and he often stopped there to eat. Fred had introduced him to the place. Three blocks to the west were some of the most dangerous parts of town in the hog ranch area, but here things were a little calmer, and a fella could relax a bit. Just a bit.

He dug into a bowl of chili, savoring the spicy flavors. One of the new things about coming west was the variety of cooking he'd experienced. There were several folks in town who'd come up from Mexico and were now running an eating establishment on Eighteenth. The food was unlike anything he'd experienced with blends of peppery spices and foods that were not at all familiar. Even the chili he was enjoying tonight had been something most unusual the first time Fred introduced him to it.

"Deputy, you want something else? Maybe some more corn bread?" the owner asked.

"No, I have to get back to work. I figure a couple more bites, and I'll be on my way. What do I owe you?"

"It's on the house tonight." The older man gave him a

smile. "Consider it an act of good charity. I always wanna be on the right side of the law."

Edward laughed. "You're one of only a few in town who feel that way." He spooned out the last of the meat and finished it off. Edward pushed back from the table and got to his feet. "I'll be by later to see that things are still quiet. Monday nights aren't usually too bad."

"True enough. Although I'm still dealing with the theft of my mule team and findin' the man responsible. A fella's got to be pretty desperate to steal mules."

"You come down to the jail and give us all the information, and we'll be lookin' for him too," Edward said, pulling on his coat.

"No, that's okay. This is a personal matter. I'll see it through."

"Have it your way." Edward buttoned up his coat and secured his hat before stepping out into the night.

Fred had left him nearly two hours ago to walk patrol in the better part of town and to swing in to check on his wife. He felt certain the baby would be coming before much longer and liked to keep a close eye on her.

"The doctor said April," Fred had told him, "but I'm bettin' March." Since this was the sixteenth of March, Fred was growing more and more anxious.

Heading west, Edward noted people coming and going. Despite most men needing to go to work in the morning, there were plenty of them on the streets and in the various gaming halls and saloons. Edward started his routine walk, checking in with the owners and taking a good glance around for troublemakers.

By the time he reached Lucky Bill's, Edward was more than a little anxious. Sometimes his senses just seemed to pick up trouble, and tonight felt like one of those nights.

"How's it going, Bill?"

The man shook his head. "The boys are feelin' mean tonight, particularly Hank Garlow and his brother. Seems like every few minutes one or the other is hollerin' about something. Usually that someone is cheating them."

"They have their guns on?"

"Probably." Bill shrugged. "Ain't seen them go more than a few minutes without weapons, even when the chief of police himself disarmed them."

"We need to enforce the rules around here. Those two are the worst offenders, but if the law doesn't stand up to them, I'm not sure we'll ever get this town civilized."

"Good luck with that. Hank is in the corner playing poker. Emory's in the back room buckin' the tiger."

"Faro's a fool's game, so that figures." Edward glanced toward the back room. "Seems quiet enough, though."

"Usually takes Hank to agitate Emory. I don't know that he'd be all that much trouble without his big brother egging him on."

"I've heard Fred say the same thing." Edward squared his shoulders. "Guess I'll go take a look around."

He moved past several men in discussion at the bar and past the makeshift tables where dice were being thrown. Smoke hung heavy over the room as most of the men were enjoying cigars or cigarettes. Seemed like twice as many men smoked after the war as before it. But then, the war had changed folks. Changed the entire country. The talk now was all about getting along and putting back together what had been torn in two. That didn't, however, mean that people were willing to forget all that had happened. There was still a lot of anger, and Edward had seen it firsthand. And given the fact it was only three years ago that the country was still at war, a person could hardly expect everything to be all right. Families had fought against each other. Friends against friends. It seemed the entire world they'd known had come unraveled. How could anything ever be the same?

Fred thought that was one of the greatest benefits of building a railroad to connect the east and west. The north and south were still nursing their wounds, and this railroad gave everyone a common interest—something positive in which to come together. Edward worried it wouldn't be enough.

Raised voices from the back caused Edward to hasten his step. He came into the faro room to find Emory Garlow holding a man around the neck. His gun was against the man's head.

"I said to shut your mouth!" Emory demanded. "You don't know nothin' about me or my brother."

Edward stepped to the center of the room not two feet from Emory. He raised his pistol to show Emory he meant business. "Let him go, Emory."

The young man fixed his gaze on Edward. His blue eyes narrowed. "I ain't finished with him yet. He owes me an apology for insultin' Hank."

"And I say you're done. I'm taking you in for carrying a gun in town. Let's go."

Emory shook his head. "You don't seem to understand, lawman, I'm makin' the call here. Not you." The man he held apparently tried to move away, because Emory yanked his head back and shoved his pistol up under the man's chin. "I'll blow your head off if you try to move away one more time."

The man held up his hands. Emory looked back at Edward. "Go on about your business, lawman. I don't need you tellin' me how to run mine."

"You are my business, Emory. Drop the gun." Edward

watched everything around him at the same time. He'd learned early in the war to take in his surroundings and judge for himself who was a friend and who was an enemy. No one in this room wanted to come to Emory Garlow's rescue. Emory knew it and so did Edward. Edward took a step toward Emory.

"Stay back or I'll shoot him."

"If you do, then I'll have to shoot you. Give it up, Emory. You're drunk, and I'm going to take you to jail to sleep it off. You'll be let out in the morning with a fine to pay. But if you kill this man, then the vigilantes will hang you tonight. Your choice."

Emory paled. Apparently the committee was more than he wanted to contend with. He let the man go but still held his gun.

"Put the gun away, Emory, and then very slowly unbuckle your holster and hand it to me." Edward kept his pistol trained on Emory's chest.

For a few moments, Edward feared Emory would try to play outlaw and shoot. The thought of barely being recovered from Hank's bullet made Edward a bit queasy, but he pushed it aside.

"What's going on here?"

Edward recognized Hank's voice and glanced over his shoulder. "It's not your concern, Hank. Emory's just going to spend the night in the jail for drunk and disorderly."

"I ain't lettin' you take him in," Hank countered. "A man's gotta let off steam now and then. Ain't no reason to haul him off."

"He's carrying a firearm in city limits. As are you. You're both breakin' the law."

"Come take it away from me."

"Since Edward's got his hands full, I'll take it." It was Fred, and Edward felt a rush of relief wash over him. "Let's finish this up, Edward."

Edward nodded. "Give me your gun, Emory."

Seeing they were between a rock and a hard place, Emory did as he was told and holstered the gun. Casting a glance at Hank, he slowly unbuckled his belt and handed Edward his rig. By the time Edward turned him toward the door, Fred had Hank's pistol and held the bigger man by the arm.

"Sometimes it's best to leave well enough alone," Fred told Hank.

"He's my brother, and I ain't about to let the likes of you and your deputy push him around." He fixed Edward with a hard gaze. "I already put a bullet in you once. Wouldn't be at all hard to put in another one. Maybe high and center."

With the Garlow brothers asleep in their cell, Edward and Fred's shift ended. The sun wasn't even up as they walked home together. Sometime during the night, thick, threatening snow clouds had moved in.

"Spring snows are the worst," Fred said, pulling up his coat collar. "Even out here where it's dryer, it still feels so cold."

Edward said nothing. He was still thinking about the events of the night. Hank now had a good reason to come after them both. "Are you worried about Garlow makin' us pay for puttin' him in jail tonight?"

"There's always that possibility," Fred replied. "The man's certainly mean enough. I guess only time will tell."

Edward realized that his time in Evansville with mostly law-abiding citizens had done little to prepare him for Cheyenne. "It's like being in the war again."

Fred said nothing for a moment. He seemed to consider Edward's words as if some detailed response was expected. "I hadn't really thought about it, but you're right. Sometimes I'm not even sure who's on whose side. Spottin' the enemy isn't very easy at times."

"You could have gotten yourself killed tonight. I could have taken another bullet and died."

"That's true. We none of us know how much time we have on this earth, but one thing is for certain: our time will end. We will die."

"Remember when you told us soldiers that we were in a fight for our lives? That every man on the field wore a mark of death?"

"I do." Fred offered nothing more.

Edward shook his head. "I feel like that here. I was just thinking how in Evansville things were calm and sensible. Most folks respected the law, and I enjoyed keepin' the peace. Out here there isn't any peace to be kept. Good folks don't stand a chance."

"They do so long as there are men like you and me, Edward. We're here to keep law and order. They rely on us for their very lives. If we continue to take a stand, things will change. Towns like Cheyenne aren't civilized overnight."

"But we could die trying. I'm not a coward, but I do like to think my life is worth something."

They'd nearly reached home. Had all of this been for nothing? Had coming to Cheyenne been a big mistake? It sure wasn't at all what he'd expected.

"Your life is worth a great deal. We find our value in who we belong to. You belong to God first and foremost, and as His child, you have His favor. You also belong to Marybeth and Carrie. They love and need you, and that makes you worth a lot. But this town needs you too. You and men like you are the only thing that stands between the innocent and those who would rob them blind and leave them dead in the streets. You're worth more than you can imagine, Edward, and I, for one, don't think you made a mistake coming west. I don't think I made a mistake either."

"But you could have died tonight."

Fred shrugged. "No one knows the number of their days, my friend. That's why we need to live them to the fullest and appreciate the blessings God has given us. There are no guarantees that we'll live to be old. But the real tragedy of it will be if we don't spend the time we've been given by living life to the fullest. What good are a hundred years if we spend them in fear, anger, and bitterness?"

"You're not talking about tonight, are you?"

Fred chuckled. "Nope." He started walking again. "And really . . . neither were you."

Marybeth woke with a start. Sitting up, she tried to listen for any sound that might suggest trouble afoot. There was silence, however. She started to lie back down, but then came the sound of footsteps outside the shed, followed by voices.

"See you tomorrow, Fred."

"Night, Ed."

The next thing she knew, Edward was unlocking the door and coming into the shed. Marybeth got up quickly and pulled on her robe. She didn't know why, but she just felt that she should make herself available.

"Are you all right?" she asked, getting the lamp lit so that they could see.

"It's been a rough night," he said without hesitation.

She nodded and went to add coal to the stove. "Are you hungry? I could heat something up."

"No, I'm fine. Maybe some coffee?"

She stirred up the embers in the stove. "I made some before I went to bed." She knew there were times when Edward would want coffee when he came in. She had taken to making sure there was a pot to warm every morning. "It shouldn't take long to warm up once the fire is going good."

She was thankful for the strained peace between them and Edward's seeming acceptance of her presence. She finished with the fire and moved the coffeepot from the back of the stove to the burner while Edward was hanging up his gun.

Marybeth wanted to ask him what had made the night difficult but remained silent. She knew the situation between them was tenuous at best. It was probably better to keep quiet.

She sat down and waited to see what Edward would do. To her surprise, after ridding himself of his coat and hat, he joined her at the table. The lamplight wasn't all that bright. Marybeth hadn't turned it up for fear of waking Carrie. In the dim glow, she could see that Edward looked troubled. How she wished she could offer him comfort. She longed to take him in her arms and hold him close, reassure him that she was there for him—would always be there for him.

For a long time, they said nothing. Marybeth didn't avoid his gaze, neither did she feel uncomfortable with it. He looked at her as if somehow he would find the answer for some unspoken question. She prayed for him, hoping he would.

Finally, when she was certain the coffee was warm, she got up and poured him a mug. Then she took down another mug and poured one for herself. She brought the coffee to the table and reclaimed her seat.

She didn't say a word but lifted the cup to her lips. The coffee smelled earthy and strong, just as she knew Edward preferred it. She sipped it slowly, refraining from grimacing at the bitter taste.

Edward took up his cup and held it for several long moments. When he spoke, it wasn't at all what Marybeth had expected.

"Have you ever been angry at God?"

She nodded. "Sure. When Pa died and Pastor Orton came to take Carrie, I was plenty mad."

He looked at her, and his expression softened. "I never thought of it . . . never knew you felt that way. You said nothing. In fact, you seemed so . . . sure of Him."

Marybeth put down her coffee. "I was sure of God. I just wasn't sure what He was up to, why He was letting things happen the way they were. I felt abandoned, and that stirred up my anger. I think that's how I've always dealt with my fear. If I'm angry, I don't feel so weak and helpless." He said nothing, and Marybeth decided to brave a question. "Are you angry with God?"

"I am. Although maybe not so much now that I realize it. I'm troubled by it and know it's not right. He's a good Father, and He's blessed me in many ways, but I just feel this hardness . . . this frustration. He took Janey and the boy and left me with nothing. I never felt so alone in my life."

"I know how that feels." She spoke before she thought it through and wished she could take back her words.

Edward met her gaze. "I know you do, and I know that I've done that to you. I'm sorry."

"Thank you for saying so. It helps that you realize what I'm feeling."

"Maybe we should both leave this place."

"Would that resolve the problem for you . . . for us?" She tried her best to keep her words tender. "You're angry, Edward, because you don't want to deal with the pain. Until you are able to let go of that pain and give Janey and the boy over to God willingly, that hurt will just go on and on. It's not enough that you love me. That won't heal your hurt. In fact, it just complicates it, and I suppose in many ways . . . makes it worse."

Marybeth was surprised by her own words. She hadn't fully realized it before, but now it seemed that God was helping her to see exactly what she needed to know in order to move forward.

"Cheyenne isn't the reason for our problems. It isn't worth the pain and the misery in my book. But a love discovered . . ." She reached out and touched his hand. "That's worth everything. I'm not giving up on you . . . or love."

23

"Would you take these pieces of cake to Melody and Clancy on your way to work?" Marybeth asked.

Edward had just pulled on his coat and hat. He glanced at the covered plate. "You didn't give them all the cake, did you?"

She shook her head. "No, I'm just sending three pieces. Since her dad got hurt, Melody's had less time to bake, and I thought they might enjoy this."

"They'll enjoy it. I know I did. You're a good cook, Marybeth."

He had been trying to say something nice to her every day since their early morning talk. He knew she deserved more, but for now this was what he could give. He could treat her with decency and respect. He could praise her accomplishments and thank her for the way she took care of him and their household. And while he did that, he was praying and asking God to help him let go of his anger. He had sought God's forgiveness as well. Being mad at God had isolated him in a way he hadn't even recognized. Edward couldn't feel at peace with anyone and be angry at God. He was glad to finally realize this.

Still, he had no idea what to do about Marybeth and his feelings for her. He didn't truly want an annulment or separation. Could he let go of his fears and be a real husband to her? Could he trust God with their future?

He reached for the plate. "I suppose I'll take it by," he said, smiling. "Clancy is probably gonna love it and want more."

"Oh, Melody is a terrific cook, as you well know. She's quite talented and will make someone a wonderful wife one day."

Edward nodded and opened the door. "I got to get goin' if I'm gonna make work on time."

It was amazing what a difference a week's time had made. Now with it nearing the end of March, the air had warmed. The days were far more bearable, and there were even spots greening up here and there.

When he reached the little tent neighborhood, Edward immediately remembered their arrival in Cheyenne. The tent they had rented was now leased to another family, and he couldn't help but wonder how they were managing in the tiny confines.

At the Doyle tent, Edward paused to call out. "Anyone at home?"

Melody appeared almost immediately. "I was just heading over to your place. Come in, Edward." She pulled back the inside flap and turned to her father. "Look who's here, Da."

"Edward Vogel. It's good to be seein' ya, son. How's the family?"

"We're all well," Edward replied. "How are you feeling? How's the back?"

"Oh, the doctor would be sayin' I still need time to recover. He won't clear me for work because he thinks the fall caused more damage than we first believed. I say I'm doin' just fine."

"Da needs to relax and enjoy this rest. He's worked hard all his life and a few weeks off won't be the end of him."

Edward laughed. "I agree with Melody." He held up the plate. "Marybeth sent this. It's cake. And mighty good cake, if I do say so."

Melody took the plate. "Your wife is a wonderful cook."

"She says the same of you, and I have to agree. That last batch of hand pies you brought over were devoured the same day. Carrie and I couldn't leave them alone."

Melody smiled and put the plate on the table. "Can you stay to visit?"

"No, it's nearly four, and I need to be at work. If you feel up to it, Clancy, I'll try to stop by tomorrow."

"And wouldn't that suit me fine," the older man answered. "Maybe ya can be tellin' me what's happenin' in the seedier parts of town. I'm sure there's plenty the papers ain't sayin'." He laughed heartily.

"That's probably true, although they love to tell all the exciting details when they can." Edward tipped his hat. "I'll see you then."

"Da, I'm gonna walk to the Vogels', and I'll be back later. Do you have all that you need before I go?"

"I'm fine. Stop fussin'."

She kissed the top of his head and followed Edward out of the tent. Melody tied the flaps loosely then smiled up at the sky. "It's so beautiful today. I hope winter is completely over."

Edward walked with her part of the way just to make sure she was safe. He knew their side of town was much calmer and less inclined to lawbreakers, but he couldn't shake off the thought that something bad could happen. All around them people were starting the work to frame houses that would one day grace the neighborhood. Piles of lumber could be seen on many of the empty lots. He wanted to give Marybeth a house of her own, but he also wanted to send her to safety. What was he supposed to do? God hadn't made that exactly clear.

"How's Marybeth been doing?"

"Why do you ask? You just saw her yesterday," Edward said, laughing.

Melody frowned. "She's just been different the last few weeks. I'd say since you got injured, if I'm honest. I suppose seeing you nearly killed was hard on her."

Edward hadn't fully considered how his getting hurt had affected Marybeth. His mind had been on his own troubles.

"I know it was hard on her," he admitted. They stopped at the corner where he would head off toward town. "I'm glad she has a good friend like you, Melody."

"It's my pleasure to be friends with both of you. You're good people, as Da says. And good people are a blessing we should never overlook."

Edward nodded. "I agree. I'd best get a move on. I'll see you both tomorrow."

"I'll set up something for you and Da to eat. He'll probably want to play checkers."

"Sounds good." Edward tipped his hat again and headed toward town.

Melody's comments about Marybeth being changed bothered him. He knew the reason she was different was no doubt his comment about sending her back to Indiana and effectually ending their marriage. His being shot hadn't helped matters, to be sure, but the conflict in their marriage was a bigger problem now.

At least he'd been able to speak with her honestly and

admit to his anger toward God. There was a part of him that wondered, however, if he'd ever be able to let go of his fear. He wanted to put it aside. He'd never been the kind of man who was overly afraid. During the war, he had performed without hesitation. As Fred had reminded him, he was usually the first one to volunteer for dangerous missions. Even after his brothers had been killed, Edward faced the enemy bravely. What had happened to his trust in God—his courage?

He walked into the jail at precisely four and found Fred talking to the city marshal, D. J. Sweeney. Sweeney won the position in a municipal election held back in January and had been hard at it ever since.

"Hello, Vogel," Sweeney said as Edward joined them. "I was just telling Fred that I had a conversation with some of the UP men. The railroad officials are anxious to get moving west. The president and Congress are pressing them to get started as soon as possible. They want this railroad completed so the country can move forward. They've been stockpiling materials since December, and those big warehouses they built are full to overflowing."

"I didn't realize they'd brought in that much." Fred gave a whistle.

"They've got their workers itching to go too. Right now, the estimated population of Cheyenne is seven thousand people. They figure that's gonna drop to less than half when the UP presses on west. Of course, plenty of men will be sticking around. This will still be the Union Pacific's divisional headquarters. And once that spur connects us to Denver, we're going to be busier than ever."

"I suppose they'll move out a lot of the buildings in Chicago and take them west too," Fred surmised. "I won't be sorry to see that shantytown torn down."

"You know they'll probably take every board, nail, and poker chip. There was hardly a building left in Julesburg after they loaded everything up and moved it here. I expect we'll suffer some of the same fate."

"As long as they take the west end with them, we'll be all right," Edward said. The thought of how things would be after the railroad moved out was actually exciting to him. He knew it was to Fred as well. In fact, all three men were probably anxious to see if the departure of the worst of their society would leave them with less crime and troubles. Surely it would.

"Another thing, I'm sure you've noticed that construction of homes is starting to go on pretty much around the clock. With the temperatures warming up, those folks who are of a mind to remain in Cheyenne are going to want to live in real houses," Sweeney continued. "Not only houses are being built either. Reverend Cook and the Episcopalians are off and running as well. They've got a sister church in Philadelphia who pledged a thousand dollars to help them build, and the reverend has been getting his parishioners to donate on a regular basis. The UP was quite impressed and donated them two lots at Nineteenth and Dodge in order to build, and they plan to start as soon as possible."

Edward thought of his desires to build. They'd been waiting for money to come from George, but so far there'd been no word from them, and frankly, he was getting worried. It wasn't like Inga not to write.

"Edward here plans to be one of those who build." Fred gave him a nudge.

He glanced at Fred and then at Sweeney. "It's true. We're anxious to get moved into a real house."

"Well, the next few months are going to really and truly

establish Cheyenne. I'm sure we'll see a lot of change. Let's hope it will all be for the better."

Once Sweeney left, Fred and Edward headed out to start the first of their see-and-be-seen walks, as Fred called them. They wanted to let the good folks know that they were on the job and that nothing bad would happen on their watch. And they wanted to let the bad folks know the same.

"Sometimes," Fred had said when Edward first came to town, *"it's enough to make a troublemaker think twice when he sees the law making special effort to walk the town."*

They both knew, however, there were those men who wouldn't care either way. They weren't bound by the law nor afraid of those who were. They were desperate men with desperate ways, and inevitably someone would suffer because of it.

"You seem a little less downcast these last couple of days. Things going better for you?" Fred asked as they turned onto Ferguson Street.

"I'm readin' the Bible and prayin' more, that's for sure. But, yeah, I'm workin' through it. Marybeth and I are speakin' a little more. I confessed my anger toward God, and she admitted she'd had her moments too."

"It's always better when you let someone bear your miseries with you. Eve has helped me get through some of the worst times. Like when I came back from the war. She was there at my side to reassure me and help me when the nightmares came."

"I didn't know you had them. I figured that, being the top man, you probably didn't have that kind of trouble."

Fred laughed. "Edward, the top man often suffers the most. He holds the lives of all the other men in his hands. I forced men—boys—to their deaths. There were times when

I knew there would be no good result from what we had to do, and yet I had no choice. I had to follow the orders of my superiors."

"I guess we all have our cross to carry."

"It's one thing to carry our cross and another to carry the weight of the world."

Edward looked at him for a moment. "What's the difference?"

"I always figured takin' up my cross was me carrying the mission God had given me. Willingly accepting that mission or task without grumbling. There's a job God has for each of us to spread the truth about Jesus and help our fellow man. For me, that's my cross. Problems and troubles are those things that try to interfere with me serving God. Those are the things Satan throws my way and expects me to pick up and carry. That's the weight of the world—remember who is prince of this place."

Edward nodded. That made sense, although he'd never thought of it that way before now.

"Jesus told those of us who are labored and heavy laden to come to Him, and He'll give us rest."

"Matthew eleven," Edward interjected. "I know it well. 'Take my yoke upon you, and learn of me; for I am meek and lowly in heart: and ye shall find rest unto your souls.'"

Fred nodded. "'For my yoke is easy, and my burden is light.' Can't say it any better than that."

"I've been worried about you," Melody admitted as she helped Marybeth wring out the clean clothes she'd just washed.

"You really shouldn't worry about me. How's your father

doing? Is he going to be ready to get back to work when the railroad pushes west?"

"I think he will be. He loves the adventure and the constant change. Not so much for me. I'm getting weary of moving all the time. I told Granny Taylor that I'm thinking hard about staying behind when the railroad moves on. Of course, Da would have to approve."

Marybeth looked up in surprise. "Would your father stay too?"

Melody laughed. "No, he wouldn't want to. I know him too well. He isn't happy sitting still. I'm not sure what he'll do when all of the railroads are built. But what's going on with you? You're so much quieter. Are you still fretting over what happened to Edward?"

"Well, it was a terrifying matter. I can't say that it's easy to set it aside. I keep praying for him to be protected, but I prayed for him that night as well."

"And he's still here," Melody reminded her.

"True, but I would have preferred he never got hurt."

"We'd like that for all our loved ones, but it's not going to happen quite that way. Granny says we live in a fallen world, and bad things will happen to all of us, even those of us under God's protection. It's just what happens in our world. We can strive to live a good life, which will take us out of all sorts of dangers, but otherwise all we can do is pray for them and trust God to know best. My da once told me that had he not nearly died as a young man, he would never have gotten right with God. He was too wild and much too spirited. He liked his whiskey and beer, and after having a falling-out with our local church leader, he was ready to forget about God. But God wasn't ready to forget about him."

"What happened?"

"One night he was running his mouth at the pub and got into a fight. One of the men put a knife in his back. Da lost a lot of blood, took an infection, and nearly died. He was alone in this world, but one of the old women who was always giving him trouble over his conduct took him in and nursed him back to health. While Da was sick in bed, she told him every day about Jesus. She prayed over him, and during the worst of it, when Da knew he was about to die, he prayed. He begged God to spare him and give him another chance. And of course, He did. That fight changed his heart and life."

"I suppose we can never tell what might happen to change everything in our lives. I certainly wasn't thinking of having my father die last year. It turned my world upside down, even more than when my mother and stepmother died. Each time was hard, but losing Pa was the hardest of all." She handed Melody a wet blouse. "This is the last of it."

Melody wrung out the blouse. "Shall I help you hang them outside?"

"If you like. I thought I'd let Carrie run around and enjoy herself a bit. It's warm enough."

"You get Carrie, and I'll bring this basket of clothes."

Hank Garlow was tired of being ordered around to give up his guns. The vigilantes were on the prowl, however, along with that stupid Henderson man and the deputy Hank shot once before. He'd just as soon kill them both—kill all lawmen. A man could marshal himself. He didn't need a bunch of fools making up rules to tell him what he could and couldn't do.

Leaving Lucky Bill's, Hank elbowed his brother. "Keep your coat down over your rig. No sense askin' for trouble.

Those vigilantes would just as soon string us up as demand our weapons."

"Glad we'll soon be movin' west," Emory said, adjusting his jacket. "I like the towns better when they're just getting settled. Once they start bringing in families and law, I'm ready to move on."

"Ain't that the truth." He nodded toward another seedy gambling house. "We haven't played at the Red Dog in a while. How about it?"

Emory didn't reply but headed for the false-front building. Hank smiled to himself. He liked the ease with which his brother took suggestions and directions. Emory was just a few years his junior, but he gave Hank the respect he deserved, and that was pretty much all Hank desired. He needed the respect of the folks around him. It made him feel important—powerful. That was the problem with Edward Vogel and Fred Henderson. They didn't give him the proper respect. The other deputies were afraid of Hank. He'd seen it in their eyes. But not Henderson or Vogel. Well, could be he'd have to do something to put fear into them. After all, he didn't want it to be said that one of Cheyenne's law dogs had bested him.

Edward and Fred finished their meal around midnight. They'd stopped in at Lucky Bill's and found it busy but without incident. Bill had bragged about having some of the best beef stew in the city, so they stayed for a couple of bowls.

"I'm full to the brim," Fred said, getting to his feet. "If I eat any more, I won't be of any use to anyone."

"Same here." Edward paid Bill while Fred drifted off toward one of the standing tables where the men were playing blackjack.

"Thanks, Bill. You were right. That stew was about the best I've had in a long time."

"We're having a good time with beef around here since several major herds have been brought in. I think cattle will do especially well up here. Lots of grass and wide-open spaces. And we've got a young guy who's opened a butcher's shop. I'd imagine Cheyenne will keep him real busy."

"No doubt about that. We'll be by later. Hope things stay quiet."

Bill picked up a bar rag. "Me too. Although I should warn you, Hank and Emory Garlow were here earlier, and they were drinking a lot and refused to give up their weapons. Said they might have to show you and Fred a thing or two."

"Figures. We'll keep an eye out. Alcohol and guns are never a good combination."

Edward joined Fred, and together they walked out onto the street. The night air was cold but not frigid like it had been.

"Bill said the Garlows have been drinking heavily, and they're wearing their guns. Talkin' about giving us a hard time."

"I've come to expect that from them. I'll be glad when they leave Cheyenne. I figure if we make it miserable enough for them, they'll go. But I suppose I could be wrong. They may just be itchin' for another fight. Some men never get it out of their system. Do you regret comin' to Cheyenne, Ed?" Fred asked.

The question took Edward by surprise. "Not exactly. I think one day Cheyenne will be a great town, but I don't know that I'll live to see it."

Fred chuckled. "I know I won't. I'm nearly fifty years old. This place is gonna need at least twenty or thirty years before it breaks out of this rowdy stage. I doubt I've got that many years left. Then again, I don't guess any of us know how many days we've got."

They turned the corner and headed toward the Red Dog. There was a lot of noise and ruckus coming from inside, and as they reached the front of the establishment, someone came flying out the doors. Edward barely missed the man crashing into him. He stepped back as the man landed in the dirt. It was Emory Garlow. Another man followed directly after him and landed in a heap in the street. Hank Garlow stood in the doorway.

"You ever lay a hand on my brother again, and I'll see you dead," he growled at the man.

Emory picked himself up and looked down at his adversary. He took a couple of missteps, then kicked the man. He nearly fell but righted himself and started to repeat his actions, but Fred intervened.

"Stop it now, or I'll haul you in."

"This ain't your fight, Henderson." Emory was clearly intoxicated. He stumbled back a step and pushed back his coat to reveal his gun. "Stay out of it."

By now a crowd was gathering onto the boardwalk. Hank seemed to enjoy the attention. He tucked his coat behind his gun, a sure sign he was ready for action. "I'm not takin' blather off any of you."

Edward carefully stepped up on the boardwalk. "You don't need to make things worse, Hank."

Emory took that opportunity to reach down and yank the man he'd been fighting to his feet. He punched him square in the jaw. The man let go a yell and headbutted Emory, sending him back to the ground. This was apparently enough to cause all three parties to put aside common sense.

As he regained his footing and breath, Emory grabbed the

man and hurled him farther across the street. Despite being drunk, Emory moved after him with the liquidity of a cat and was on top of the man before anyone could even move.

The men around them were yelling support for both sides, but Fred was having none of it. He put himself in between the two, but it was Emory he grabbed hold of. "I told you to stop it or I'd haul you in. Guess you're goin' to jail."

Shots rang out, one right after the other. Edward pulled his gun and ducked around the side of the building. Everyone ran for cover as the firing went on with someone emptying out one revolver and then another. Edward pressed forward to get a look around the edge of the building. It was Hank. He was shooting everywhere. When the shots finally stopped, Edward peeked around the corner of the building, his gun drawn.

"Hey, you could have hit me," Emory protested as he got up from the street.

"Wasn't aiming at you," Hank replied, reloading his revolver.

"Drop it, Hank," Edward said. He rushed the man and knocked the gun from his hand. "Enough!"

Edward noted there were two men still lying on the street. One was the stranger Emory had been beating. The other was Fred.

"Take hold of them both," a man's voice called out.

Edward recognized several members of the vigilante group. They took charge and grabbed Emory and Hank. Stepping forward, Edward saw that even more vigilantes had arrived.

"I saw the whole thing," one of the men declared. "It was murder, pure and simple."

"Killed both in cold blood," someone else yelled out to a rousing chorus of agreement.

Both? Edward looked again at the men on the street. Fred still hadn't gotten up. In fact, he wasn't moving at all.

Edward hurried to his side and dropped to his knees to roll Fred over. Someone rushed forward with a lantern. Edward could see a single bullet hole in Fred's forehead. His eyes were closed and his body still.

Fred Henderson was right. He wouldn't live to see Cheyenne become a decent place to live.

24

E dward knelt by Fred for a long time. All around him
chaos was breaking out, but he didn't care. The vigilantes could tend to it. He stared at his friend and former
commander. This couldn't be happening. Fred couldn't be
dead. What was Edward supposed to do now? What was he
supposed to say to Fred's wife and boys?

"You okay, Deputy?"

He looked up, hardly seeing the man standing beside him.
He blinked a couple of times, but his mind wouldn't let him
respond. Fred was dead.

The man reached down and pulled Edward to his feet.
"Are you hit?"

"No." Edward shook his head, then looked back down at
his friend. "He was just trying to stop the fight."

"I know. We saw the whole thing. It was murder. Hank
was shooting wild and killed Fred while Emory put a bullet
into the other man. They will both hang tonight." The man
glanced down. "Do you know this fella?"

"No."

"Well, someone will. Don't worry about it."

Another man knelt beside Fred and felt for a pulse. Edward didn't recognize the man but watched him in wordless silence. It was as if his entire world had gone quiet. He could see down the street that a large group of men were dragging Hank and Emory off to their fate. And still Edward couldn't move.

The other man rose. "They're both dead."

"Thanks, Doc. I'll have them taken to the undertaker," the man who'd been talking to Edward said. He looked at Edward. "You know the deputy—his family?"

"I do," Edward replied, but his voice sounded so distant.

"Then you get the job of tellin' 'em what happened. Sorry." The man turned and motioned to some other men on the side of the street. "Joe. Arnie. Grubber. Come help me get these two over to the undertaker."

Edward battled the shock of having watched his best friend die. He'd seen men, good friends even, die in the war. He'd been on battlefields where hundreds lay dead, but nothing had prepared him for this moment.

As two of the men lifted Fred and carried him away, Edward fought the desire to run after them and force them to stop. But he found it even harder to move.

"I'm with the *Leader*," a man said to him as Edward watched them take Fred and the other man away. He glanced down as if to make sure Fred was really gone. There was a pool of something mixing with the dirt and mud. Most likely . . . blood. Edward was glad that the light wasn't good enough to reveal it well.

He looked back at the reporter, who was even now asking him questions about what had happened.

"I can't talk to you," Edward said, pushing the man aside. He started walking back toward the jail, but then he veered off, knowing that he couldn't go back there. Not yet. He had to go tell Marybeth what had happened. He had to see her. To touch her. To know she was all right.

He walked faster and faster until he was running. Running as fast as his legs would travel. He felt the burning in his calves as he pushed himself harder. The situation was impossible—heinous—unreal.

How was he supposed to tell Fred's wife that he was dead? He could scarcely believe it himself. Fred's house was just ahead. The lights were off without a sign of anyone being awake. Of course, it was the middle of the night.

Edward slowed his pace and skirted the house. He went straightaway to the shed, knowing he'd find Marybeth there. She would be stunned and saddened by the news, but she would also help him tell Eve. He just couldn't do that alone.

He unlocked the door and let himself into the dark room. Marybeth stirred and, without saying a word, came to him.

He pulled her into his arms and felt his chest tighten. He buried his face against her hair and moaned in sorrow. The moan grew to a cry, and he forced it to silence so he wouldn't wake up Carrie.

Marybeth held him tightly. She obviously knew something was wrong, but she said nothing. As Edward began to tremble, she led him to the rocking chair and pushed him down. She lit a single candle and placed it close by before coming back to him. She pulled up the crate beside him and took hold of his hand.

"What has happened?"

⌒

Marybeth wasn't sure why her husband was trembling and crying, but she feared the possibility. Her heart warned her that the news would be horrendous. Her mind confirmed this, knowing that Edward wasn't one to break down easily. It terrified her to ask the question, but she posed it again.

"What happened? Tell me."

He opened his mouth as if to speak, but words didn't form. Tears continued to pour from his eyes, but he made no sound.

The truth dawned on Marybeth. Fred. Fred must have been hurt. She gently stroked her husband's hand. "Is it Fred?"

He stared at the stove for a long while but finally nodded.

Marybeth's heart sank. Edward wouldn't be acting this way if Fred were merely hurt. "Is he dead?"

Edward met her gaze and nodded. Marybeth felt sick. She couldn't have heard him right. This couldn't be happening.

"Are you sure?"

He nodded again and then buried his face in his hands and wept.

Without a word, Marybeth went and dressed. She knew they would have to go and tell Eve the truth. She hated the idea with every fiber of her being. Eve was due to have a baby soon. This would probably send her into labor. Then, of course, there were the boys. How would they explain to them that their father wasn't ever coming home? Those boys adored Fred. It would break their hearts.

She grabbed her brush and ran it through her long blond hair. With nimble fingers she plaited a single braid down the back and tied it off with a ribbon. She looked in on Carrie. She was sleeping soundly. Carrie routinely slept through the night, and even when Edward returned home, she never woke. Marybeth didn't like the idea of leaving her alone, however.

She woke Carrie up and helped her into her coat. There

was no sense in making her get dressed. It wasn't going to make a difference. Hopefully at some point Marybeth could get Edward to go for Melody. They would need her help with the children.

"Go play?" Carrie asked, yawning.

"No, we need to go talk to Mrs. Henderson and the boys. You must be a good girl. You can go back to sleep when we get there if you like."

Carrie said nothing but held her arms up to be carried. Marybeth drew her up and held her tightly. This wasn't going to be an easy time for anyone.

When she came back around the curtain that separated their sleeping area from the rest of the room, Marybeth found Edward calmer. His eyes were still damp, but he was no longer crying.

"Ready?" she asked.

He nodded. "As much as I can be."

They walked the short distance to the Hendersons' house and paused at the back door. For a moment, Marybeth wondered if they should go to the front of the house but knew that would probably just be harder.

Edward knocked on the door and waited. After a few minutes, he knocked again. Finally, on the third time, light appeared beyond the mudroom. Eve came to the door.

"What is it? What's wrong?" She looked at Marybeth. "Is Carrie sick?"

Carrie was already back to sleep, and Marybeth shook her head. "Let us in, Eve. We need to tell you something."

Eve backed up a step. "Is it . . . is it Fred?"

Edward moved to take hold of her. Marybeth followed him into the house and waited for him to lead Eve to a chair.

"What's happened? Where is he? Is he all right?"

Marybeth put Carrie in the front room on the sofa. She heard Eve continuing to question Edward and then a strangled cry broke from her.

"No! No! No!"

Marybeth hurried back into the kitchen and came to Eve's side. She knew there was nothing she could say to soften the blow. Eve hugged her body as if to ward off anything bad from touching her.

"It's not true. It's not. Fred can't be gone."

"I'm so sorry, Eve," Edward said, pulling up a chair in front of her. "It all happened so fast. There was no time to warn him or for him to take cover."

"Who . . . who did it?"

"Hank Garlow. The vigilantes have him now. He's probably already been hanged. His brother too. He shot another man."

She met Edward's gaze. Her head tilted slightly to the left as she seemed to shrink away. Her eyes rolled back, and Edward caught her just before she started to fall against the table.

"We should probably put her in bed," Marybeth said. She grabbed the lit lamp and headed toward the door, pausing there to wait for Edward.

Edward lifted Eve and followed Marybeth to the bedroom. She straightened the covers and pulled them back while Edward deposited Eve on the mattress. Eve didn't wake up, so Marybeth put the lamp on top of the large chest of drawers and went to the pitcher and bowl. There was a towel hanging on the stand, and she took that up and dampened it.

She sank down beside Eve and began to wipe her face with the cloth. It was only a few minutes before Eve opened her eyes. She looked at Marybeth and broke into tears. She pushed Marybeth's hands and turned away.

There was nothing else to be done. Marybeth knew there were no words that could lessen Eve's pain. All they could do was be by her side.

⁓

By morning, Eve had cried herself out. She slept for no more than an hour, then rose and asked Marybeth to help her dress. Marybeth could see she was determined to be up and so didn't argue. To her surprise, Eve had a black dress in her wardrobe.

"My mother taught me early on that you never know when you might need to dress for mourning," Eve said as Marybeth helped her into the skirt portion of the gown. Thankfully, it had an adjustable waistband.

"I needed this when I was carrying Samuel and my grandfather died." She helped Marybeth position it over her swollen abdomen. The top part of the gown fit rather snugly, but Eve didn't seem to care. She told Marybeth where to find her black shawl, and once it was wrapped around her, she looked prim and proper.

"Edward went to fetch Melody. She's going to take care of the children while Edward and I go with you to the undertaker."

"My poor boys," Eve said, sinking onto the edge of her mattress. "What in the world am I going to tell them?"

"The truth. Their father died a hero."

"They won't understand him being gone. They won't understand any of this." She fisted her hands. "I hate this town. I've always hated it. I won't bury Fred here. I'm going back to Indiana. I'm taking him too."

"You should probably wait until after the baby is born," Marybeth suggested.

"No! I won't give one more thing to this devil's town." She looked at Marybeth. "I've paid dearly enough. I'll have this baby on the train before I'll give birth in Cheyenne."

Marybeth could see the pain in her eyes. Pain mixed with anger. She couldn't blame Eve for the way she felt.

"Perhaps we can wire someone from your family, and they could come here to accompany you and the boys. You certainly can't travel alone."

"Yes." Eve seemed to consider this for a moment. "I'll send a telegram to my father and mother. They'll manage it all. They'll know what's best."

Melody came into the room and locked gazes with Eve. "Edward told me what happened. Oh, Eve, I'm so sorry." She came and knelt beside Eve. "I'll do whatever I can to help you. Da said not to worry about a thing. He'll be by to check on your coal and water situation."

"Thank you. Thank you both. Hopefully once Fred . . . once he's prepared, I can pack the boys up and take the train home."

Melody looked over her shoulder at Marybeth. Her expression was one of questioning.

"Eve plans to return to Indiana to bury Fred and . . . live. She doesn't want to stay in Cheyenne."

"I don't blame you." Melody took hold of Eve's hand. "We're all here for you, Eve. We're praying for you and the boys, and we'll do whatever we can to get you through this sorrowful time."

"I hate to interrupt," Edward said at the door, "but the boys are up and Carrie too."

Melody dropped her hold on Eve and got to her feet. "Would you like to talk to the boys alone?"

Eve squared her shoulders. "I should. Yes. Bring them here."

"I'll take Carrie home and get her dressed," Marybeth said. "Then I'll come right back and fix breakfast."

She didn't wait for a reply but followed Edward out into the hall. She met his eyes and saw a reflection of sadness that equaled her own. Without pause, she wrapped her arms around him and hugged him tightly. She could hear his heart beating steadily. His breathing was rhythmic . . . constant. He was alive.

"I'm sorry for the wasted time. I'm sorry for not loving you as I should," he whispered against her ear. "You deserved so much more than I gave. Forgive me, please."

"There's nothing to forgive," Marybeth replied, pulling away. She held his gaze. "Nothing."

Edward didn't get a chance to speak. Melody was coming down the hall with the children. Eve's boys were laughing and running in circles around Carrie. She was giggling and clapping. Marybeth wished their happiness could go on and on.

"Carrie, come here. We need to go home and get you dressed. Then we can have some breakfast."

The little girl perked up at this. "Eat more." She clapped again and the boys clapped too.

Dear Lord, why couldn't the children go on being happy and carefree? Why did Fred have to die now? Why is this life so cruel?

25

Marybeth spent the week after Fred's passing helping Eve pack up the things she wanted to keep. There wasn't a lot that she cared about, considering all that had happened.

"Most of the things we have are things we picked up here. They don't hold sentimental value. We were going to wait until spring to send for the rest of our things. I'm glad they're in storage back in Indiana," Eve told her.

"I wish you didn't have to go, but I certainly understand. After all, you have family to care for you, and that is so important. Especially with the baby coming."

Eve folded one of the boys' shirts. "I don't think I could go on if not for them. My father and younger brother should be here tomorrow, and I know when I see him, I shall fall apart. I've only stayed strong for the boys."

The boys had taken the news hard at first. Samuel cried a lot, and David wandered around asking for his papa. Having Carrie around to play with seemed to soften the blow. David and Carrie were rather oblivious to the loss, but Samuel felt it quite keenly and often paused in play to come to his mother for comfort.

"I wish there was something more I could do."

"Maybe you can help me find someone to buy this place. I'd like to have it resolved before I leave," Eve replied.

Marybeth hadn't considered that Eve would sell the house. She and Edward were living on the Hendersons' property and would probably have to leave if someone else bought the place.

"Perhaps we could buy it," she said, thinking aloud. "I've been waiting to hear from Edward's brother-in-law about the sale of my house back in Indiana, but maybe it would be enough to buy this place."

Eve looked at her for a long moment. "Money isn't important. My family is rich. I want you to have the house. I'll set up the papers and transfer the deed to you and Edward."

"No, we couldn't take it. We will buy it. I just have to wait for George to come through with the money."

Eve took a seat and laid the shirt across her expanded stomach. "No. Please listen to me. This would be an answer to prayer. I haven't known what I was to do with the place. Fred loved it so much. He designed the house and was so much a part of building it when we came here last summer. He would love that it went to Edward. It's what I want to do."

"I don't know how Edward would feel about such a thing ... but I can talk to him." Marybeth still didn't like the idea of Eve merely gifting them the house. It might not matter to her, but she and Edward had been taught to pay their fair share. As much as the idea of Eve giving them a house bothered Marybeth, she knew it would bother Edward even more.

"Let me talk to Edward," Eve said matter-of-factly. "I think I can convince him."

"But, Eve, you must think of the future and your children. You'll need money to raise them properly."

Eve gave her a sad smile. "As I said, my family is rich. I don't mean just well-off. My father is worth millions. Fred was always very insistent upon paying his own way, so we spoke very little about it, but money simply doesn't matter."

Marybeth fought to keep from gasping. She'd had no idea of Eve's father being so wealthy. She supposed it was of very little consequence if Eve gave away her home. Perhaps this was truly an answer to many prayers.

Edward had been relieved to get a telegram the afternoon before from his brother-in-law. After months without word, it helped to ease Edward's worries. It seemed George had sent a letter, but apparently it had been lost or misdirected. The news was mixed. The entire family, with the exception of Inga, had come down with measles. The children had passed it from one to the other, and finally George and Father had taken ill as well. George followed the brief explanation with the words "all recovered." Edward was happy to know that much.

George went on to say a letter was soon to follow. The only other bit of news was a single two-word statement: "House sold."

It was a relief, he supposed. Marybeth would feel better knowing there was money to start building their own home. But with the way things stood, Edward wasn't sure he wanted to stay there. Fred was gone, and Eve and the boys would soon leave. The railroad would pick up and head west in another few weeks, and Cheyenne would completely change.

They would still need lawmen. The thought seemed to echo words Fred had said one evening when they'd been discussing the coming change. Edward had pledged to Fred that he wasn't going anywhere. He liked Cheyenne's location and intended to make it his home. But without Fred there, Edward wasn't so sure he wanted to stay. If Eve had intended to remain there, Edward might have had the incentive to stay and help her with the boys. He and Marybeth were doing all they could to keep Eve and her sons company. But they'd soon be gone.

The Garlow brothers had been hanged the same night they killed Fred and the other man, Clement Sawyer, who had just hired on with the Union Pacific to help with bridge building. So there wasn't even a reason to stick around and see justice served. Punishment had been exacted swiftly and without prejudice, as Edward had been told by City Marshal Sweeney. Both had committed murder. They had served justice to the brothers side by side on a gallows erected for just such purposes. The bodies had been left hanging for forty-eight hours as a message to other worthless cutthroats who might think of copying their work. Edward never bothered to go see them before they were cut down.

He glanced at his pocket watch. Eight o'clock. The sun was well up, and the town was buzzing along with plenty of activity. When he'd ended his shift, Edward had been in no hurry to rush home and wake up Marybeth with the news of the telegram, but now he figured he should.

Marybeth wouldn't question his late arrival. He'd told her of his need to mourn Fred in his own way. He'd warned her that he'd be late getting home some mornings, and so far it had been every morning since Fred's death. Edward felt somewhat guilty, but she had understood. She always seemed to understand. She was just that way, and Edward knew he didn't deserve her patience with him. Marybeth was the best thing that had happened to him since Janey, and he hadn't even let her know how much he appreciated her.

He made his way from town to the Henderson house, knowing he'd find Marybeth there with Carrie. He'd have tonight off, so there was no need to rush to bed, and he needed to tell her about the telegram and see if Eve needed anything.

Marybeth opened the door shortly after his knock. She smiled and reached out to pull him into the house.

"I need to tell you something," she said, seeming almost excited.

"I need to tell you something too." He reached into his pocket and pulled out the telegram. "George sent this."

"Is something wrong?" Her hand went to her throat.

Edward realized that telegrams were usually only sent during times of trouble—or death. "No, it's all right. Nothing is wrong. They did all have measles, except for Inga, but they're recovered now. I just thought you should know the house has sold. George didn't say how much he got for it, but he's sending a letter with all the pertinent information."

"That seems most fortuitous," Marybeth said, lowering her arm. "Eve is selling this place."

Edward glanced around the front room. He hadn't thought about what Fred's widow would do with the house in Cheyenne.

"But I already told Marybeth that I won't sell it to you." Eve had come into the room without Edward noticing. "Fred would have known that I would leave Cheyenne as soon as possible. He would also have known that I had no need for the money because I have a large inheritance. More than we could ever need. I want you and Marybeth to have this house as a gift. Fred would want that as well. I know he would. He was so pleased with building this place, and to sell it to a stranger wouldn't be right when I could give it to someone Fred loved so much."

Edward didn't know what to say. For a moment, he couldn't even think. How could he simply accept an entire house as a gift?

"No, I can't . . . can't do that." He shook his head. "It wouldn't be right. I won't take advantage of you in a time of grief. Besides, if Marybeth wants to, we can probably afford to buy it now. I don't know what my brother-in-law sold her house for but—"

"Please." Eve drew near. Edward could see her eyes filling with tears. "This is important to me, Edward. I'll speak to my father when he gets here tomorrow and see what needs to be done, but I'm leaving the house to you and Marybeth. I need to do this. I know it's what Fred would want."

That night after Carrie had gone to sleep, Marybeth and Edward sat at the table and talked about all that had happened. It wasn't easy to face the truth of Fred's death, nor even of the gift Eve wanted them to have.

"We can't just take a house and pay nothing," Edward said.

"I said the same thing. But I have also been thinking. Eve is right. Fred would want this. Eve doesn't need the money, and I guess my thought is that if her father approves . . . you should let her do this."

"But people will say I took advantage of a grieving widow."

"Do you honestly care what people say, Edward? We know that isn't the case. Besides, no one needs to know anything about it. For all anyone else would know, we bought the place. We don't need to lie about it, but neither do we need to shout it from the rooftops."

She reached across the table and took hold of Edward's hand. "Fred loved you, Edward. You loved him. He was an important mentor in your life and the dearest friend you had."

"Except for you." Edward looked up and stared into her eyes. "I meant it when I told you I hate the time I've wasted and the way I've treated you. Life is so brief, and we should do what we can to help each other and be a blessing. I was willing to share my sorrows with you and to share yours in return, but somewhere along the way I set aside sharing the joy and . . . love. I didn't think I deserved it after Janey."

"I know." Marybeth squeezed his fingers. "I've been praying you would see that God put us together for reasons other than keeping Carrie safe. We cared for each other as friends, and we shared a common grief. I was more than blessed that you were willing to take Carrie and me as your own—even in name only."

"But that was never fair to you. I see that now."

"It wasn't fair to you either, but you had to work through your sorrow over Janey and your anger at God. I was worried that you'd be angry again with Fred's passing, but you don't seem that way."

"No, I'm not. Fred and I had many a conversation about life and death, and it made me really think. He wasn't afraid to die. During the war, he told us men that we would all die one day. Could be tomorrow, could be decades from now, but death wasn't something we had to fear. He helped us to see that we needed to spend our days living—not dying. So even on a battlefield with no guarantee that we would even see the next hour, Fred taught us to live to the fullest." He rubbed his thumb across Marybeth's knuckles. "I want to do right by you, Marybeth. I love you, and I know you love me."

He rose and pulled her up to join him. Marybeth knew he would kiss her. His embrace was tender, and his kiss so very gentle. When he pulled away, Marybeth drew a deep breath. She felt her heart skip a beat.

"I love you with all my heart, Edward. I always will."

He took her hand in his, then blew out the lamp.

⌒꙳

"I'm glad to finally meet you," Eve's father, Jasper Hollister, said, shaking Edward's hand. "Eve tells me that you and your wife have been there for her every step of the way. I appreciate that more than I can say."

"Fred was a good friend and mentor," Edward replied. "In some ways, he was an older brother."

Hollister nodded and motioned Edward to join him in the front room. "Eve's taking a nap, and your wife has taken the children for a walk. I thought it would give us some time to speak without interruption."

Edward took a seat on the sofa and waited for Hollister to sit. The tall man looked to be around sixty or so with graying hair and bushy eyebrows. He wore a thick mustache and was dressed impeccably in a dark suit.

"I'll get right to the point. My daughter has told me that she wishes to gift this house to you. She feels certain Fred would want this, as he had great admiration, respect, and love for you."

"I told her I couldn't just take her house. We would like to buy it. However, we don't know how much we have from the sale of Marybeth's house in Indiana. I could speak to the bank about a loan. We do own a city lot. I'm told it's worth quite a bit now. Or if you want to arrange something between us, I am open to that as well."

The man frowned and shook his head. "No, son. I will not loan you money to buy this house. I believe you should allow Eve to give it to you. As she has told you, she is not in need of the money and, frankly, never will be. This means a lot to her to be able to do this, and I am determined to convince you to let her."

"But I feel certain that I should pay. Some might think that I was taking advantage of her otherwise."

"Then, if necessary, we will make it known that it was a part of Fred's last wishes. Eve tells me that he wanted nothing more than to help you thrive out here. She feels confident that if he had written up a will, you would have been included."

Edward didn't know what to say. It was one thing that Eve, in the midst of her heartbreak, should suggest such a thing, but now her father was insisting as well.

"Son, I know you're a God-fearing man. Eve told me that you are strong in your Christian faith. I am, as well. I believe that there are times when God gives us an opportunity to be blessed by others, as well as be a blessing. Please, I'm asking you as the father of a grieving child, let Eve bless you this way. It will help her healing. It will make her feel as if Fred's life mattered to someone beyond her and the boys . . . that he won't be forgotten."

"He'll never be forgotten by me. House or no house," Edward assured. "However, your words do convict me. I remember my mother saying something similar. She said sometimes we had to set pride aside and allow others to help us. Not because it would accomplish something great for us, but rather because they were answering God's direction in their lives and doing what He had appointed them to do. She said it wasn't right to interfere with God's work."

"Exactly. I couldn't agree more." His expression softened. "So will you let my daughter bless you and your wife?"

Edward felt a wave of peace and nodded. "I will, and I will always remember the real price of this house. Fred will never be forgotten. I'll tell my children about him."

Marybeth, Edward, and Carrie waved good-bye to Eve and the boys as they boarded the eastbound passenger train. Eve's father had taken care of all the house business with a local lawyer, and now the Henderson house was legally the Vogel place.

It was hard to fathom the changes in her life. Marybeth had a real home and a real husband, all within a matter of days.

"Boys go bye-bye," Carrie said, continuing to wave.

"Yes," Marybeth said, giving Carrie a kiss on the cheek. "They are going far away." She knew Carrie didn't understand and in the days to come would be lost without them. "I'm going to have to find you some new playmates."

"Seems like there are children living in the house across the street," Edward offered. "What with winter having kept everyone indoors, maybe it's time to get out and meet our neighbors."

The train jerked forward and began its slow start to the east. Carrie called out good-byes again and again and waved with furious vigor. Marybeth could hardly hold the rambunctious two-year old, so Edward took her and mimicked her wave. This seemed to delight Carrie all the more. To her, this was a grand celebration.

And maybe it was. Marybeth couldn't help but consider the situation as good, even if bad men and their actions had brought them to this place. Fred could never be replaced in their hearts, and losing Eve as a friend wouldn't be easy.

The train was finally picking up speed and would soon disappear from sight. Marybeth knew that in the future Eve would write to her and let her know about the baby and how the boys were doing. She would be all right, because her family would surround her with love and see her through this sorrowful time. Marybeth couldn't help but smile as she watched Edward and Carrie. They were her family, and she finally had a home again. She no longer felt the fear that had once nagged at her. They would have a good future. She was certain of it.

Edward caught her gaze and grinned. "You ready to go home?"

He had once asked her that after her father's funeral, and she had felt as though there were no home to go to. Now things had changed, and she knew what awaited her.

Marybeth laughed and took hold of his arm. "I am."

If you enjoyed *A Love Discovered*,
read on for an excerpt from

A

CHOICE CONSIDERED

AVAILABLE IN JULY 2024.

1

What do you mean they stole the fire ladder?" Melody Doyle asked her father over breakfast.

"Well, just what I be sayin'," her father replied. "Judge Kuykendall has run an ad in the paper sayin' somebody stole it and he wants it back immediately."

"Seems like sneaking off with a large ladder would be difficult—and even harder to hide." She poured hot coffee in her father's cup.

"For sure it would be, now." He downed half the cup in one gulp, then folded the paper. "No doubt someone will be findin' it. Hopefully before the next fire. Oh, I forgot to be tellin' ya, I'm gonna go to the prizefight tonight."

"Are you sure you're feeling up to it, Da?"

Ever since late January when her father fell at work, his back had been giving him nothing but trouble. He couldn't even get clearance from the railroad to return to work because of the problems it was causing him.

"I'm sure to be just fine, daughter. Don't ya be worryin' none."

But Melody did worry. Da wasn't his usual self. All her life he had been the very image of strength and resilience. These last few days, however, he seemed so weary, and Melody was certain he was in pain.

She knew her father was frustrated after taking that fall at work. He'd been quite high on the ladder when he'd lost his balance and hit the ground on his back. The doctor said it was a wonder he hadn't hit his head, but Da had only laughed and said if he had, then there wouldn't have been any injury at all. He was a hardheaded Irishman who'd definitely gone through worse, but for some reason, this fall had taken its toll.

"There is something I was hoping we could discuss." Melody pushed back her empty plate. "Do you feel up to it?"

"For sure I do. Don't be worryin' about me. I won't be coddled."

She smiled and reached out to place her hand over his. "You've never allowed anyone to coddle you, and I won't insult you by trying to start now. In fact, what I want to say is about as far from coddling as I can get."

"Then speak. What would be on yar mind?"

For as long as Melody and her father had lived in Cheyenne, they'd called a tent home. It was the way of most section hands and their supervisors since the railroad kept them moving along the line.

Melody hadn't really minded in the beginning. It was fairly comfortable—at least as much as they could make it. The entire tent wasn't much bigger than ten-by-ten, but it was all Melody had known for some time. Now, however, she was more than ready to enjoy the comforts of a real house with windows she could look out of and a nice large fireplace. Da seemed most content when he was living like a nomad, but not Melody.

Melody straightened. "I want to stay in Cheyenne. I know the railroad is moving out and that your job will take you west with it, but I've had my fill of moving from place to place. I like Cheyenne and the people we've come to know. Marybeth and Edward, the Taylors, Dr. Scott. They're all good people, and I want to be a part of their lives. So I'd like to remain here when you go.

"And you won't be that far away. They won't get down the track more than a couple hundred miles, and you can always take the train back here on the weekends. I could find a nice place to stay and have room for you as well. Just think how pleasant it would be for you to leave the chaos of the end-of-the-tracks town and come back here to rest. You wouldn't get to go to church with me since services are still held in the evening, but at least we'd have some time together."

"So ya have yar heart set on staying in Cheyenne? I cannot say that this is surprisin' to me," Da began.

She nodded. "It's been on my mind since Julesburg."

"I cannot be holdin' against ya the desire to settle yarself near friends. The folks ya named are good and godly people." He tossed down the other half of his coffee and held out the cup for more. "But I cannot have ya stayin' here without a man to protect ya. There will still be dangers even after the rowdies pull out."

She refilled his cup. "But our friends will keep an eye on me. Marybeth even said I could come and live with them. I could stay in the house or in the little shed out back where they were living before the Hendersons sold them the house."

Her father shook his head. "No, ya'll be needin' a husband, Melody. I've been feelin' that way for a long time now. Ya need a man of yar own and children. Yar made for love and family—like yar ma."

Melody only had vague memories of her mother. She'd died when Melody was barely ten years old. Now almost sixteen years later, the memories were cloudy. She could hardly remember what her mother looked like, although Da said she was the spitting image of her mother.

"And while I know yar old enough to decide for yarself, I'm still yar da."

"I respect that, Da. I don't want to do anything against your wishes. I just hadn't thought of marrying anyone. You'll soon be heading west, and finding a husband in that short time is going to be difficult. After all, there's no one special in my life."

"Not that I don't have men askin' me all the time if they can be courtin' ya. Of course, they know there's a risk in approachin' me, but that's the first part of the test. If they're brave enough to come and discuss it, it shows strength of character." Da chuckled. "Yar a beauty like yar mother, and ya could have yar pick of suitors. We've only to put out the word."

"Advertise for a husband? Is that what you're suggesting?" She was surprised she didn't feel more appalled by the idea.

"And for sure it could work. We could be lettin' folks know that yar of a mind to marry and live here in Cheyenne. I could take this time away from work to inspect each man and listen to his story. Then I could be pickin' a few suitors for ya to choose from. Ya know for yarself that I have God's gift of discernment. I can be tellin' when a man is truthful or false."

Melody shrugged. "I suppose we could give it a try. It's not like I must marry any of them. I can always head west with you if none of them appeal."

"And for sure ya could and ya would, for I'll not be leavin' ya here without protection and security. After all, how would ya make yar way and pay for all that life costs ya?"

"Well, I supposed I'd get a job. I can clean house, and I'm a fair cook, as you well know."

"Aye, that ya are, and I know ya enjoy workin'. It's havin' ya alone that torments me."

Melody knew he was just concerned about her well-being. She patted his hand. "If you want to pick out some suitors for me, then I'm not opposed. I love and trust you. I don't want to stay here to be rid of you. I'm hoping, in time, you might even want to come back and settle here as well. My children will need their grandda."

"Could be. But ya know me wanderlust." He beamed her a smile. "Yar a good daughter, Melody, and God has given ya sound judgment. If ya have a young man who has caught yar eye, ya might be lettin' me know. I can talk to him and give ya my opinion. After all, the choice is gonna be yars."

She got up and kissed his cheek. "Thank you, Da. I know that together we should be able to figure it out."

He nodded and picked up his paper. "Now, didn't ya say ya were gonna go visit Marybeth?"

"Aye. After I do up the dishes, I'll be on my way."

He nodded and picked up the paper again. "*Is é do mhac do mhac inniú, ach is í d'iníon d'iníon go deo.*"

Melody smiled at the old Irish saying. Your son is your son today, but your daughter is your daughter forever.

"Aye, Da. I'm yours forever."

"And so Da said he'll put out the word that I'm looking for a husband. I figure we have about forty-five days to find one because the doctor said Da can rejoin the workforce in June." Melody glanced from Marybeth to Granny Taylor. These two women were her dearest friends in the world.

"That doesn't give us a whole lot of time," Granny Taylor observed. "Are you sure you want to choose a husband this way?"

"It wasn't my idea. Da won't let me stay if I'm not married."

Marybeth had been frowning since Melody had first told them of the situation. "Maybe Edward can speak to him."

"My Jed could do the same." Granny Taylor picked up her knitting. "I can't abide for you to marry without love."

"Nor I. The very thought is abominable," Marybeth added. "You deserve love, Melody. You above all people."

The latter comment made Melody laugh. "Why me above all? I'm nothing special."

"But of course you are," Granny Taylor replied. "You are God's own child, and your heart is one of the kindest and most loving. You deserve a husband who will adore you— love you and make you happy."

"I won't marry a man unless I think I can love him in time." To be honest, Melody had been somewhat concerned about this very issue. She could always refuse to marry any of the men her father chose. It wouldn't be the end of the world if she had to push on with Da. She could always make her way back to Cheyenne. Still, the thought of leaving the friends she'd made nearly broke her heart.

"But I want more for you. I want passion and romance," Marybeth said, sounding as if she might soon be moved to tears.

"Marybeth, you married to save your little sister from being taken away from you. You married a man for convenience."

"Yes, but I loved him. I didn't even realize just how much, but I knew that I loved him at least as a friend."

"Love is important, Melody. Isn't there anyone who has caught your eye? Made you think he might be the one?" Granny asked.

Melody thought about it for a long quiet moment. "No, there's no one. I know we live in a town where the men probably outnumber the women forty to one, but I've honestly not found myself thinking that way about anyone. You forget, I've been with Da all the way on building this railroad. I've seen the antics of the men working the line. I know a lot of them, but they're like brothers or wayward relatives." She laughed. "Definitely not men I would consider as a husband."

"We need to get to praying about it, then," Granny said, once again setting her knitting aside.

She'd picked it up and put it down so many times that Melody thought it a wonder she ever got anything accomplished. Still, she was right about praying. Prayer was the answer for getting answers, as Granny Taylor was always saying.

"I hadn't even thought to pray." Melody smiled and folded her hands. "That's why I come to you, Granny. You always know the right way to handle a matter."

"Not only do we need to pray, but we need to be keeping our eyes open. I'm sure Jed might know a fella or two who would make a decent husband."

"I can also ask Edward. He spent most of his time with Fred Henderson . . ." Marybeth's words faded.

"We all miss Fred, to be sure," Granny Taylor said. "And we'll miss Eve and the young'uns."

Fred had worked with the town marshal's office and hired Marybeth's husband, Edward, to be a deputy in Cheyenne. Unfortunately, Fred had been shot and killed not even two weeks back, and his sweet wife had fled the town she hated with her sons and a baby on the way. The loss was still keen, and none of the women had quite been able to move on.

"I find myself still expecting Eve to come through the door

at home, since it was her house to begin with," Marybeth admitted. "She was such a dear friend."

"You can't blame her for leaving. This town would only serve to remind her of what she lost." Granny shook her head. "I am heartily sorry for that woman. Left with two little boys and a babe soon to be born."

"She's got a good family," Marybeth threw in. "They love her most dearly and will see to it that she has everything she needs. They're quite wealthy."

Granny gave a sigh. "But money can't bring back the one thing she truly longs for. We need to remember her in prayer as well."

The women were used to getting together to pray on a regular basis. Often they would talk with one another for an hour or more before speaking to the Lord, so Granny's comment was expected.

"Yes, and we should pray for my da," Melody requested. "His back is hurting him something fierce. He doesn't say much about it, but I know he's in pain."

"And pray for my Jed. His arthritis is causing him grief in his hands. A mechanic with bad hands won't be much use to the railroad. And while we've saved a good bit of money, it won't last that long if he finds himself out of work. Of course, we could go live with one of the children and make ourselves useful to them."

"I'd hate to see you leave Cheyenne." Having Granny Taylor here was one of the reasons Melody wanted to stay. She was a sort of mother figure to the younger woman, and after so many years without her own mother, Melody cherished Granny's advice.

"Say, don't you have a birthday coming in a few days? The thirteenth, isn't it?" Granny asked.

"Yes, I'll be twenty-six." Melody hadn't been overly worried about it. Her father always remembered and took her out to dinner for the event. And he always had a gift for her. His gifts weren't bought without thought either. He was most meticulous in what he gave her.

Granny laughed. "Just a youngster. Well, we should plan a party."

"I don't need a party, Granny."

Marybeth's frown finally left her face, and she offered a grin. "No, she needs a husband. Maybe we could have a birthday party and invite all the eligible bachelors in town."

Melody chuckled. "That would save Da the time and trouble of running them down for himself."

"Maybe he could just take out an ad in the paper," Marybeth suggested.

"Or announce it from the pulpit at church," Granny countered, more than a little amused by the entire matter. "Goodness, perhaps we could just put up an auction block in the middle of town."

Melody laughed but wasn't all that certain that her father wouldn't jump at the opportunity to try any of their suggestions. What exactly had she agreed to? The thought of marrying a stranger was starting to sink in. Goodness, what would the rest of Cheyenne think when they learned the truth? And what would the men of Cheyenne think? Would they think her wanton? Or perhaps unreasonable and difficult since she hadn't been able to find a man on her own?

Things were about to get very interesting in the Doyle world. No doubt about it.

Tracie Peterson is the award-winning author of over one hundred novels, both historical and contemporary. She has won the ACFW Lifetime Achievement Award and the Romantic Times Career Achievement Award. She is often referred to as the "Queen of Historical Christian Fiction," and her avid research resonates in her stories, as seen in her bestselling HEIRS OF MONTANA and ALASKAN QUEST series. Tracie considers her writing a ministry for God to share the Gospel and biblical application. She and her family make their home in Montana. Visit her website at TraciePeterson.com or on Facebook at facebook.com/AuthorTraciePeterson.

Sign Up for Tracie's Newsletter

Keep up to date with Tracie's latest news on book releases and events by signing up for her email list at the link below.

TraciePeterson.com

FOLLOW TRACIE ON SOCIAL MEDIA

Tracie Peterson   @AuthorTraciePeterson

More from Tracie Peterson

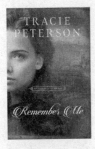

Haunted by heartbreak and betrayal, Addie Bryant escapes her terrible circumstances with the hope she can forever hide her past and with the belief she will never have the future she's always dreamed of. When she's reunited with her lost love, Addie must decide whether to run or to face her wounds to embrace her life, her future, and her hope in God.

Remember Me
PICTURES OF THE HEART #1

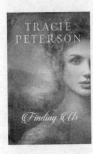

While taking photos at an exposition in Seattle, camera girl Eleanor Bennett meets a handsome stranger, Bill Reed, who recognizes the subjects in one of her portraits as a missing woman and her child. As they hunt for the truth, Eleanor and Bill will have to band together to face the danger that follows.

Finding Us
PICTURES OF THE HEART #2

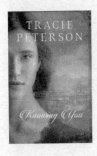

May Parker is captivated by the Japanese exhibits at the Alaska-Yukon-Pacific Exposition, longing to know more about her mother's heritage. When she's reunited with childhood friend Lee Munro, they become entangled in a dangerous heist involving samurai armor, and their love is threatened. Will they be able to overcome the odds against them?

Knowing You
PICTURES OF THE HEART #3

⬧BETHANYHOUSE